ALSO BY *ROBERT FLYNN:*

NORTH TO YESTERDAY (*1967*)

This is a Borzoi book, published in New York by Alfred A. Knopf

IN THE HOUSE
OF THE LORD

In the House of the Lord

ROBERT FLYNN

ALFRED A. KNOPF New York

1969

THIS IS A BORZOI BOOK
PUBLISHED BY ALFRED A. KNOPF, INC.

Copyright © 1969 by Robert Flynn

All rights reserved under International and Pan-American Copyright Conventions. Published in the United States by Alfred A. Knopf, Inc., New York, and simultaneously in Canada by Random House of Canada Limited, Toronto. Distributed by Random House, Inc., New York. Manufactured in the United States of America.

Library of Congress Catalog Card Number: 68-23961

FIRST EDITION

For JEAN

CONTENTS

Days of Youth   5

Days of Our Fathers   51

Days of a Hireling   131

Days of Prophecy   184

Days to Come   232

IN THE HOUSE
OF THE LORD

I said, O my God, take me not away in the midst of my days: thy years are throughout all generations.

THESE ARE the days of Pat Shahan, disciple of Jesus Christ, prophet of the Most High God, who by the hand of the Almighty saw signs and banners, fire and rain, dreamed dreams of drunkenness and duty, was nailed to a cross, descended into hell, and heard the voice of the Lord in the midst of his days.

Days of Youth

> *Oh that I were as in months past,*
> *as in the days when God preserved*
> *me; when his candle shined upon*
> *my head, and when by his light I*
> *walked through darkness; as I was*
> *in the days of my youth, when the*
> *secret of God was upon my tabernacle . . .*

IT WAS BRIGHT, warm October. It was the time of the Great Crusade. It was the day of Desperate Deeds. It was the afternoon of Banner Sunday, when, between the Trumpet Call and Shout that was to shatter the walls of Jericho and the climactic Let Your Light Shine In A Dark World candle lighting that was to usher in a new day of hope and understanding, Ray Elliott was to wave the world's largest All Conquering Banner of Jesus Christ over the city.

Pat Shahan stood in the dusty weeds of the littered fairground watching the excited crowd, hearing the roar of the airplane. But the Lord did not come down. The walls of Jericho did not come down. It might have been something he heard—a falter in the roar of the plane or a sudden hush in the noise of the crowd, or it might have been something he saw in their faces that told Pat everything had gone wrong. But even before he saw the falling plane or heard it crash at the edge of the fairgrounds, he had a vision of what was to come. Ray Elliott dead, himself to blame.

He was running although he had not intended to, caught up in the compulsion of the crowd, elbowing and fighting his way over the rough, rutted ground, through the dusty weeds and bits of scattered trash, drawn to the fire that burned without consuming. Feeling the heat from the plane stinging his face, he stopped although others pushed past him. But he did not want to see what was in the cockpit, and already he could smell burning oil and rubber and something else.

Turning on his heel, Pat walked away from the plane, pushing through the crowd that still surged toward the rising column of smoke. He had reached the parking lot before he heard the sirens.

Although he was responsible for transporting the bullfighter, the actor, and two football players back to the hotel, Pat got in the car and drove away. He had had enough. He stopped at the hotel only long enough to finish packing the two bags containing the six suits and twelve shirts he had required for the week. He stopped again at the outskirts of the city to buy gas. The attendant, observing the bumper stickers, asked him his connection with the Great Crusade.

"No connection," he replied.

He drove through the bright, sunny afternoon, scarcely aware of the golden fields on either side of the road or the signs that glittered with warnings and promises. SLOW. CURVE. UTOPIA RIGHT LANE. ELYSIAN FIELDS NEXT EXIT. ARCADIA 68 MILES. And into the night with its flash and wink of colored lights. GAS. SAVE. EAT. EXIT.

"What was it I wanted that I would go to the Crusade to get?" he asked. "A chance to preach?"

"I SEE YOU DOWN THERE, TOM PAINE, BURNING IN HELL. I SEE YOU IN THE FIRE, BOB INGERSOLL."

Who in hell was Tom Paine? No, that hadn't been it. He had known he wouldn't get to preach when he had left for the Crusade. He had gone in the hope that lightning might strike. That by being a part of something as big and glamorous and well-publicized as the Great Crusade he might share a measure of the glory. That something might happen that would change him from a dull, pedestrian preacher into a prophet of God. He wanted to do something important, to say something significant. He would never be Bishop because in his church there were no Bishops. He would never be canonized because he was a Protestant. He would never be a martyr because no one cared that much.

Pat wanted to be a prophet. He wanted to see visions. Pat Shahan, prophet, seeing the fire that burns without consuming. He wanted to be a savior. Pat Shahan, messiah, leading the exodus from the Great Crusade. He wanted to hear the voice of God. And occasionally he did, although it usually sounded like his own voice, or Lillian's voice, or sometimes even his mother's voice.

"DID YOU CAST OUT THOSE DEVILS, PAT?"

"No, Lord, that's what the public wanted."

"DID THEY ASK FOR TRUTH, PAT?"

"Yes, Lord, we gave them a slogan."

IN THE HOUSE OF THE LORD

PROVIDENCE. HOLY CROSS. DOLOROSA. NORTH FIFTH. The house was in darkness when he turned into the driveway. Lillian wasn't expecting him until tomorrow. "That's all right," he said. "I didn't expect a light in the window. After all, a man returning from the wars can't expect much except to be allowed to come home at all."

Taking the bags from the car, Pat set them down in the carport and deliberately tore the stickers off the bumpers, peeling them off in strips. GREAT. COME. SING. HEAR. REPENT.

Pat tried the door. It was unlocked, although he always told Lillian to keep the doors locked while he was away. For the kids if for no other reason. Switching on the light in the kitchen, he carried his bags through the back door, closing and locking it. He checked the front door and switched on the light in the hall before carrying his bags into the bedroom. Lillian, looking soft and sleepy, turned over and looked at him, blinking against the light. "What time is it?" she asked.

"Eleven thirty," he said. "You didn't lock the back door."

"I guess I forgot. I thought you weren't coming until tomorrow?"

"I left early."

"Because of Ray?"

"That was part of it."

"Did you see it?"

"I was practically in it," he said, wanting to appropriate some of the importance for himself. "I had talked to Ray just before take-off. He couldn't get the sign up. He couldn't get the damn thing off the ground. It was going to be the biggest sign ever towed by a single engine plane, and he couldn't get it off the ground."

"I called Rachel as soon as I heard. It was all over the radio. She seemed to be taking it pretty well. One of her friends was going to spend the night with her."

"Did you tell her I asked Ray to pull the banner?"

"You did not."

"I was the one who told him the Crusade wanted a pilot."

"That's a long way from asking him," Lillian said, getting up to unpack his bags and hang his suits in the closet. "Any of these need cleaning?"

"Just the brown one and the one I have on," Pat said, taking off his coat and sitting on the side of the bed. "It was the worst mess I ever got into. Conceived in grandeur, planned in pride, executed with hypocrisy, and climaxed with one great big plane crash." It was a description he had worked on all the way home.

"I told Rachel you would be by tomorrow. She's going to make the arrangements in the morning."

"Does she want me to help?"

"I don't think so. You know one of their relatives is connected with a funeral home. I think it's his cousin. She said it would probably be afternoon before they are all home."

"What am I going to say? That Ray made the Crusade a big success? That it was conceived in Hollywood, planned on Madison Avenue—"

"Tell her Ray did what he thought was best and that you're sure good will come of it."

"Crap."

"I wish you'd stop saying that. Every time you go off on one of these things you come back like that."

IN THE HOUSE OF THE LORD

"Spiritually rejuvenated. Revived all to hell."

"You see. I wish you hadn't even gone."

"I had to go."

"You didn't have to go."

"I had to go," Pat said, loudly and insistently. "I am thirty-five years old, almost forty—"

"And you are pastor of a larger church than you ever thought you'd be."

That was true. He had never expected to be a success, and his prosperity, his ability to get ahead of better men frightened him a little. Yet he had expected to do something significant by the time he was thirty-five, something meaningful, and that failure was galling.

"Did you see Dr. Espey?" Lillian asked.

"Yes, I saw him," Pat said. "He even spoke to me." It was Dr. Espey who had found him a place in the Crusade. Dr. Espey had been Pat's childhood pastor, had baptized him, asked him to preach his first sermon, and performed the ceremony when Pat and Lillian were married. And now they were pastors in the same city. Only Dr. Espey was pastor of the old, downtown, first family church, and General Chairman of the Great Crusade, which was held each fall in a different city.

Pat had presumed upon their acquaintance to humbly beg Dr. Espey for a place in the Crusade. Dr. Espey was chagrined that Pat could think man had anything to do with selecting the participants in the Crusade. God selected. The Executive Committee, of which Dr. Espey was also chairman, merely invited those God had chosen. Pat had thought God might have nominated him. Dr. Espey had been suspicious. He had been doubtful that Pat would "fit in." He hadn't approved of Pat's recent attitude, and as Pat must know, "a minister's attitude is as important as his theology." But because Pat was his "Timothy," his son in the ministry, after a few humiliating delays Dr. Espey had gotten Pat on the Crusade's Hospitality Committee. "You don't know where we can find a good pilot, do you?"

"What did Dr. Espey have to say?" Lillian asked, coming over to sit beside him on the bed.

"He said, 'We're even now so don't ask for any more favors.'"

"He did not."

"He didn't say it, but he meant it."

"Did you get to preach any?"

"No, I was private valet, bell hop, and chauffeur for Rex Hamilton, television actor, Victor Martinez, bullfighter, and two nondescript football players."

Being on the Hospitality Committee had consisted of keeping the participants happy, present at the meetings, and morally circumspect. "I had to provide food for two gluttons, photographers for an egomaniac, and keep an eye on the bullfighter, who looked a little flaky to me."

Pat got a Crusade brochure from his coat pocket and handed it to Lillian. It was an attractive pamphlet explaining the purpose of the Crusade, giving the schedule of events, and decorated with striking photographs of the principal speakers—a state senator, an ex-convict, a Mexican bullfighter, an eighty-year-old cowboy, a second-rate television actor, and three professional athletes, plus smaller, more commonplace photographs of the benign, near-sighted ministers and firm-jawed, hard-eyed evangelists taking part.

"I think we should have had at least one dope addict for class," Pat said.

"Your picture isn't in here," Lillian said.

"I didn't want it in there," he said, and it was almost true. He would have been embarrassed if his picture had been in the brochure, yet he was disappointed that it was not.

"I'm sorry it was so awful for you," she said, putting her arms around him and laying her head on his shoulder.

"It was a hard war, but I came back alive."

"I missed you," she said, unbuttoning his shirt and putting her head on his bare chest. He kicked off his shoes without untying the laces and lay down with her, holding her gently in his arms. There was more of comfort than of urgency in their love now. What had once been merely heat was now also light, what had been self-forgetfulness was now also discovery. What had always been pleasure was also sometimes joy. But for Pat there was something yet to attain. In all their reaching, and probing, and searching there was an awareness they had not discovered.

What was it they searched for as they struggled toward the light? In the beginning it had been a search for something beyond themselves; but they had found that early in their marriage; and now they reached for something beyond their sum, bigger than unity, a break-through, a swelling of oneness until it burst into something else.

He sought Revelation. He sought Vision. "When you love," he thought, "God is what you make." Yet he knew that they were slowly ebbing away, fading apart, and that once again he had failed. There was a perfection, a knowledge he had not reached. He listened to her breathing, aware that she was at peace, that she was free of him now, having escaped into sleep, and that he would never know her completely nor possess her for long.

She was gone, asleep in his arms, leaving him to face the night with its voices. All the unspoken doubts and fears that he had shut out of his mind during the long drive home now pressed about him in the darkness, shouting to be heard.

"What's it all about?" They asked. "What does it mean?"

"It means you can believe anything you want as long as you're not serious about it," he said.

"Where was God that such a thing as this could happen?" They asked.

"God is the unknown soldier," he said.

"But how could God allow such a thing? What does it mean?"

"It means that God is where you live," he said.

"What was the Great Crusade like?" asked a snap-jawed reporter.

"The Great Crusade was conceived in iniquity and aborted in sin—"

"What did you think of the Great Crusade?" asked Dr. Espey, his bald head furrowed with sincerity, his weak eyes peering intently through the rimless glasses.

"A moral victory," Pat said.

"WHAT WAS IT LIKE, PAT?"

"Lord, you would have been ashamed."

"WERE YOU ANGRY, PAT?"

"Lord, I didn't even get my picture in the brochure."

"Why did you participate in the Crusade?" They asked.

"The Great Crusade was without a doubt the outstanding evangelical witness of our decade. I was proud but humble to have a part in it."

"What did you do?"

"I gave up my raincoat to Rex Hamilton. I carried cold water to two football players. And I walked the second hundred miles keeping an eye on Victor Martinez."

"Why did you ask for a place in the Crusade?" asked Dr. Espey.

"Because I didn't go to Korea."

"WHY DID YOU GO, PAT?"

"Lord, for once in my life I wanted to be part of something big. Something significant. Something successful."

"WAS IT SUCCESSFUL, PAT?"

"Lord, it was tremendous. It was efficient, organized, publicized. They had surveyed the area to find out what the people wanted; they had selected speakers to appeal to each sex, age group, and cultural environment; they had contests to see who could get the most people there and prizes for those who put up the most posters. The football stadium was packed, Lord. We didn't bring down the walls of Jericho, maybe, but we set attendance records every night. Rex Hamilton said it was the best box office he had ever had. I'll bet ten thousand people came out just to see Ray launch the world's biggest banner. Only Ray couldn't get it off the ground."

Pat's face prickled again from the searing heat of the burning plane, and he turned on his side, staring in the darkness, trying to shut out of his mind the sight of something black and crumpled he thought he had seen moving in the flames and the smell of something other than burning oil and rubber. He seemed to have lost the grace of sleep, and no position of his body seemed natural or restful.

"What does it mean, Pat?" They asked. "What did you discover?"

"A man's banners are more than he can bear."

"Cliché," They said.

"A man's dreams are earth-bound."

"Not spiritual enough," They said.

"His aspirations fall to earth and writhe in flames at the edge of the trash-strewn fairgrounds."

"Pat Shahan," They said. "That sounds just like Pat Shahan."

Who was it supposed to sound like? he thought. The voice of doom? Gabriel's trumpet? They wouldn't know the voice of God if they heard it. And if he had a vision, he wouldn't have the words to express it.

Angrily, Pat seized the covers and rolled over. Lillian stirred beside him, and guiltily he replaced the covers over her and tried to close his mind to the images and voices that swarmed about him. Usually he tried to visualize the leaves of a book being rapidly flipped, so rapidly that he could see nothing except the blur of the pages, but tonight even that didn't work. Over the snap and purr of the turning pages he could hear their voices, and out of the fluttering leaves came the words.

"Who. made. you. a. preacher?" They asked. "By. what. authority. do. you. these. things? By. what. sign? Who. gave. it. to. you?"

Once again to ask the question that had to be asked—the question that had no answer. The question that had to be asked because he wanted to be an honest man who sold himself nothing. That had no answer because he was the only authority who could rule on the validity of his experience. His was a double obligation. As a spiritual leader he must find answers for his people, but as a seeker who had not arrived he must question the validity of those answers.

"Who made you a preacher?" They asked. "By what sign?" And once again he was driven to establish a working agreement, to find an understanding. At best what he had was a truce. At best what he knew was uncertain.

"God," he said. "God called me to minister."

"How did God call you to minister?"

"Well, I was out in the pasture one day, not doing anything, just walking along. I remember it was in November, and I was swinging a stick, hitting the dead brush and weeds. And it seemed to me—I mean, there wasn't any flash of light or roll of thunder or anything, but it seemed to me that God was speaking to me—"

"Were you frightened? Did you fall on your knees and cry out?" They asked.

"No. It—seemed very natural. No, it seemed—very wonderful. I went right on with what I was doing, walking and swinging a stick, but it seemed wonderful. Meaningful. I can still remember that I felt alive and that death seemed just as wonderful. Everything was the same. It seemed wonderful to sing and shout and dance, but it was just as wonderful to walk along and strike at the weeds. And I remember—"

"But what does God's voice sound like?" They asked.

"Sometimes it's like my mother's voice, and sometimes like my father's voice, and sometimes like the voice of Dr.

Espey. And sometimes—sometimes it sounds like my voice."

"Why don't you quit?" They asked. "You left the Crusade, why don't you leave the church?"

"One day in June I was driving a combine in a wheat field that stretched as far as the eye could see. Clouds kept piling up in the northwest, and it looked like rain any minute. In the east smoke from a burning wheat field spread along the horizon threatening the whole harvest. A gust of wind blew my hat off, but I didn't stop because with fire and rain threatening the harvest there was no time to worry about a hat. I remember I kept thinking: 'The wheat. I've got to save the wheat. Only the wheat is important.' And that thought kept driving me on so that I forgot about my hat. I forgot that I was hot and tired, that I wouldn't be able to keep my date that night, that there had been no time for lunch. I was doing something desperate, something real, and I knew then that saving the wheat, making the harvest was—"

"Symbol thinking," They said.

"When I was a boy, one of my chores was to keep plenty of fresh water in the horse trough. I used to take a stick and rescue all the bees that had fallen in the water, but I noticed that there were never any wasps in the water. The wasps floated on top of the water and the bees drowned. I asked my father about it, and he said it was because bees had hairs on their legs so they could gather pollen and that the hairs broke the surface tension of the water so that they couldn't float. The very thing that made them useful caused them to drown. That didn't seem right to me—that what was useless could float while the good and productive struggled in the water. I couldn't believe there was such injustice in the world, and as young as I was, I decided that no matter the struggle, I would fight injustice, and I would—"

"But who asked you to?" They asked.

"I remember walking home from a football game, the first game I ever played in—for three plays and a kickoff, I think. I was cutting across the alfalfa field and the moon was so bright it was like the lights were still on, the crowd still there, and I began running across the field, feinting with my hips and stiff-arming tacklers and I was crying—from the excitement I guess. I just burst into the house and started shouting, "I got to play, I got to play."

"Is that all?" They asked.

"Yes," he said. "Yes, that's all." Other men saw shafts of light. Other men had earthquakes and rushing wind, but for him God spoke only by the voice of others, through fire on the horizon and in the buzz of bees' wings.

"WHY ARE YOU A PREACHER, PAT?"

"Lord, I didn't want to work for just anybody. I didn't want to just make a living. I didn't even want this—the car and the clothes and the good salary. I just wanted to do something important."

"Are you sure that you want to be a preacher?" Dr. Espey had asked. He was younger then, about forty-five, but just as bald, as emphatic, and as positive that he had a private arrangement with the Lord.

Pat hesitated. He did not want to begin his ministry with a lie, but how could he be sure? Who could tell him, and by what authority? Dr. Espey was so certain, so sure. To him God must have given a special sign and before that confidence Pat quailed. Dr. Espey watched him through the rimless glasses and only his eyes were friendly. Pat dropped his head and nodded. "Yes," he said.

"You are absolutely certain that of all His people God has called you to be a special servant?"

Again Pat nodded his head, embarrassed by his own immodesty, appalled at his presumption. Dr. Espey leaned back in his chair, still not satisfied, not convinced. He waited for Pat to persuade him, but the only words Pat knew seemed shabby and dishonest. He sat mute with the silence deepening between them.

"Very well," Dr. Espey said. He would accept Pat's response, but that question, that scarcely discernible fear that Pat would dishonor both his trust and the Lord's did not leave his face even after Pat's ordination.

"Why do you want to be a preacher?" asked his father, who didn't think much of preachers. His mother had insisted that Pat tell his father. "You know your father always planned on you taking over the farm. You've got to tell him that the Lord has other plans for you, and that you're going to have to have some help to get through college and the seminary."

"Why do you want to be a preacher, Pat?" his father asked, and again Pat sought the words to express a nameless and wordless urge. How could he make his father understand when he couldn't even explain it to himself? How could he make his father believe when Dr. Espey doubted? They stood beside the corral like silent strangers, feeling alone and forsaken.

"I'll have to go to college and the seminary," Pat said. "At least seven years."

"That'll cost a lot of money," his father said.

"Yes, sir."

"I don't have it," his father said. He looked over the corral at the flat, characterless land that was his birthplace, his only home, the security of his old age, and his legacy for his son. "This is all I have," he said, and Pat knew he might have said: "This is all I have ever had," or "This is all I will ever have," or "That's a lot to ask, son."

"Is that what you want to do?"

"Yes, sir."

During Pat's first year at college his father sold a portion of the farm. The shinnery, a brushy corner of the pasture that Pat loved best, was the first to go.

"Who are you to be a minister?" They asked. "What do you know about man? Have you ever faced death? Have your sins driven you to despair? Do you know the taste of misery? Do you know the smell of the ghetto? Have you ever seen night fall in a prison? Have you suffered?"

No. He knew very little about man. To Pat, his life seemed as flat and as lacking in color and drama as last year's sermon, as the stained-glass figures posing in the church windows. Pat Shahan, one glass hand holding his garments about him, the other extended in invitation.

"I remember as a child sitting in a patch of stickers near the corn field playing with a yellow kitten. I would put the kitten in the stickers, and it would try to walk back to me as I was the only chance of escape. But it would get stickers in its feet and shake its paws and meow until I'd pick it up and pull out the stickers. And I'd say, 'It wasn't me that did that, it was someone else.' Then I'd put it back in the stickers. I knew it was wrong. I knew that I was hurting the kitten and God was angry with me, and yet I did it because I wanted to. That is my earliest memory."

"How do you know that was real?" They asked. "How do you know you didn't just dream it?"

"It was real," Pat said. "I know it was real because I am still that boy."

"But who are you to be a minister?" They asked. "What do you know about God? Have you ever had a vision? Have you ever seen the Lord high and lifted up, His train filling the temple?"

No, he had never seen God high and lifted up, His train filling the temple. He had seen Him low and cast down, His need filling the world.

The pages turned, the airplane burned along the edge of the fairgrounds, the kitten gingerly picked its way through the stickers, drowning bees made concentric circles in the water, fire and rain loomed on the horizon, in the alfalfa field the moonlight was as bright as destiny, and in the gun park cleaned, oiled, obsolete guns pointed their useless muzzles at the sky.

"WHO ARE YOU, PAT?"

"Lord, I'm the figure posing in the church window."

Pat Shahan, with beautiful feet, carrying the gift of God across the moonlit field. Pat Shahan, blessed of the Lord, with uplifted eyes seeing the fields white with harvest. Pat Shahan, savior of the bees, one hand holding back the fire

IN THE HOUSE OF THE LORD

and rain, the other forming a bridge over which the bees can walk to safety.
GOD IS THE IMAGE I CAST.

Pat Shahan, in an ecstasy, dreaming of drunkenness and joy, of power and glory, opening his eyes upon the dark impotence of this world. Anya, his seven-year-old daughter, was standing beside the bed. "There's a cow on Captain Kangaroo that's five years old," she said.

"Wake me when she's seven," he said, pulling the covers over his head and reaching again for the moon and fire and destiny of the horizon. When he opened his eyes again, she was there on the other side of the bed.

"Mother said if you want any breakfast you have to get up now."

Only this time it was six-year-old Penny who stood beside the bed. Stretching, he pretended he was going to get up, but when he opened his eyes again Penny was still there. "Mother says you have to get up."

"Sharper than a serpent's tooth," he said, "is a faithful child."

"Mother told me to wake you up."

With a groan he sat up and waved her out of the room. "Sleep is the mother of the world," he said, "offering rest in one bosom and escape in the other."

Pat Shahan, clothed in his earthly members, made his way into the bathroom and stepped on the scales. Without his glasses he had a little difficulty reading the figures. A little over 180. He had carried 170 in the Marines and had looked slender because of his six feet height, but this was fat and he was beginning to look soft and puffy. "Thou shalt not expect a halo about thy head," he said, "if thou hast a balloon about thy belly."

Pat washed his face in cold water and combed his hair. Getting thin on top but scarcely noticeable. Not for three or four more years. A little puffy around the eyes with the beginning of a roll of fat around his middle and under his chin. "But yet virile, still dangerously seductive," he thought.

"Reverend Shahan, what is the last thing you do before you begin to speak directly from God's heart?" asked the large, breathless President of the Ladies Auxiliary. "Whisper a prayer?"

"The last thing I do before I speak the word of God is to check my fly," said the Reverend Pat Shahan. "Nothing is so distracting to worship as an exposed expositor."

Slipping into a robe, Pat sat down on the side of the bed, uncertain as to what he should do. He wanted to call Rachel Elliott as soon as possible, but it was still early and who knew whether or not the poor woman had been able to sleep. If she had lain awake all night waiting for dawn, then what a relief to be able to talk to someone. But if after a night of tossing, she had just gotten to sleep, what a crime to wake her.

Despite his good intentions and despite the desire of his people that he assist them at such times, he nevertheless felt like an intruder. Only with fear and trembling did he insinuate himself into the circle of the bereaved. With misgivings he picked up the telephone and dialed Ray Elliott's number. The receiver was lifted on the second ring and a voice he did not recognize answered.

"This is Reverend Shahan. I wonder if I could speak to Mrs. Elliott?"

"Oh, Reverend Shahan. How nice of you to call," said a voice which was too bright. Too animated. "Just a moment."

"Hello, Pat, I'm glad you called," Rachel said. Her voice was flat, tired, but under control.

"Rachel, I just wanted to call and tell you how terribly sorry I am," he said, announcing his apology for a calamity he could not change. "Lillian and I, and I'm sure all the members of the church, are ready to do whatever we can," he said, offering help when there was nothing to be done. "We wanted you to know that we share your grief," he said, taking a portion of that which was not diminished by division.

"I'd like to come by and be with you a moment," he said. "Whenever would be most convenient for you."

"We're going over to Pete's this morning. It's quieter there and the children won't be alone."

"Rachel, would you like me to help with the arrangements?" Pat asked. He tried never to let the bereaved, often helpless with grief, go to the mortuary alone. How often had he seen widows in a state of shock sold elaborate and costly funerals they could not afford.

"No," Rachel said. "Pete is going to help me. You know he's a mortician. There are several arrangements to be made. It will probably be afternoon before the children and I are back home. I'd like you to come when we're all together."

"What if I stop by on my way home from church?"

"That would be fine. Thank you, Pat."

Pat hung up the telephone and sat for a moment on the side of the bed thinking of nothing. "Got to get going," he said. "Promises to keep. And miles to go."

Opening the door of the closet, Pat considered what to wear. Monday. He would spend most of the day in his office. An older suit. He would make a hospital call. White shirt, cheerful tie. He would see Rachel Elliott. Dark suit, not too new, and make it a dark tie. Would Mrs. Weatherby be in the hospital again? Probably. Then he should wear the dark blue suit that had belonged to the late Mr. Weatherby. The black shoes that were comfortably broken in but not too worn, with above the calf socks so that his bare leg wouldn't show while he was talking to Rachel.

Tie clasp. There was a plain gold cross, a grain of mustard seed sealed in plastic, the tablets of the commandments made of clay from the Holy Land, the praying hands, a silver fish, an artificial pearl dove, and a tiny leather Bible on a chain—all of them gifts from his parishioners. The fish wasn't too bad, and it had been given to him by Mrs. Wright. But then he would have to wear the cuff links too, and they were awkward when he was writing.

Pat picked up the cuff links and then paused for a moment. There beside all the gift tie bars and tie tacks and cuff links were the ammonia capsules and the bottles of dust supplied by the mortuaries. Should he take an ammonia capsule for Rachel Elliott? She seemed composed enough on the telephone but one never knew. "A minister is always prepared," he said. Picking up one of the capsules, he dropped it into his shirt pocket.

Dressed in the vestments of conservative righteousness, Pat trod down the hall seeking justice and mercy. Lillian and the children were already eating by the time he got to the table. Cold cereal. He hated cold cereal, but he kept silent for the love of God.

"Did you call Rachel?" Lillian asked.

"Yes, she's taking the children over to their relative's house. Pete somebody. He's going to help her with the arrangements. I'm going to see her this afternoon. Anything in the paper about Ray?"

Lillian handed him the paper and there on the front page was an account of the tragedy. LOCAL MAN DIES IN FIERY CRASH. GAVE LIFE FOR CRUSADE SAYS PROMINENT MINISTER. Quickly Pat scanned the story. Ray Elliott had crashed while trying to tow the world's largest banner advertising the Crusade. A moment of silence was observed Sunday night at the last meeting of the Crusade in memory of Ray Elliott, war hero. Afterward it was announced that Elliott's pastor and close friend Reverend Pat Shahan was in the audience, and he was asked to come to the platform and say a word in memory of Elliott. Dr. Espey, prominent local minister, announced that Reverend Shahan had returned home immediately after the accident to comfort Elliott's widow and to pledge to her that those present at the meeting "would lift the charred banner from the weeds of the fairground and each in his own way carry its message to the city." The service ended with a dramatic ceremony in which those pledging to carry on Ray Elliott's work lighted candles and left the stadium singing.

Pat read the account with mounting frustration. Something had happened and he had missed it. Once again he had been left out. He had even been given a chance to speak and he had not been there.

But what had happened? A man had died attempting a publicity stunt. Afterward there had been a moment of silence—he had observed hundreds of them for political leaders, prominent churchmen, wealthy church members—and a candle-lighting ceremony—he had seen dozens of them and it was impressive in the darkness if it was the first you had seen and you were young and impressionable. It might be exciting to read about in the paper, but if he had been there he would have been dismayed at the familiar, shabby bag of tricks.

And what would he have said? The mental picture he had of himself standing before thirty thousand people and stammering his way between truthful blasphemy and soul-saving hypocrisy was painful to contemplate. Could he have said that Ray had given his life for the Crusade? No. Without naming the idiots who had planned the fiasco, he would have had to say that Ray had died like a damn fool.

There was much about the Crusade that he had thought stupid and unnecessary, but Ray's death had seemed a sacrilege. It had made a kind of sense at first to tow a sign over the city. After all, the Crusade was being publicized on billboards, posters, radio, and television. But when they had waited until the last day of the Crusade to fly the sign, and when the flying of the sign itself had been publicized and people invited to see the event, and when the sign had become the world's largest banner, and the event had become a ceremony, a symbol, a crusade itself, then he had been unable to comprehend it. He had no words with which to give it meaning. Only Dr. Espey could think of something to say on such an occasion. That he had left the Crusade and rushed to Ray's widow to pledge to her that they—but it had been midnight when he got home. What was Dr. Espey thinking of? Puzzled, Pat lay the paper aside and looked at Lillian.

"Did you bring us anything, Daddy?" Anya asked.

"Do you think I have to get you a present every time I go away?"

"I was just asking," Anya said, shrugging, pretending not to care, yet certain that he had a surprise.

"Miss Prince said that if your daddy went away, even if he went a long, long way, and was gone a long, long time, and if he didn't have time to get something, or if he didn't see anything for little girls to play with, or he didn't have any money or anything, it was all right if he didn't bring you anything," Penny said.

"Did Miss Prince say that?" Pat asked Penny, who had very strong opinions but who always ascribed them to the voice of authority, her teacher, Miss Prince. "Well, if Daddy had the money and did get you something, what would you want it to be?"

"A horse," said Anya.

"If it weren't a horse."

"If it wasn't a horse—let's see—is it something to eat?"

"What would you like for it to be?"

"A doll," said Penny, who had a limited imagination when it came to gifts. She asked for a doll for every occasion and her grandmothers, aunts, and parents always heard her. She had a closet full of dolls she never played with and every year after Thanksgiving there was a little game of trying to persuade her to give the dolls to some Christmas gift drive. ("What if there were a little girl who had never gotten a Christmas present and had never had a doll and had always wanted—" "What's her name?")

"What if it were a record like *The Wizard of Oz?*"

"Oh, boy, a record," said Penny.

"Can we listen to it?" asked Anya.

"May we?" corrected Lillian.

"May we listen to it?"

"Not now, it's time for school," Lillian said.

"You can hear it when you get home," Pat said.

"Aw, Daddy, we just got it and we don't even get to listen to it," Anya said.

"Gollyeee," said Penny, who wasn't really upset about not getting to hear the record but felt she should be.

Anya, who was upset, walked out of the room dragging her feet. "Thank you for stepping on my foot, Anya," said Penny. "Miss Prince said that when someone steps on your foot or bumps into you or something you should say 'thank you' and that will make them feel bad."

Pat looked at Lillian. "That wasn't Miss Prince. That was her Sunday School teacher," Lillian said. " 'A Christian is thankful for whatever problems God puts in his way.' "

Pat groaned. They were going to turn his children into spineless spinsters who said "thank you" to every disappointment, who considered every betrayal, every failure a visit from God—patient-faced women who never struck back, never cursed their fate, never raised their voices in protest. "Thank you, Lord, for Sunday School teachers," he said.

"Well, I've got to get the kids off to school," Lillian said, leaving the table.

Pat poured himself a fresh cup of coffee and carried it into the study. This was his quiet time. He had carefully instructed the church members that this was a sacred hour for him—to pray for them, to read his Bible, to seek God's guidance, and to prepare his heart with something to say on the Lord's day—and they had been very thoughtful in reserving the time for him. Just as carefully he had instructed Lillian and the girls that he needed the time alone to think, and they occasionally remembered.

Pat was disappointed that the windows of the room didn't open on a busy street downtown, where his people on their way to their work could see the light in the window and know that their pastor was on the job.

"See that light in the window," They said. "That's my pastor praying for me. Somehow it makes it a little easier to go to work just knowing that he's there. It's like—well, it's like he and God were on my side pulling for me."

"Crap," Pat said, sitting down at his desk and putting on the glasses that he needed for reading but never wore in the pulpit nor while visiting his people.

Often his period of meditation was wasted time as he sat and stared at the bookshelves, or thought of the things he should have done yesterday or said last Sunday, or daydreamed about the great sermons he was going to preach so that men fell silent and birds divided themselves into four companies and flew away to the uttermost parts of the world, or the wicked women he was going to rescue from their sins so that they fell on their knees and kissed his feet. Sometimes he wondered if the time wouldn't be more usefully spent sleeping a little longer, or of more lasting benefit if he spent it with his children. And sometimes he wrote speeches and sermons he would never deliver.

"A Christian family is a family with children" he said to the Planned Parenthood Association. "Of course there are some couples who want children, who pray for them, but are not so blessed. They are like Peter, who toiled all night and got nothing."

"My mother could not cook," he said, addressing the Princeton divinity students. "I think that was when I first began to see through the American dream. If mother cannot bake an apple pie, might not God be dead?"

"Man is naturally religious," he said to the World Conference of Theologians and Jews. "Worshipping by instinct, by wish, by impulse, naturally seeking something higher, purer, more worthy than himself. Seeking the embodiment and perfection of those things which he himself desires but is incapable of being. Man is born a theist. You have to harry him into being an atheist. The lions of Rome turned pagans into Christians. The American badger makes atheists of them."

"I have been surprised by people but not disappointed," he confessed to the A.B.C. network. "I have found them to be much like myself. Hypocritical scoundrels. Vain, egotistical fools. Those who are a little better than me I admire. Those who are a little worse I deplore. Those who are much worse than myself I denounce, and those who are much better I detest."

Sometimes he worked on the address he was going to make some day when he was invited back to the seminary as an honored alumnus. "After the palm branches had been thrown in the street and trampled underfoot, after the cheering had stopped and the muttering had begun, after the crowd had lost its enthusiasm and had gone off to seek new diversions, Jesus got off his ass and went to work. Gentlemen, I recommend that you go and do likewise."

But today no sermon ideas came, no speeches while accepting the Nobel Peace Prize, no stating of the obvious in a profoundly obscure way. With a confusion of emotions, Pat picked up the Bible and opened it to the predetermined chapter. He tried to begin each day with a reading from the Bible, not only for sermon ideas and insight, but also because it gave a form to the period of meditation, a semblance of structure to his day. But in taking up the Bible he felt like a football player donning shoulder pads or a soldier picking up his rifle, liking the familiar heft and feel of it, yet reluctant to once again bear its weight.

The Bible was an old one, the binding cracked, the pages worn and water-stained, given to him by his mother on his ninth birthday. She had asked him what he wanted, and he asked for a Bible. He could not remember what his father had given him for his ninth birthday.

When he was twelve his father had given him a calf to raise, and when he was fourteen his father had given him an old, double-barreled, thumb-buster shotgun. The calf, grown into a cow, he had sold to go to college, the shotgun he had traded for a second-hand typewriter, the gift for his ninth birthday he had forgotten. But the Bible his mother had given him he still had.

On the title page of the Bible, written in ink in his mother's full, round, self-conscious hand was: "To Pat from mother on his ninth birthday." Scattered through the margins of the Bible, written in his own stiff, angular hand were secret vows—"From this day forth I, Pat Shahan, solemnly swear that I will not think evil thoughts or do them," formulas for Christian living—"What I am + what I can do = enough." Answers to disturbing questions—"What must I do to be saved? Jn. 3:16." "Who is God's washpot? Ps. 60:8." And inspiring quotations of devout men. "Waiting on God is never wasted time." "God helps those who help themselves."

Pat never used the Bible his mother gave him for study, because it was too old and worn, or in the pulpit, because it was too sentimental, but he always used it for his morning meditations, because it gave his life a kind of continuity and served as a link to the boy who asked for a Bible for his birthday and read it from beginning to end before he was ten.

What had he been looking for? What compulsion drove him through the tedious lists, the obscure laws, the archaic words? And what had it meant to him? He could remember a mystery, a puzzled excitement, a baffled awe. Now, trained in Greek, Hebrew, psychology, archaeology, and Biblical criticism, he had difficulty finding that kind of excitement, and there were times when the Bible meant nothing at all.

Today he had difficulty keeping his mind from wandering, and putting the Bible aside with relief, he bowed his head to pray. He began well enough with a rush of fervency, but soon he began listening to himself, self-consciously picking words and phrases, restating his petitions so that they sounded better—more humble and more pious.

The door opened behind him and with a rustle of her skirt, Lillian tiptoed into the room, bringing him another cup of coffee and pretending that her presence didn't disturb him. Running his hand under her dress he patted her bottom, and she leaned over and kissed him.

"Did you get the kids off?" he asked.

"Late as usual," Lillian said. "Anya couldn't find her shoes, behind the bathroom door where they always are, and Penny forgot to take her money for the trip to the zoo."

"Do you want me to take it by?"

"She can take it tomorrow. She has until Wednesday to get it there. Anya said to tell you she knows how to spell Mississippi. Working on Ray's funeral?"

"Yeah."

"Rachel said she'd like something about flying in the funeral service. Because he was a pilot. Something like 'they shall mount up on wings with eagles.'"

"As eagles."

"Well, I've got to get busy. I'll let you get back to work."

He held her for a moment, not wanting to go back to work. Everyone thought Lillian was wrong for him, wrong for a minister's wife. Even he had thought it. But she had been right for him. He would have to be blind not to see that, faithless not to believe it.

When the rustle of her skirt had passed and the door had closed behind her, Pat took up a sheet of unlined paper and a ballpoint pen to jot down whatever ideas came, with the hope that something would strike fire in his mind, and at the end of the day the ideas would come together and he could make a brief outline and then sleep on it. The next morning he would make a longer and more comprehensive outline, pray over it, and find suddenly and miraculously when he stood before Rachel Elliott with the body of her husband between them that the little notes had been transformed into brilliant words that made sense and meaning of death, into poetry that comforted grief, that out of the waste and ugliness of death a shrine of meaning might be built. Pat stared at the paper. No thoughts came.

Did he have to be a hero? Pat thought. Was that it? Did he have to prove that he could get the sign up? And did Rachel hate him for that need, because the need to be a hero was greater than the need to be a husband and father?

"Your husband was a hero, Rachel. Not only in Korea but in the Great Crusade too. He was doing what he thought was right. You have that to remember. You have that to cling to when you are lonely."

Taking up the pen he wrote "Ray Elliott did what he believed to be right."

"These things are hard to understand, Rachel, but a man must do what he feels is right. Of course there was some risk involved. Anything important involves an element of risk."

"Ray Elliott lost his life in the service of his God," Pat wrote, "because God's service always demands our best, sometimes our all."

"No, I don't think it had anything to do with Ray's

war record. No, I haven't killed anyone. I was in the Marines, you know, but I didn't kill anyone. No, I don't guess I would understand. Yes, I guess I was lucky. Yes, yes, I was lucky. Extremely lucky. I was in a replacement draft, but just before embarkation I was called out of the formation and reassigned to an antiaircraft battalion. 'You're out of it,' Captain Angers said. I never knew why. Luck I guess."

"Ray Elliott was not a lucky man," Pat wrote and then scratched through it. "Ray Elliott was a hero," he wrote and studied the words. Not tried to be a hero or acted like a hero, he simply was a hero. Lean, athletic, the kind of man who seemed born to be a hero.

Because they had both served in the Marines, Ray had always been friendly but Pat could never get close to him. Ray never hesitated, never quibbled, never ducked, and Pat couldn't be comfortable with that. While he stewed over the right thing to say, the right thing to do, Ray did it and it was right, as cleanly and naturally as throwing a bullet pass or hitting a line drive to left field.

Until the Crusade. How had he made a mistake like that? Ray was not the kind of person who allowed himself to be used. If he towed the sign, it was because he wanted to. But how could he have so miscalculated the risk? Pat wondered if, for just a second, Ray had not questioned whether his plane was powerful enough to lift the huge banner into the air, whether he had the ability to do it. If so, he had not given the slightest indication of it. He had smiled and waved for the photographers and had kidded Pat about having to ride herd on a television actor. "You mud Marines always get the glory details," he said.

Pat wondered what Ray thought in that moment when he knew he wasn't going to make it. Did he curse God? Did he blame those who stood safe on the ground and watched? Did his life flash before his eyes? Did he give up, or did he, with the supreme confidence of a hero, never admit that he couldn't pull it off, still in the game until the whistle blew and the lights went out?

"For a brief moment Ray Elliott looked death in the face, perhaps seeing, beyond the mask of death, the face of God, and Ray Elliott did not flinch or cry aloud—"

"Crap," Pat said, somewhat amazed at the ability of his mind to come up with an endless variety of false, mindless phrases. Was that his "stock in trade"? His "gift" for the ministry? The sign of his "calling"? The outrageous ability to bury the reality of the event under a deluge of words? Total recall of the slick, meaningless, all-purpose, every-occasion words ministers lived by? "God's will, providence, truth, love, eternity, justification, reconciliation, regeneration, preservation, the Lord bless, the Lord comfort, the Lord forgive, in His hands, in His name, in His good time, someday we will understand, all things work for good, bye and bye."

With shame Pat remembered how easily the words came and how little they cost him. He remembered describing the joys of death to a woman who was dying. In his days as a student minister it had been his duty to visit Lucy Gillespie, who was dying of cancer. Young, immortal, full of optimism and cheer, he had called at that small but respectable frame house on an unpaved street to describe the glories of heaven to the terrified Mrs. Gillespie who clutched at his hands and begged him to ask God to heal her.

Pat, knowing that she was beyond medical remedy, felt that instead of demanding a miracle of God she should accept her fate. In that small, closed bedroom, smelling of sickness and stale linen, surrounded by the small children, who, caught up in their mother's terror, clung to the bed and cried, he had held Lucy Gillespie's thin, dry hands that were surprisingly tough and strong, and talked cheerfully of the absurdity of death and the glories of the resurrection. He, knowing nothing of life or death, had presumed to conquer her fear with words which were not his own, which he did not understand, while her husband stood at the door, ashamed of the revulsion he felt for his sick, frightened wife, yet unwilling to come in. Yet somehow in the words that came so easily to his tongue, in the tears that cost him nothing, Lucy Gillespie found the grace to die with courage.

He could not renounce the words. To do so would be to stand mute before the events of life—birth, death, suffering, joy. Life was accompanied, events were celebrated by little rituals—a handshake, a sigh, a tear, a closing of the eyes, a folding of the hands, with hello, goodbye, gloria patri, Father, Son, and Holy Bible, we beseech, adore, praise Thee, I have sinned and done evil, mea culpa, into Thy hands, hosanna, hallelujah, Amen. Formally or informally the shock and reality of the event were made significant, transformed into meaning by the threadbare and careworn rituals of life.

What were the words, the rituals that would give meaning to Ray's funeral and would comfort Ray's widow? Where was the magic that could mend a broken heart?

" 'Precious in the sight of the Lord is the death of his saints,' " he wrote from memory. What did that mean? How many times he had used that scripture in funeral services such as this one, and he didn't even know what it meant. Perhaps it was a bad translation.

" 'Died Abner as a fool dieth? Thy hands were not bound, nor thy feet put into fetters: as a man falleth before wicked men, so fellest thou.' " He knew what that meant. But he needed something with wings in it. What did God have to say to Rachel Elliott with wings in it?

As he thumbed through the concordance at the back of the Bible, he was surprised at the number of references listed. "Wings seem to have a special significance to the writers of the scriptures as is evidenced by the more than eighty times the word is used in the Bible. There are some fifty references to flying."

"The desire to fly has been one of the age-old dreams of man. To soar above the bonds and toils of earth. To rise above yesterday. To fly on the wings of the morning, to mount up on wings as eagles. Ray Elliott knew that dream."

That had possibilities. As he jotted the idea down on paper, the telephone rang. He did not pick up the telephone on his desk, knowing that Lillian would answer it in the kitchen, but he stopped anyway, certain at this hour of the day the call was for him, a cry for help, a plea for understanding, a petition for forgiveness, a request for counsel, prayer, money.

Lillian opened the door. "Dr. Espey," she said, making a face.

Pat nodded and slowly took up the telephone, preparing himself. Dr. Espey was not a man to speak with carelessly. For almost forty years Dr. Espey had been a minister and in that time had risen from an obscure beginning to a position of unofficial power and undeniable prestige as pastor of the oldest, wealthiest church in the city. He had had an undistinguished academic career at inferior schools and had begun his ministry in small farming towns. But what he had lacked in education and scholarship he compensated for in the force and openness of his opinions and his willingness to express them. Carefully he made a reputation for himself as a defender of the past.

When he was thirty, Espey had ferreted out in his own alma mater (a small, disreputable church school) a heretic who claimed his words were just as valid as those of theologians of the past, and had succeeded in driving the man out of the college and into a prestige eastern seminary. Encouraged, Espey had persisted in his attacks on suspect professors until, when he was thirty-five, his alma mater had given him an honorary degree as Doctor of Divinity.

As Dr. Espey he began making a reputation for himself as a man who was often wrong but who wasn't afraid to tell you what he thought or to fight you in the public press. "He may be wrong," people said, "but he's honest."

As a reward for his honest differences of opinion and perhaps also as a result of his proclivity for public disputation, Dr. Espey had become a prominent and distinguished minister and an unofficial spokesman for his church. Reporters found that Dr. Espey always had an opinion on any subject and was ready to express it. Whenever they wanted a quotation, they turned to him, and Dr. Espey, though often wrong, was always ready and always honest.

Motioning Lillian out of the room, Pat set his face into a smile and answered the telephone.

"Hello, Pat, how are you?" The voice was warm and personal as always and despite himself, Pat responded to it. "What did you think of the Crusade?"

"Well, I—I thought it went all right. Considering."

"I wasn't too pleased with it myself. I don't believe it measured up to our expectations. I don't think we failed, but I don't believe we succeeded as well as we might have. In fact, we had a meeting right after the last service to see how we could improve it. I wanted to talk to you about it, but of course you had already gone."

"I left early," Pat said. "Just after the trumpets had blown."

"I know what a shock it must have been for you seeing your friend die, and, of course, we all knew that you would want to see his widow as quickly as possible."

There they were, assigning him reasons, explaining away his actions, and there was no way he could escape it. They couldn't allow him a little honest wrath, a little moral indignation that man was so foolish, so fragile, and died as quickly and inconclusively as a dream.

No matter how loudly, how vehemently he insisted that Ray was a member of his congregation, an acquaintance, a man he spoke to after services, they would believe Ray to have been his dearest friend. No matter how often or how clearly he confessed that he left the Crusade because he was sick of it and that Rachel Elliott did not want to see him yet, they would remember that he had rushed to her side to pledge that her husband had not died in vain. They would describe him as noble no matter how profanely he explained that he had been looking for an excuse to quit the Crusade.

He had almost left the first day when he found out what the duties of the Hospitality Committee were. "It doesn't matter how menial it is, Pat, it's all important if it's done for the glory of God," said Dr. Espey. He had packed his bag the night Rex Hamilton had preached on "Making the Scene For Jesus." (A. Put on a happy face. B. Be sure your costume is neat and proper—what would Jesus wear? C. Act like the best person you know.) "It has relevance for some people, Pat," Dr. Espey said. "No minister can speak to everyone." He had finally left the Crusade because he was simply appalled at the littleness and waste of the whole enterprise, which had been epitomized by Ray's death.

Sunday, all over the state, ministers would be telling the story of Ray Elliott and what God was trying to say to them through this tragedy. "God is telling us that we must lift up that charred and tattered banner and carry it to the world." Nothing he did, nothing he said would make any difference. They could not comprehend any other motives than those they had assigned him, they could not comprehend any other message than the one they had assigned God.

"Did you see the paper, Pat?"

"Yes, sir," Pat said, mentally kicking himself for talking like a junior partner.

"Since you weren't there I felt that someone should say a word on behalf of Ray and I thought you would want me to. Of course I didn't know what to say as I didn't know Ray very well, but I felt that he would have wanted us to finish the job, being the kind of man he was. Didn't you find him that way?"

"Well, he usually finished whatever he started."

"Yes, that's it, a man who finished the job. That's the way I saw him. Pat, I'm sorry about the assignment you got for the Crusade. As far as I'm concerned it doesn't matter where I serve as long as I'm serving God, but I think we could have used you more wisely. Put you to better use elsewhere. In fact, we talked about using you for one of the speakers next year."

Pat began reconsidering his opinion of the Crusade. True, it had been badly handled this year, overpublicized, overglamourized, overorganized, but next year could be better. As one of the speakers he could have a part in making it better. The Crusade was worth saving. Perhaps this was his task, his mission, to reorganize and reform the Crusade, to make it relevant to the people and the times, to move it out of the fairgrounds and into the alleys and crossroads. "That sounds pretty good," he said.

"What we were thinking of—and this is just talk—was having a special service next year for Ray Elliott. A kind of commemoration. Maybe stage a pageant showing the highlights of his life—shooting down those Japanese planes and all—and maybe have a flyover, and then we thought, and this is all off the tops of our heads, about having you tell the story of Ray Elliott and how he died and then maybe end with a bugler playing taps. What do you think of that?"

Pat was appalled. Ray had done his best for the Crusade; why couldn't they just let the poor man die. Why did they have to use him? Pat knew that if he spoke at the commemorative service he would have to wear Ray Elliott around his neck for the rest of his life. "Tell us again that wonderful story of how Ray Elliott died waving a flag for the glory of God." "What did you think when you saw the plane was going to crash?" "Is it true the crowd heard him singing 'Nearer My God to Thee' as the plane fell?" "I heard when they removed his body from the plane they found that a Bible he was carrying in his pocket hadn't even been scorched."

"I think it would be better if it were just dropped," Pat said. "If we make too much of his death people are going to start asking why he took such a risk."

"Then we'll tell them. He did it for the glory of God. I have no doubts about that, Pat. I talked to the man before he took off. He was an earnest, sincere young man who wanted to do something for the Lord and flying was what he could do. Didn't he strike you that way?"

"Well, he was earnest." They would never let such an opportunity pass. A war hero whom Providence had spared at Midway and Korea in order to die towing a sign at a church meeting. What an illustration of the uncertainty of a man's life! What a parable of sacrificial service to the cause of God! What a lesson in humility! What a symbol of the futility of man's aspirations! They would use it.

"I think we're going to go ahead with our plans for the service, Pat. There's nothing official about it, you understand, but I think you should be our speaker. You think it over. I guess I'll see you at the Council meeting tonight. We'll talk about it then. I suspect you're having a little trouble with the funeral," Dr. Espey said, as though he were pleased about it.

"I was working on it."

"I know it's not easy when it's someone you love. Let me know if I can help you. I'd be happy to read the eulogy if you'd like. It would be less personal, less emotional that way. By the way, I want to commend the Hospitality Committee for the fine work you and the others did. Rex Hamilton in particular asked me to pass on to you his highest regard."

"Thank you," Pat said before he remembered that he was not a junior partner and that he was offended at being commended as an errand boy for a television actor.

After inquiring about Lillian and the children, Dr. Espey hung up, leaving Pat puzzled. Dr. Espey did not make social calls, and he did not make unofficial plans, and he had never before gone out of his way to be helpful. He wanted Pat to speak at the commemoration service of the Crusade next year, and he wanted to read Ray's eulogy. But why? Was he going to launch next year's Crusade at Ray's funeral?

Shrugging his shoulders, Pat turned back to the task at

hand, finding a scripture with flying for the funeral oration.

"'If I take the wings of the morning, and dwell in the uttermost parts of the sea, even there shall Thy hand lead me, and Thy right hand shall hold me.'"

That might work. "While a city watched, Ray Elliott took the wings of the morning—"

"If accurate," said They, who always heard too little or too much, who clearly remembered the many mistakes and stupidities, forgot the moments of truth and honesty and were never even aware of the rare moments of insight and revelation.

"Ray Elliott took the wings of the morning and flew to the uttermost parts of the sea."

"Too poetic," They said.

"Where he has gone we cannot say. What state he is in we do not know. But this much we know, yea, this much is certain, wherever Ray Elliott is, he is in the hands of God."

"Commonplace," They said.

"Ray Elliott is dead, killed in a flaming plane crash at the edge of a carnival fairgrounds, his body burned to flinders. But something of Ray Elliott remains. What it is and where it dwells is beyond our understanding. Our hope, however, our faith, is that wherever that something is, there is God."

"Too indefinite," They said.

"The lesson for us is this—he who would rise to the frontiers of tomorrow must not be tied to the banners of yesterday."

"Cynical," They said.

"A prophet is not without honor save to his own paymaster."

"Crude," They said.

"The ministry is somewhere between heartburn and hemorrhoids, being both a warmth in the heart and a pain in the ass."

"Crap," They said.

Having disposed of They for a time, Pat leaned back in his chair and closed his eyes. What good was a funeral anyway, he wondered? Did they ever help? Had his father's funeral helped him? Or his mother? He could not remember the scripture that had been read, or the eulogy, or a word that Dr. Espey had said. Instead he remembered that the choir had sung sad, mournful songs and that Dr. Espey had not thought his father to be a good man.

He had been shocked the first time he discovered that there were people who thought his father was wicked because he did not go to church. "I'm praying for your father," Dr. Espey had told him when he was a boy. "Maybe you can say something to your father, get him to come to church."

Pat had tried, although it wasn't easy talking to his father about going to church. He had followed him out to the shop, where he worked over the forge, and had stood around, desperate and embarrassed, trying to think of a way to tell his father he was not a good man. Unable to think of anything he rummaged around through the tools and scraps of metal lying about, nicking his thumb. With relief he started to the house to wash it when the inspiration came to him to write the message he could not speak.

"God our Heavenly Father is love," he wrote, squeezing

the blood out of his thumb to write with. "The soul that sinneth, it shall die. Christ died for us. This is the blood of Jesus Christ that was spilled for you." And when his father went to the house for lunch, Pat slipped into the shop and laid the message under the hammer on the anvil.

He was playing by the windmill when his father called him to the shop. "Did you write that?" his father asked without looking at him.

"Yes, sir," Pat said, beginning to cry.

"Why?"

But Pat said nothing. He looked at the dirt floor of the shop and he cried. How could he look at his father? How could he tell his father he was not a good man?

"I never cared much for church," his father said. "But I've always tried to do right."

"But you don't believe in God."

"Yes, I do, Pat," he said. He put his hand on Pat's head and tried to explain something, but Pat couldn't understand because it was about the First World War and the trenches of France and the first three men over the top falling back dead or wounded, the third falling in his arms. And how as the fourth man he had had to have something to get over the top of the trench. And how when he had reached for it, it was there.

Pat didn't understand because Dr. Espey had never told him about anything like that and because it had nothing to do with singing hymns, going to church, and naming the name of God. But he had remembered it following the hearse out to the flat, treeless north Texas cemetery, and he had wondered when his father was dying if, when he had reached again, God was what was there.

He remembered that one of the pallbearers had thrown a cigarette out the car window and that it had rolled across the narrow, black top farm road in front of him and that he had known then that he would never forget that sight. He remembered that it was bitterly cold and that sleet had rattled against the plastic raincoats and canvas sides of the shelter. He remembered that he had been pleased that the day was gray and cold and that the sleet cut the hothouse flowers banked on the coffin and rattled the pavilion of death.

Pat looked at his watch. Fifty minutes. He had meditated enough. He would put it aside for a while and this afternoon or tonight he would come up with something to say at Ray's funeral. Something that Rachel and the children would cherish and remember, something that Ray's friends would learn.

Pat stood up, empty-handed, and looked about him. He always felt like that, that he should have something to carry to work—a sword, a banner, a cross. Everyone else carried something with them as they went to work—a brief case, lunch box, newspaper, rifle. A man leaving the house empty-handed looked insignificant, without authority. The man you noticed on the street was the man carrying a sample case or a sack of groceries. Old men carried canes, young boys carried school books, but Pat Shahan went to work without a scepter, without a rod, without a shield, a man who dreamed of drunkenness but was never drunk.

Pat stopped at the door of the study, and for a moment he thought of leaving the light burning in the room so that some oppressed man passing down the street might see it and know—

He reached up and snapped off the light. It was time to go to work, to go to the church. Time to play the magician. Time to pluck healing out of the air, to find forgiveness in a child's ear, to draw pearls of wisdom from a whore's mouth, to pull from his empty pocket an endless handkerchief with which to dry the tears of the world.

"Pat Shahan," he thought. "Great mother of the world, with salve in one teat and balm in the other."

"DO YOU LOVE ME, PAT?"

"Yes, Lord, I love you."

"PAT BUTTS."

Pat Shahan, master of magic, casting out demons, receiving strangers, blowing his ram's horn, dividing his garments with beggars.

GOD IS WHAT I GIVE.

Days of Our Fathers

> *Woe unto you, scribes and Pharisees, hypocrites! because ye build the tombs of the prophets, and garnish the sepulchres of the righteous, and say, If we had been in the days of our fathers, we would not have been partakers with them in the blood of the prophets.*

THE CHURCH was an imposing red brick building with a spire and a cross, located on one of the busy thoroughfares to downtown, and looked exactly like three others in the city. But it was substantial and stately the way the seminary professors said it was supposed to be—"as though it were intended and planned, and as though it were going to be there for a while"—and its green shrubs, landscaped lawns, and spacious parking lots offered a brief respite from EAT, BUY, SAVE, SHOP, ENJOY.

"A church is a sanctuary," had said Dr. Randolph Hoffman, round, sour-faced professor of Pastoral Ministry, and those who passed beneath the shadow of the church felt sheltered by it, perhaps even dominated. "A quiet refuge," Dr. Hoffman had said, smacking his thick lips, and pedestrians seemed to huddle together and drop their voices when passing. Even the traffic seemed quieter in the moment that it passed the church.

"A bit overdone," thought Pat.

"The building is just the house for the congregation," Dr. Hoffman had said, "just the shell, but like the shell of a turtle it gives shape and expression to that which is within."

"It's a good, solid church," Dr. Espey had said, trying to interest Pat. "Rather middle class but with a few first families for foundation."

"Country-club turtle," Pat whispered as he walked past the three large, copper-covered doors, ornately decorated with grape vines and pastoral scenes but which were kept locked except on Sunday, and entered through a small, plain side door that was marked only with the black and yellow sign that designated the church as a Civil Defense shelter.

The church office was off the foyer and Pat walked noiselessly over the thick brown carpet and rapped lightly on the door so as not to startle Mrs. Wright when he opened it. As though anything startled Mrs. Wright.

Mrs. Wright was typing out cards and stacking them neatly on the desk. She was a little woman, scarcely fifty, but already she had lost that bloom, that appealing softness which belonged to woman and had become the taut efficiency which belonged to business. Mrs. Wright finished typing the card and placed it on the desk before turning to look at him over her glasses with the expression efficient women have for inefficient men who don't get to the office until after nine.

"Hello, Pastor, how was the Crusade?" she asked.

"Well, it went smoothly enough until Ray's accident," he said, pulling at his tie so that she would notice he was wearing the tie bar and cuff links she gave him for Christmas. As though Mrs. Wright missed anything. "It was very well organized. By the way, have any reporters called about Ray?"

"No. Wasn't that awful. I called Rachel. I knew you would want to talk to her first thing this morning, but she said she would prefer that you wait until this afternoon. There's something she wants to talk to you about that she's not ready to talk about yet."

"Yes, thank you," Pat said. Mrs. Wright was not only officious; she also made mysteries out of molehills. Nevertheless, it gave him an uneasy feeling. "If any reporters do call, you'd better let me handle it. How have things been here?"

In her unhurried manner Mrs. Wright informed Pat of the important things that had happened to his people in his absence. Who had died, or married, or been born, who had sinned, or been sick, who had called the church office to complain. The variety of things that could happen to God's people seemed endless and oftentimes trivial; nevertheless they wanted their pastor's concern, approval, or reprobation. Mentally Pat made a note of the problems he could put off until later and those that would take care of themselves. The others he would have to take care of immediately.

While Mrs. Wright talked, Pat scanned the mail. As usual most of the mail was advertisements—how St. Andrew's got organ music in a church that couldn't afford an organ, collars that never needed laundering, hymnbooks for crisis times, bells that inspire, folding chairs, folding doors, folding walls, folding tables that never rock and roll, water fountains that purify, portable vacuum cleaners for pennies a day, rest-room fixtures, kitchen appliances, stack cribs for the nursery, self-counting coin holders, distinctive lecterns, tamper-proof hat and coat racks, world's finest mop wringers, insulated stained glass, toilet plungers, impelling light fixtures, beautiful fabricated memorial tablets, programed offering envelopes, and functional office supplies. The number and variety of goods required by the church was awe-inspiring.

Pat dropped the advertisements on the desk and Mrs. Wright picked them and began filing them away for future reference while he looked over the rest of the mail. There were two letters from former members telling how they missed the old church and how well they liked the new one, a letter from a listener whose life had been changed by a radio address, an invitation to speak on "Jesus, The World's Greatest Salesman" at a businessmen's luncheon, a crank letter condemning him for his modernistic sermon on Jonah (Pat hadn't preached on Jonah in three years), and two requests for recommendations.

Pat looked at the names. Jerry Barnes and Mac Winston. Mac Winston had been a seminary classmate, the only classmate Pat would have wanted for his own pastor. But Mac was no longer a pastor. He had left the ministry a few years earlier but could settle on nothing else to do. Pat had written him recommendation after recommendation, each time thinking that Mac had found a place for himself as he went from public school teacher to law student, Y.M.C.A. recreational director, textbook salesman, Boy Scout field representative, and assistant editor on a small devotional magazine. Now he wanted to work with a federally supported youth opportunity program. Pat stuck the letter in his coat pocket.

Jerry Barnes. Yes, he remembered Jerry Barnes because Jerry had come to his house late one night to confess that he had been taking money from his employer. Except for that he would have remained a respectable face that Pat saw once a week, sitting halfway back on the left side of the church. The money had been returned, the affair had been kept quiet, and Jerry, swearing he had learned his lesson, had moved to another city to make a fresh start. That had been three years ago. Now he was asking for a recommendation. Had he been caught with his finger in the till or was he moving up to better things?

Pat knew that if Jerry had not confessed to him he would have recommended him without hesitation. Yet, to use Jerry's confession against him was at least as unfair as to recommend him without question. Pat hated recommendations, as it was impossible to deal honestly with them. To accurately appraise someone was damning, as anything below superior was considered a black mark. It was like a game, having to estimate how much he would need to exaggerate to come out even with the employer, who would underestimate his opinion anyway. And how could he evaluate a man he hadn't seen in three years? In three years a man could become a saint or a rapist. But not to answer the request would be to blacklist Jerry.

"The truth is a hard thing for a minister to handle," Pat thought.

"As a minister you will be asked to write all kinds of recommendations," Dr. Hoffman had lectured. "A minister's recommendation should be scrupulously honest, in the knowledge that a good man is never harmed by the truth."

"A minister's word is his bomb," Pat thought.

"I don't make recommendations for fear I might be misunderstood," Dr. Espey had said. "But I will make it known that you are willing to serve in the Great Crusade."

Pat handed the letter back to Mrs. Wright. "See if you can find out how I can get in touch with Jerry," he said. "I'd like to talk to him before I write anything."

Pat dictated the letters that needed to be written—to the sick, the absentees, the visitors, new parents, the Program Committee, which had invited him to participate in the Crusade—indicating what he wished to say and leaving it to Mrs. Wright to find the suitable pietistic phrases.

Mrs. Wright gave him a list of people who had requested appointments, pastoral visits, or telephone calls. Pat groaned aloud as he looked at the long list, but instead of expressing sympathy, Mrs. Wright answered the telephone and discovered that Anna Mae Rogers wanted to speak to the pastor.

"She's having dizzy spells again," Mrs. Wright said, handing Pat the telephone.

Miss Rogers had been having dizzy spells every since Pat had known her, and he was certain she had been having them ever since she had first realized she was never going to be a sweetheart, never going to receive a proposal or a ring, never going to have children, never going to be a grandmother, would in fact, never be any of the things she dreamed of and cried for. Large, cheerful, motherly Anna Mae, who at times seemed to run the church by herself, had dizzy spells and nothing seemed to help except large doses of sympathy and attention.

"I've just been afraid to come to church," she said, puffing. "Afraid I would just pass out. And all those steps to climb and standing up to sing. And the church is always so hot."

Anna Mae was a nuisance, taking up more of his time than any other member of the church, but she was a genial nuisance and Pat had compassion for her. "Now you just lie down, Anna Mae. Are you lying down? Do you have your feet propped up? Miss Prince says you must prop up your feet." Anna Mae responded wonderfully to authority and Miss Prince was as good an authority as any. "Now breathe into your paper bag. Do you have it there with you? Now you just take it easy, Anna Mae. We wouldn't want anything to happen to you. We're counting on you to help us with our community service again this year."

Anna Mae loved community service, when she could be busy from morning to night doing things for others. That seemed to soothe her somewhat, and when her breathing returned to normal Pat hung up.

"Okay, let's go over that calendar again," he said. "I'm going to have to cancel some of these appointments for today."

"Most of these were made before you went to the Crusade," Mrs. Wright said. "They've been waiting over a week. I didn't put them down unless I thought they were important."

"I'll just take the list to my office and if there are any that can wait until tomorrow I'll let you call them," he said, stepping out of the office.

"Women," Pat said, thinking of all the hard-faced, shriveled-souled secretaries who filed away the joys and heartaches of the world.

"You don't like women."

"Yes, Brother Paul, I like them," he said, thinking of all the demanding, breathless, heavy-bosomed Anna Maes whose shapeless dresses hung unevenly over their sagging flesh.

"You hate old women," Brother Paul insisted.

"Well," Pat said, hedging, "I like girls."

"What is so useless as an old woman?"

"A sick wife?"

"Old ladies are hard for a minister to handle," said Brother Paul.

"Young women are hard for a minister to handle," said Pat, "Yet, lest ye burn—"

Pat's study was at the other end of the church, an unsatisfactory arrangement, since it separated him from his secretary and required extensive use of the intercom system. But it did make it possible for Mrs. Wright to head off a lot of people who only wanted general information or someone to talk to. Anyone who got past Mrs. Wright either had good cause to see him or superb determination.

Pat crossed the foyer and walked into the darkened sanctuary. The only light came through the stained glass windows. He paused for a moment to feel the hushed silence. The stained glass was not good, the pews were old and creaked when the congregation rose to sing, the carpet was worn and stained. Yet, there was something—familiar as love, peaceful as death.

Sometimes when Pat sat behind the pulpit confronted with the routine of Sunday services and the listless, insular faces of the people, he felt impotent and alone. At such times it seemed to him that God's people were for the most part ugly, overfed, overindulged, frightened by change, disinterested in problems, concerned only with soaking up all the church had to offer of comfort, assurance, pacification, and the utilization of their leisure time. The women seemed apathetic, stiff with stays, content with safety. The men seemed sleek, self-important, threatening financial ruin to one another. The young people were either earnestly convinced that their secret pleasures and minute sins had everlasting significance, or irreverently certain that only youth possessed immortality and innocence.

The organ music would begin and the service would start. Above the hymnbooks he would see the ravaged faces of those who every day confronted death—and what could he say to them? That God was also Lord of the dead? The haunted faces of those who carried the constant shame of being imperfectly made—that even flawed vessels revealed the Creator's hand? The stunned faces of those who, beyond guilt and grief, were appalled, amazed at the wickedness within them and the power they had to bring suffering and destruction upon all that they loved—what tongue could recite? The restless faces of those who could not find contentment, but whose demons drove them sometimes into the tombs and sometimes into the fire—what language held peace?

In his mouth were plain words, commonplace even to

himself. In his mind were the shabby, shopworn ideas of seminary classrooms, denominational presses, ministerial conferences. In his hand was the thick, heavy, ostentatious Bible. He knew what he felt. Sentimentality. Nostalgia. Pride in his position before men.

Yet, when he stood, and in the silence of the church, spread upon the pulpit the opened Bible and began in his high-pitched, ministerial voice to read, he sometimes found that the cold stone of routine was rolled away, that the Presence dwelt among them, and sometimes to the consternation of all, he caught a fleeting glimpse behind the masklike faces.

There was Emily Graham, sour, embittered, her life poisoned at the source by something he had never been able to touch. Mrs. Clark, a widow, whose only son had discovered in a Freshman philosophy class that there was no God and that life had no meaning. For almost a year, with the sacrifices she had made to send him to college still evident in her hands, she had waited for a letter while he searched for being in the cellars of New York.

There was Al Worley, who sat near the front of the church although some complained that there was the smell of liquor on his breath. There was Jimmy Nevins, who always tried to do God's will—God's will consisting of something meaner and more difficult than whatever he was doing at the moment. Dragging his family with him, Jimmy Nevins plodded down the glorious path to financial ruin.

Sam Sorrele, who sat halfway back and on the aisle, although some complained because he was the editor of *The Informer*, a throwaway newspaper that was full of inflammatory racial and religious inaccuracies.

There was Marjorie Zinkgraf, who for over twenty years had patiently and faithfully lived with her second husband, the paraplegic veteran she had married shortly after the Second World War. Her first husband was killed when he stepped on a land mine in France. Rumors said that Marjorie had been living with another man at the time.

Walter Miles, who after forty years had not forgotten the half-wit girl who had borne his illegitimate child and drowned it in a toilet.

Ann Ostergaard, a small, dark girl who cowered in a back corner of the church, whom he had spoken to only half a dozen times and then only to ask about her invalid mother. "How's your mother, Ann?" he always asked when he saw her because he didn't know anything else to say.

"She's fine," Ann would always answer, although there was something else she did not say.

As he preached to them he sometimes saw the dull, featureless faces come alive. With what? Hope? Joy? Renewal? Remembrance of mothers and old hymns, of Christmas stockings and manger scenes? Perhaps it didn't matter, only that for a while the faces were alive and real and not masks over dead souls.

Nor was he disillusioned by the fact that sometimes the cares they forgot were fashioned by their own hands, that sometimes the burden which was lifted could have been borne by a patient child, that sometimes the sins which they were forgiven were not the sins which blighted their lives.

Occasionally their faces would be lifted, renewed, and they would chatter happily on their way out of church, and be courteous to each other in the parking lots. Occasionally they would be halfway through Sunday dinner before the mask came down again, shutting them off from the injustice of the world, the appeals of ubiquitous need, the cannibalistic necessity of their own families.

Pat stood in the solemn sanctuary, waiting. There was peace. Silence. Nothing else. No one spoke.

Pat walked through the darkened sanctuary, up the three carpeted steps, opened the door of his office and looked inside, aware of the seminary's disapproval.

"The Pastor's study should be arranged so as to give the appearance of neatness and order at all times," Dr. Hoffman had said. "Nothing is so reprehensible in a minister of God as a habit of untidiness.

"A Bible should be kept open on the desk to indicate an attitude of industrious study and meditation. A poem or suitable inspirational thought or motto may be placed under the glass desk top for easy reference, and at appropriate moments may be read or preferably recited for the benefit of the visitor. A studio-type picture of the pastor's family may be suitably placed on the desk to make inquirers, particularly female inquirers, at ease. Such pictures should be appropriately formal without being severe. Informal portraits and candid snapshots are to be discouraged, as are pictures of the minister with distinguished personages, or taking part in public ceremonies. Such pictures are more suitably hung in the church library or parlor.

"Preferably the window should be at the minister's back. Experience has taught that thoughtless persons may be discouraged from overextended visits by careful manipulation of the blinds.

"The pastor's library should be kept in his study rather than in his home so that the books may be observed by the church members as well as being near at hand for the pastor's ready reference. The books should be arranged according to subject. Their number and size should be impressive, and they should be neither new nor brightly colored in appearance. Brightly colored books have the appearance of being light in subject matter and frivolous in approach, and new books suggest not only that they are unused but also a certain transience in belief. Truth is of old and looks best in faded binding.

"Wherein possible, a minister should keep a number of inexpensive devotional books on hand to distribute to appropriate inquirers after first writing a suitable inspirational message inside where it may be seen whenever the book is opened. The message may be composed in advance but should be inscribed in the presence of the inquirer. The effect is, of course, enhanced if the book of devotions has been written or edited by the minister himself."

Pat's office suggested an untidy mind. There was only one window, of stained glass, placed there so the church would look symmetrical from outside. The Good Shepherd in search of the strayed lamb, in memory of Jesse Latham, a man Pat had never heard of. There wasn't even a Latham in the church, yet there was his memorial, forever in search of strayed lambs with no way of arranging the light so as to discourage a persistent petitioner, confessor, or inquirer.

Pat's library was kept at home, and the study bookshelves contained yawning gaps. The books on the shelves were either new reference books or yearbooks and handbooks, full of facts and figures, names and addresses important in the life of the church. There were no inexpensive devotional books to be given away, no portrait picture of his wholesome family at devotions, no open Bible, no inspirational message, no motto regarding his humility, his work, or his attitude toward people, no poem encouraging him to sail on, live by the side of the road and be a friend, build a bridge because he would not pass this way again, or keep his head while everyone else was losing theirs. It was his office, imbued with his own careless, inefficient style, and he felt at home in it.

Pat sat down behind his desk, feeling a pleasant sense of being on the job, of being occupied with something important. Taking Mac Winston's letter from his pocket, he laid it on the desk and read it again. Mac thought he had finally found a place to serve.

In the seminary, Mac had been one of the brightest and most curious students, but none of the professors had time to answer his questions or listen to his ideas. They were too busy preparing for sabbaticals or writing papers for publication.

Most students fretted, cut classes, and talked irreverently about putting in this time—three years until they could get their "union card," the diploma. Mac went from class to class, from professor to professor looking for something that didn't appear in the syllabus; and when in desperation he had cornered a professor in his office, he had been asked how far his knees were from the ground. "Not over twenty inches, would you say? That's how far you are from the truth."

And when Mac had only looked bewildered, the professor in exasperation had explained that he should get on his knees and ask God for the truth.

Mac had been given his diploma, but despite his high

grade average he had not been permitted to study for the doctoral degree because of his "attitude." Nevertheless, Mac had gone to his first pastorate with eagerness. It was a small, rural church, the frame building standing forlornly in a cotton patch at the side of the road. Mac had repaired the church, taken care of his people's needs, and preached simple, thoughtful sermons. Yet, after three years the church members didn't feel "warm" about him, the church had not grown in size, and his superiors agreed that he "lacked inspiration." Mac had held on for one more year before leaving the ministry to teach in the public schools.

Pat picked up a pen determined to write a recommendation that would assure Mac of being engaged in the kind of work he wanted. Mac was unselfish, honest, industrious, intelligent, humble. Then what was wrong with him? He was a failure in the ministry, unhappy out of it. Mac had left the ministry because he could no longer endure the insignificance and hypocrisy, only to discover that neither could he endure the sham and futility of education, law, recreation, or publishing. And now he wanted to try government welfare.

"A man must find the area where he has the greatest tolerance," thought Pat, who had patience with Anna Mae's need for attention, Mrs. Wright's need to be important, Al Worley's need for alcohol, even Sam Sorrele's need for dirt and scandal. He would even endure men who were Christians out of loyalty and ministers who believed in the church rather than God, but he could not abide lawyers who believed in courts rather than justice, or educators who believed in schools rather than education, or doctors who believed in medicine rather than healing.

Pat summarized Mac's qualifications and closed by observing that "Mac Winston's entire career has been spent in the service of others." Relieved to have that out of the way, he turned to the list of people he was to see, looking for those he could shift to another day. "The Book of Tribulations," he called it. "Ten Plagues for the day."

Mr. Hyde had called concerning the Thanksgiving baskets and wanted Reverend Shahan to return the call. It annoyed Pat that he should have to call every year and reassure Mr. Hyde that the church would cooperate in giving the baskets of food when the church had been giving them since long before he became pastor and doubtless would continue as long as there was Thanksgiving and a church on the corner.

Pat disliked the thin-haired, neat little man who held the power of the government over the poor, and the cause of the poor over the city, and always spoke as though he were being quoted by *Life* magazine. "The enemy is not poverty but an economic system which permits poverty." "We do not deal in surplus foods and used clothing, we deal with human dignity and self-respect." "The first obstacle to overcome is the illusion that a man can be poor and happy."

Wanting to be done with Mr. Hyde as quickly as possible, Pat called to inform him in a brisk, businesslike manner that if Mr. Hyde would supply the church with the names and addresses of needy families, the church would give the usual number of food baskets at both Thanksgiving and Christmas, and hinted that the church might possibly aid an additional dozen families if it were necessary.

Mr. Hyde was of course profoundly gratified but wished to notify Reverend Shahan of a change in procedure. Instead of the church members distributing the baskets this year, Mr. Hyde and his staff would distribute them.

"That's rather antiseptic, isn't it?" Pat asked. "I mean, what's the point in us giving if it's going to be so cold-blooded, without any contact with the people to whom we are giving?"

Mr. Hyde appeared to have heard this objection from other ministers, as his answer seemed planned and stiff with repetition. The families had been screened and certified to be worthy of help so that the church would not be guilty of giving a crust of bread to communists, atheists, or other degenerates. The churches would get full credit as the donors and each recipient would be instructed to be grateful.

Pat silently cursed Mr. Hyde, whom he considered not only officious but also prissy. A professional wet nurse. "Social welfare, wet nurse of the world," he thought, "with tea in one breast and tests in the other."

"I'm not talking about whether or not they deserve help. If they need help they deserve it," he said, expressing an opinion he was not certain his parishioners shared, and which was far more liberal than he had ever been in public pronouncements. "And we're not giving the baskets to publicize the church," he said forcefully because he wasn't sure it was true. "We give because we need to give. We need to share what God has given us," he said, making a mental note that he could use that in a sermon. "What I'm trying to say is that there's not much point in giving if we're just going to pour it down a chute. We could just as easily mail the baskets. There has to be some kind of human contact—communication, expression of love."

"Perhaps it is more blessed to give but it is more difficult to receive," said Mr. Hyde. "To be the object of charity is embarrassing, to accept gifts from strangers is humiliating. My co-workers and I deal with these people every day and when we give them a basket of food or a box of used clothing they know it is not from us and that we do not expect nor require a demonstration of gratitude. We do not ask the underprivileged to love us for a can of soup."

"Are you saying that we do?"

"Some do, yes. Perhaps not your church, Reverend Shahan, but some churches give baskets at Thanksgiving and Christmas full of good wishes and brotherly love, exact a demonstration of gratitude, and never return until the next Thanksgiving. It is difficult to accept charity from those who are concerned for you only at Thanksgiving and Christmas, and to be grateful to those who you do not admire."

Pat was infuriated. If there was anything that angered him more than listening to a sanctimonious, irreligious prig, it was having to admit that he was right. It was his church Mr. Hyde was talking about. Hastily assuring Mr. Hyde that the church would cooperate in whatever manner was necessary, Pat hung up.

" 'Perhaps it is more blessed to give, but it is more difficult to receive.' " Not bad. But Pat didn't really believe that pinch-mouthed Hyde had thought of that by himself. It sounded more like a directive from Washington. "READY REPLIES TO COMMUNISTS, COLUMNISTS, AND CHRISTIANS."

Nevertheless, Pat knew that he had seen a portent, a sign, if only he could understand what it meant, if only he could

find the words with which to communicate it to his people.
"It is more blessed to give but more difficult—"
"WHY DID THE CANNIBALS EAT MY MISSIONARIES, PAT?"
"Because they were fat?"

Pat turned back to his duties for the day. He was to call Reverend Gonzalez, who was trying to organize a Protestant bloc at the Council to oppose blocs by the Catholics and Jews.

The Council, an interfaith, interracial body of leading laymen and clergymen, had originally been organized to steer the city through the crisis of public-school integration. The crisis had never materialized and integration had been an accomplished fact for several years, but the Council still met once a month. Pat had only recently become a member, but as best he could determine, it had evolved into a clergy-dominated watchdog committee with no official capacity or authority which concerned itself with the defense of the poor and defeated.

The city was in line to get a shower of gold from the government if they could come up with an acceptable cause. The Council had been delegated to find a cause, and all the churchmen were nominating their pet projects in order to do the most good for everybody. Each group believed that its plan was the only one broad enough to include everyone and that they were the only ones honest enough to handle the money without corruption and distribute it without prejudice.

Pat leaned back in his chair and closed his eyes. This was an important matter to the city, and yet he was reluctant to become involved in it. It seemed the only way to be certain the money was wisely used was to step in and take personal control, and that was what everyone else was trying to do. Every meeting of the Council had become an exercise in gab and grab. The faith and unity they had achieved in a decade of cooperation had disappeared in the rattle of the first coin. "The gold spike has become a wedge," Pat thought.

Not knowing what to do, Pat decided not to call Reverend Gonzalez but to wait until he had more information, perhaps wait until he got to the meeting.

He was supposed to call Harry Nelson. Harry had seen a chapel in California with a revolving neon cross that attracted the troubled and homeless to a minister who waited inside all night to feed, pray with, or counsel those who desired such aid. Harry was a severe, old-fashioned man who always came to church wearing double-breasted suits and starched shirts with high, stiff collars, his hair neatly parted in the middle and combed straight down the sides. He had no family and few needs and wanted to spend the savings of his lifetime to buy a revolving neon cross for the church.

Pat had pointed out that the church was not downtown, that the cross would be visible only to a half-dozen residences at the back of the church, as the spire would shield it from the front, and that if any troubled or homeless people should be attracted by the cross, all they could do would be to look at it, since the church was closed every night except Sunday and Wednesday and was locked up by nine thirty on those nights.

The old man was adamant. He had saved fifteen thousand dollars, and he could think of nothing else he wanted to do with it, since a revolving cross was something you could see for years, while fifteen thousand dollars worth of food, medicine, underwear, or shoes would disappear in a moment, and be enjoyed only by those who received them, leaving no blessing for the giver.

Pat was revolted by the idea of the neon cross grinding round and round on top of the educational building, forgotten and unseen. He had visions of the workmen of another century climbing to the roof top and discovering the cross, still lighted and still turning but completely forgotten by the church.

To Pat the revolving cross was not only a sinful waste of money, but a sacrilege as well—a desecration of the meaning of the cross and the meaning of witness. But he couldn't reason with the old man, who had orders directly from God to buy the cross, and no one else would stand in Harry's way since it was his money. That made it inviolable. "The Eleventh Commandment," thought Pat. "Thou shalt not tell a man what to do with his own money, it being indecent, undemocratic, and nobody's damn business."

"WHAT IS THAT, PAT?"

"Why, Lord, that's your church. Don't you recognize it? There's the J. Roy Folts Memorial Window, the Dorsey Adams Chapel, the Amos-Upton Gymnasium, the E. Turner Whitener Educational Building, the Faye Cunningham Spire, the—"

"WHERE IS MY NAME, PAT?"

"Your name, Lord? Well, it used to be—let's see, it's

either on the corner stone or the communion service."

No, he would not call Harry Nelson. And if the old man called him, he would say the kind of cross the church needed cost at least twenty thousand and send Harry back to pinching pennies again and hope the Lord called him home before he saved it.

With a sigh Pat saw that Emily Graham had made an appointment to see him. That meant another long morning listening to Emily's tale of misery, and his heart had been wrung dry. He had heard it all before. How she had cared for her father while her sisters' husbands got on their financial feet. How afterward her sisters had been too busy promoting their husbands to take care of their father so she could marry Eddie. How Eddie had come driving up to the house in a yellow Buick from Byars Used Car Lot to say he could wait no longer and was going to marry Leona Byars. How, after all she had given up for him, her father had died leaving everything to her two sisters. How they had put her out of the only house she had ever lived in and even accused her of killing her father.

It was a tragic story, and human, and even familiar. He had listened. He had wept. He had prayed for her. He had pulled his hair and beaten his breast. He had talked to her sisters. He had given her the best advice he had, but Emily refused to be reconciled to the past. Her sacrifice for her father, her sisters' betrayal, Eddie's yellow Buick, her father's will were the most real and vital events of her life. She could talk of nothing else. At least twenty years must have passed since Eddie drove his yellow Buick up to her door, and yet none of those years had meaning for her. She could not accept the past, live in the present, or believe in the future. And Emily Graham was coming to him again.

"Okay, Emily, get down off that cross, you've posed long enough. But God isn't going to do that, Emily. He wouldn't do that even for Jesus. You got up there so you can just get down by yourself and give somebody else a turn."

After Emily Graham had finished telling her wounds and collecting whatever tears she could squeeze out of him, he was to counsel a young couple before he married them on Saturday. Why did he always insist on counseling them before he married them? Because he was convinced it did them good? Because it made him superior to know something they were supposedly forbidden to know and he could play the expert, the authority? Because in the seminary they had told him he was supposed to?

"One of a pastor's most delightful duties is marrying the young couples in his church," Dr. Hoffman had lectured. "There are three parts to a minister's obligation when called upon to perform a wedding ceremony. First, there is the Preparation, a counseling session at which time the pastor should cover the spiritual, intellectual, and physical aspects of marriage. The Consummation, that is, the wedding itself, plus the rehearsals and receptions. And what I like to call the Expectation, a pastoral visit after the newlyweds have begun looking forward to the beginning of their family. At that time it is fitting to present them with a book of children's prayers, suitably inscribed by the pastor. Of course, this effect is enhanced if the book has been written or—"

Pat had done it, too. But what marriage had been successfully launched by his counsel? What home saved by his timely advice? What was there to say that was memorable or even meaningful? Had anyone said anything meaningful to him?

Dr. Espey had made marriage seem a necessary though occasionally agreeable qualification for the ministry. His mother had disapproved of Lillian but had approved of marriage. His father had approved of Lillian but had disapproved of marriage. Then he had relented a little. "Do you love her?" he had asked.

They were sitting in the lobby of the small hotel where Pat's father had been living since the divorce. The farm was gone and with it any semblance of home. Now there was only the hotel where his father lived and the apartment where his mother lived. Pat was trying with Lillian to create a home for himself and was startled to find that his father did not object to Lillian, or their youth, or their lack of financial security. He objected to marriage itself. Pat had never before heard an adult disapprove of marriage and he was momentarily confounded. Perhaps it was because of this that his father relented and asked if he loved Lillian. Yet how could he ask it since he had divorced the woman he loved? How could his father believe in love when he could not live with the woman he loved?

Pat could not remember what he had answered his father. Perhaps he had said nothing as it was not easy to believe in what he felt for Lillian if he could not believe in what he saw between his parents. Or perhaps he had said: "What is love, father? Tell me if you know. Am I the product of a loveless match? Am I the child of failure?"

Rachel Elliott. He had to console Rachel Elliott. And her children. Sometime between now and this afternoon he would have to find the words that would comfort Rachel.

Would she be pleased to know that Dr. Espey might read Ray's eulogy? That there might be a commemorative service at the Crusade next year? He would keep it in reserve like the vial of ammonia to be used only if necessary.

Evan Moore. That was an appointment he had made himself. He should have taken care of it before he left for the Crusade but there hadn't been time.

Evan Moore was twenty-four years old, a bachelor, a research chemist, and a Sunday School teacher of sixteen-year-old boys. One of the boys told his father that Evan had kept him after everyone else had left a Sunday School class party at Evan's apartment and had made an indecent and perverse proposal to him. The boy's father was threatening to cleanse the church not only of Evan but of everyone else that didn't meet his standards of masculinity, up to and including the pastor. He was sending his boy to Sunday School to teach him manners, not to make a sissy of him.

Pat didn't know Evan very well; still, it seemed incredible that he could have done such a thing. He had encountered homosexuals before. He had been shocked to find them in college. (Did homosexuals take math?) In the Marines he had heard rumors of them in the Navy. (Were homosexuals patriotic?) He had been distressed to find them in the seminary. (Did homosexuals become pastors? Did they pray? Perform marriages? Comfort the sick?)

Nevertheless he could not believe there was a homosexual in his Sunday School. Not Evan. And although the situation was extremely dangerous, as the church was always vulnerable to scandal, it was difficult to take it seriously. Surely it was a misunderstanding that would be cleared up as soon as he talked to Evan.

"Pastor, I swear to God, I don't know what you're talking about. All I said was 'Study to show thyself.' "

And what if Evan couldn't explain it away? What would he do then? Read the Bible to him? "Thou shalt not covet thy neighbor." Pretend innocence of the whole affair? "I'm surprised that you don't go to St. John's, Evan. It's much closer to where you live, they have a fine pastor, a great choir, and a good bunch of boys."

Be sympathetic? "I'm as broad-minded as any ordinary, normal man."

Philosophical? "Brotherly love is a virtue, Evan. But anything can be carried to excess."

Diplomatic? "Evan, we think you've done a fine job with the class and we're going to move you up to greater opportunities—a class of girls."

But what if Evan really were a deviate? What would he do then? Take him out of the boys Sunday School class for sure. But was he still welcome in the church? Certainly no one cared as long as he kept his problems to himself, as long as his deviation was only a rumor or suspicion. But if Evan had in fact labeled himself and in doing so had disrupted a Sunday School class—

Pat believed the members of his church were for the most part tolerant. But there were some—if the boy's father ever came to church and found Evan, there would be trouble. If Sam Sorrele heard that the church was sheltering homosexuals, he would write an exposé in *The Informer*. And there were some, mostly boys, who, if they knew, would at every opportunity seek to humiliate and embarrass Evan. Then wouldn't it be best if Evan went to another church?

But was it Evan's fault? Did he choose to be that way?

Was it his parents' sin? Or the way he was born? Should the church hold him responsible for the way he was? Punish him for it? Should they try to talk him out of it as though he were an adulterer, try to reform him as though he were a bigot, surround him with women buddies to sit with him when he was tempted as though he were an alcoholic? Or was such a person beyond the aid and comfort of the church?

"In God's house there is room for every sinner," Dr. Hoffman had lectured, "and a place of service for every member."

Surely that was a bit idealistic. Supposedly, the church was for those who needed God, but more realistically it was for those who needed to worship publicly. Ideally, the church was a refuge for guilty, conscience-stricken men. Practically, it was a shelter for those with socially acceptable needs. And where in the church was a homosexual going to serve?

"The doors of the church as the arms of Jesus are spread wide enough to include every sinner no matter how low and every sin no matter how vile," Dr. Espey had said to Pat's father.

Surely that was hypocritical, because Espey's church accepted only polite sinners like seducers and embezzlers and high-class alcoholics. They accepted no one mean enough to be dirty, no one low enough to steal for bread, no one wicked enough to be born black.

Pat decided that regardless of the outcome of his meeting with Evan, he would insist that Evan stay in the church and if some people didn't like it they could leave. And if they don't leave? Then they'll just have to accept Evan. And if they don't accept Evan? Oh, but they will after I have explained the meaning of the church. I am an idealist. A ruptured idealist.

"What, sir, is a ruptured idealist?"

"That, sir, is a pastor who expects the best of his people, but keeps his eye open for a position with another church. A man who walks with his head in the clouds, but keeps his eyes on the ground lest he become entangled in his own entrails."

The intercom buzzed and Pat picked up the telephone. "There's a girl on the telephone who wants to talk to you, but she won't give her name," Mrs. Wright said, her voice heavy with suspicion.

"All right," Pat said. "Put her on."

"Hello, Reverend Shahan? You don't know me but I need some help. I think I'm in trouble."

The voice was that of a young girl and sounded vaguely familiar, but Pat could not place it. "How old are you?"

"Almost sixteen."

"Sandra?" The startled sound at the other end of the telephone told him he had guessed correctly. Sandra Sue McCord. He had held her hand when they removed her appendix. She had babysat with his children. He had presented her with a Bible for Sunday School attendance and memory work. And now she was pregnant and not quite sixteen.

"Oh, God," he said as she began telling him her story. She had babysat for a couple and the man had stopped when taking her home. Pat did not want to know. "Sandra, listen. Stop crying and listen. Where are you?"

"At home. I said I was sick so I wouldn't have to go to school."

"Have you told your parents?"

"Oh, no, I can't. Please, I can't."

"You have to, Sandra. I'll come over and help you."

"Not today. Please not today. This is my father's birthday. I'll die. I'll just die."

"Will you tell them tomorrow? When your father gets home from work? Would you like me to be with you when you tell them?"

"Yes. Why did this have to happen? It wasn't my fault. I couldn't help it. Please don't blame me. Please."

"All right, Sandra. All right," he said, reassuring her even after she had hung up. Sandra Sue McCord. Not even sixteen. How could such a thing have happened? She was such a nice girl. Modest. Intelligent. She made up stories for his children. Dependable. How could she be to blame?

And her parents. The finest people in his church. Not wealthy, or prominent, but decent, honest people. And they loved Sandra. What had they done wrong?

She had almost perfect attendance in Sunday School. She had heard him preach many times. He had had a special service for the young people and talked on "Sins of the Flesh." She had been at church camp where he had lectured for three days on moral responsibility. She had been in his home and seen the love and joy that was there. And in taking her home he had always talked to her as a friend, listened to her problems, given her his best advice. How had he failed her?

"WHOSE SIN WAS THIS, PAT?"

"Lord, it wasn't my fault."

Pat Shahan, sign of the times, receiving strangers, hearing complaints, examining wounds, assigning guilt.
GOD IS WHO YOU BLAME.

The intercom buzzed. "Evan Moore is here to see you," Mrs. Wright said.

"Yes, send him on back," Pat said, taking the horn-rimmed glasses out of his coat pocket and putting them on. What face should he wear? Anger? Disgust? Ridicule? Begrudging sympathy? Pale compassion? Pat selected professional disinterest.

"Come in," he said forcefully when he heard the knock at the door. He didn't get up but Evan reached over the desk and shook his hand anyway. "Have a seat," Pat said, indicating a chair that was not too near the desk, noticing that his cuff links flashed when he gestured and that Evan moved the chair slightly forward when he sat down.

Why had he worn those damn cuff links, which glittered every time he moved his arms and drew attention to his hands, which had once been hard and sunburned from working in the fields and digging foxholes and gunpits but were now soft and pink and almost plump. Self-consciously, Pat dropped them on his knee below the desk and looked at Evan, curious as to whether or not he knew why he had been asked to come.

Evan was of medium height, and although slight, he looked muscular for a chemist. However, you wouldn't be afraid of him on a dark street. His black hair was straight and his features were fine but not effeminate. His voice was soft and tremulous with excitement and he seemed slightly ill at ease, but perhaps that was because the office was strange to him. He also seemed happy to be there, as though he intended to enjoy his visit. However, Pat was not fooled by that. He had known too many people who enjoyed confessing the most odious sins.

"How was the Crusade, Pastor?" Evan asked in his shy but boyishly enthusiastic way.

"Well, it was interesting," Pat said, reaching inside his coat and scratching his armpit in a crudely masculine way. "You meet a lot of characters at a thing like that. There was this television actor I think you might have found interes—" Why had he done that? Why hadn't he talked about the football players instead? —"rather amusing. He was—Evan, the reason I asked you to come—what I wanted to talk to you about was your Sunday School class."

Evan was eager to talk about the Sunday School class. As the teacher he had never missed a single class, he had always been prepared, he tried to visit the boys in their homes, he called them each week to encourage them to come, he tried to sit with them during church services—

Pat watched Evan as he talked, making vague gestures with his hands. He suspected that Evan had tried too hard, been too conscientious, and that all the attention he had given the boys only made the parents suspicious. "Evan, do you feel that the boys like you? That they respect you?"

Evan made vague empty gestures with his hands. He wasn't sure. Maybe some of the boys didn't like him. He didn't know why except that some people just didn't like him. "I know it doesn't seem like we have very good attendance, but some of those boys on the roll don't even live here any more and others live so far from the church they can't come unless their parents bring them. And some of the boys just won't come any more. I go to visit them, I call them every week. I thought maybe if I gave them a party—"

"How many came to the party, Evan?"

"Five. I don't know why the others didn't come. I called them, I sent them an invitation—"

"Where did you meet?"

"At my apartment," Evan said, naming a once fashionable but now run-down section of town. Pat wondered what some of the parents must have thought letting their boys out of the car in front of the unpainted, dirt-streaked apartment house—what the boys must have thought walking up the uncarpeted, dimly lighted stairs. "I guess I could have used the gym," Evan said, "but I thought maybe if they got to know me—"

"Oh, Evan," Pat said. Evan was so vulnerable, such a big, fat target that it was impossible for his shots to miss. "But I am responsible for the church," Pat thought. "For the good of several hundred people. I must not be weak because the wicked suffer. I must not be gentle because sin is hard."

Pat leaned across the desk, frank but kind. "Evan, after the party at your apartment, the father of one of the boys called and said that something had happened to upset his son and that he was never going to let the boy go to Sunday School here again."

For a moment Evan shook his head, making empty gestures with his hands and then he seemed to cave in. For a moment Pat thought he was going to cry.

"I tried to call you right then to give you a chance to

explain, but I couldn't get you and I had to leave for the Crusade. Can you explain, Evan?"

"It wasn't at the party," Evan said. "It was afterward. One of the boys stayed. I thought it would be all right. It would give us a chance to know each other and—"

"Why did he stay?"

"I don't know, he just wanted to."

"But Evan, there must have been some reason for him staying after the others left. Did you ask him to stay, encourage him in any way?"

"I told him he should go on home, that his folks would be worried about him. But he said he didn't want to go home. He just wanted to talk to someone. He wouldn't talk to his parents. He said that he didn't like his father, that he was a mean man. I told him he should talk to his father, make him understand."

"Did he leave then?"

"No, he said he didn't want to go home, he wanted to stay with me."

"Did you let him?"

"I didn't make him go right then, but I told him it didn't look right. His folks might not like it, or some of the other boys might misunderstand, but he said he didn't care. I told him what might happen—how things got twisted up—"

For a moment Evan was unable to speak and then he told Pat how he and two other boys had been playing in the shower after a high-school gym class and didn't hear the bell. The teacher sent another boy after them, and the boy thought he saw something naughty.

"We weren't doing anything, but the teacher reported

us and the principal talked to our parents. It didn't seem to bother the other two boys very much. I mean, they just laughed about it. But my father—he whipped me and said bad things about me. He never let me forget it. He thought —see, I wet the bed until I was fifteen and when I got upset I would throw up, and my father—"

Pat shook his head, amazed once again at the abyss one discovered when he went beyond the routine of shaking hands and inquiring after another's health. A twenty-four-year-old man was ashamed because he had wet the bed in his youth, haunted by his father's suspicion.

"Did you tell the boy that? About wetting the bed and everything?"

"Not everything. I just tried to tell him how people could misunderstand."

Pat began to understand what might have happened when the boy's angry and worried parents had asked him where he had been and what he had been doing. Talking? Talking about what?

"Evan, did you think how that might sound to a sixteen-year-old boy? Don't you think you could have helped him more by sending him home?" Evan didn't say anything, and he looked as though he might cry. Had it been another man Pat might have put his hand on his shoulder to comfort him. "Evan, I have to know. Did you encourage him to stay?"

"I don't know. I told him he ought to go, that his folks would be worried, but I didn't make him go. I know I should have but—he wanted to talk—"

"Don't you have any friends you can talk to?"

"There's a girl across the hall. I talk to her sometimes.

And there's a man at work—we play chess at lunch every day."

Pat listened unwillingly as Evan told him of his loneliness. He had lived in the city for almost two years but had been unable to make friends. Even in the church the only people he knew were boys in his Sunday School class. Evan was completely cut off from normal companionship. Pat didn't like the sound of the old chess player so he decided to back the girl across the hall. Maybe if Evan brought her to church a few times people would forget all the other—especially if she were a knockout.

"Evan, do you ever date this girl across the hall? Bring her to church?"

"Oh, no, she's just a friend."

"Well, it's not right, but in this society if a man your age isn't married he has to appear in public with a woman on his arm or people start looking at him funny."

"I've been married," Evan said.

"Oh, I didn't know—was that before you came here?" Pat asked, hoping that Evan was either a widower or had been divorced for adultery.

"Yes. She went back to her mother."

"And you're divorced?"

"It was annulled."

Pat leaned back in his chair, seeing warning signs everywhere. It was like one of those busted plays in football where everyone in the stadium seemed to be throwing red flags. Evan might not be homosexual, but he was certainly no normal American male always in danger of committing statutory rape.

"How long were you—did you live together?"
"Three weeks."
"Have you ever sought professional help?"
"While I was in college I took some tests. They said not to worry about it. I was—all right."

Pat believed him. He was just a pathetic little man lost somewhere in between the sexes, unable to belong anywhere. Maybe something had been left out of his mother's milk. Maybe all he needed was vitamins. Hormone shots. Confidence. He should set himself a goal each day so that he could achieve it and feel a sense of accomplishment. Make a pass at a female lab assistant. Work up to the big things. Evan had probably started off by marrying the local frigidaire. "Psychology," he thought. "The big lay. Release and achievement."

"I know I haven't done very well with the Sunday School class. Only two boys showed up yesterday. I took the class for selfish reasons. Because I was lonely. I want to resign."

"Evan, I think under the circumstances that's wise. Not because you've done anything wrong, but because there's been a misunderstanding and I think this will help straighten things out."

"Do you want me to go to another church?"

That was a question Pat had hoped he wouldn't have to answer. He had hoped Evan would make his own decision. He could not ask Evan to leave, but could he advise him to stay? A Sunday School class had been disrupted. Some of the boys probably would never come back. He had no way of knowing how disturbed the church membership might be by the gossip and suspicion. But could he protect the ninety and nine by sending the one away?

So far the church had failed Evan. He did not have a single friend in the congregation. Dare Pat believe when they heard the gossip they would come to Evan's assistance? There was much to recommend that he make a fresh start in another church, particularly since he had no emotional ties to this one. It was not the church of his youth, or of his family and friends. Probably nothing dramatic, nothing memorable had happened to him here. It seemed to Pat that it would be easier to leave, but would that mean defeat to Evan? Rejection?

"Evan, please try to understand this. I think it might be difficult for you here. I think it might be easier to make a fresh start somewhere else. But if you want to stay, if you think we can help you, then I want you to stay."

"I guess I'll go some place else," Evan said.

"Is it because we failed you?"

"I don't belong here."

"Evan, I want you to know that I wish you the best of luck. That I'll be praying for you. That I care what happens to you. I just wish—" Seeing Evan pulling himself together to leave, Pat stood up and offered him his hand.

"Evan, this friend of yours—the old man. Is he—I mean, do you think he's the kind of friend—"

Suspicion clouded Evan's large brown eyes. "What do you mean?" he asked.

Why? Pat asked. Why did I do that? Destroy his last bridge. Cut off his only escape. It reminded him of his training in the Marines to bayonet the bodies of the enemy to be certain they were dead. To leave nothing to chance—nothing undone. "Stick 'em if they don't stink," the D.I.'s said. Had he instinctively gone for the jugular?

"You think there's something wrong with him?" Evan asked. "That he thinks—"

"Evan, I'm sorry," Pat said, awkwardly trying to restore what he had so eloquently destroyed. Evan seemed scarcely to hear as he groped blindly for the door.

Pat caught the doorknob in his hand to stop Evan from leaving. He had to offer him something—some means of relating, some place of belonging. "Evan, stay in the church. Give us a chance to help you."

"I'd better go," Evan said, his voice coming from deep in his throat as he tried to keep from sobbing.

"Evan, I'm sorry. Please give me another chance."

"I don't know anybody here. It was—just a place to go."

Pat released the doorknob and Evan opened the door and stepped outside the office. "Thank you, Pastor," he said politely, perhaps out of habit.

"Thank you for coming," Pat said foolishly. "And thank you, Lord, for sending him," he said, sitting down with a sigh. He had failed Evan and he was acutely aware of it.

Perhaps he should be thankful that the church had not meant more to Evan. Just a place to go. But where would Evan go now that he no longer had this place? And how many times had Pat longed for a place to go? He thought of the special loneliness of a barracks full of sleeping men, of spending Christmas day in the deserted streets and closed shops of a strange town, of walking along crowded beaches, through noisy amusement parks. What was he looking for? A place to go. A friendly face, although it be a strange one. Someone to sing with though the song be new. Someone to pray with though the prayer be silent.

Pat wondered how many others came to church for a place to go. Al Worley, because alcohol did not make one sing. Sam Sorrele, because bigotry did not make one happy. Walter Miles, because there was much to forget. Ann Ostergaard, because there was no place else.

Pat remembered sitting in the house and listening to the laughter of children playing in the snow. What had he wanted? To belong to that happiness. To be included in that thoughtless joy.

"DID HE ASK FOR BREAD, PAT?"

"Yes, Lord, I gave him a stone. And Lord, thank you for the opportunity."

Pat Shahan, menace of God, battering the walls of Jericho, defending the faith, dividing the sheep from the goats.

GOD IS MY ROCK.

"The minister of God is dressed not in the gowns of judgment but in the robes of mercy," Pat said, addressing the awed and envious seminary students. "He is not the defender of the past but the frontiersman of tomorrow. He is not the sign of the times but the intimation of the eternal. He stands on the watch tower not only to warn of fire and rain but also to keep a light in the window. He does not guard the treasure but gives it away. He runs not for the glory of running but to set the captive free. He knows that to speak with the voice of God is not to wave the banners of tradition, nor to shout the slogans of righteousness, but to call nations to justice and societies to repentence. He believes that to wear the mantle of the prophet is to—"

There was a rap on the door and Pat started, reluctant to leave the glory and security of his inspired audience. "Yes, what is it?" he asked.

Orin Kilgore, church clerk and treasurer, opened the door and stuck his head in. "Got a minute?" he asked.

"Sure, come in," Pat said, looking away so as not to reveal his irritation. Why didn't Orin just open the door and walk in like anyone else instead of working his way in head first.

"Glad to see you back, Pastor," Orin said, crossing the room to shake Pat's hand. "How was the Crusade?"

Pat winced at the question. "I think it went pretty well," he said, trying to measure the Crusade in Orin's cup, weigh it on his scales. "They had very good attendance, and when I left they had just about broken even on the budget and they had one more service to go. I imagine they'll come out with enough to cover any incidental expenses and maybe some advance promotion for next year. You heard about Ray?"

"Too bad," Orin said, sinking into a chair. "You know he was one of our most faithful members. I sent some flowers to Mrs. Elliott and there'll be a nice wreath for the funeral. I'd like to send her something a little more personal—a book of poems or something, but the way the budget is right now—"

"Whatever you want to do, Orin," Pat said, not wanting to have to decide whether or not the budget could afford a book of poems for a widow. "How have things been here?"

"Well, we're down a little in receipts. Not as well as we did last year. In fact, we've been consistently down over what we did five or six years ago when we had the Every

Member Canvass, the Over The Top Push, Victory Sunday, and all that."

Pat was annoyed at what he took to be personal criticism. He didn't get the money in the way E. Harrison Ledbetter, former pastor, had done. It was Pat who had abolished the campaign, the canvass, the pledge, the parade, the whole ritual of temple tax collecting. He had decided if God's people couldn't give freely without coercion then they shouldn't give. Unfortunately, that was exactly what had happened. Some people felt no necessity of giving to the church if they weren't threatened with punishment or promised a reward.

"After spiritual awareness, intellectual ability, and physical well-being, a minister's greatest virtue is financial responsibility," Dr. Hoffman had said. "This means close, personal supervision of the budget. No pastor shall stand faultless before the Savior of all men on the Day of Judgment who has neglected his financial duty to the church. First, he must challenge his people to adopt a sacrificial budget. Second, he must lead his people to faithfully subscribe the budget. Third, he must personally supervise the budget. And last of all, he must diligently teach his people the spiritual rewards of sacrificial giving—giving until it hurts.

"Let us consider the first: subscribing the budget. Survey after survey has convinced us that the best method of subscribing the budget is through the skillful utilization of the Pledge Card. And by skillful utilization, I mean get the card out, get it signed, and get it back."

Orin shifted uncomfortably in his chair. "I know you don't like that kind of thing, but it gets the money."

"Get the card out, get it signed, get it back," Pat said.

"I know budgets are difficult for a minister to understand," Orin said, "but when Dr. Ledbetter was pastor we could count on subscribing the budget on Victory Sunday and oversubscribing it on Clean Up Sunday."

"If you had a Victory Sunday why did you need a Clean Up Sunday?"

"Well, not everybody kept their pledge. Some people had hard luck and some people just wouldn't do what they said they would. We had to oversubscribe the budget by fifteen to twenty per cent to come out even."

"Good old Christian pragmatism."

"You can call it what you want to, but it worked," Orin said cheerfully. "The thing is, we are approaching the end of the year and those months aren't very good. September and October—everyone is a little short because the kids are starting back to school and education costs so much these days. November is Thanksgiving and everyone is planning on a big dinner or going out of town. And then Christmas, and people just don't have any money during Christmas. There's just too many gifts to buy and charities to give to. January—people still haven't gotten over Christmas."

Pat sighed and leaned back in his chair. "We're in trouble," he admitted grimly, thankful that he was wearing the late Mr. Weatherby's suit. He didn't want Orin to think he was overpaid.

"Well, you were gone last week and that hurt us. It sort of takes the pressure off when the pastor's not here. Some people feel that they don't have to come if the pastor's not here, and if they don't come, they don't feel that they have to give. Then too, a lot of folks are sick."

"How bad is it?" Pat asked. He hated watching dollars and always tried to ignore finances, hoping that everything would work out, but Orin Kilgore loved crises. Disaster was sweet in his mouth, and more than anyone else he loved to alarm the pastor.

"I've kept a close eye on things, and so far I've kept us out of trouble. But I thought maybe you'd ask the church staff to watch their spending until I'm sure we're going to make it all right. Even for budgeted items. That includes you of course."

Pat studied the treasurer for a moment. "I've already pledged the Thanksgiving and Christmas baskets."

"Well, it's in the budget," Orin admitted. "But don't give any more than you have to. I've already spoken to the other staff members, but if you'd talk to them also it'd give it a lot more weight. You might say something to the church, too, if you would. They'll give but you've got to stay after them all the time."

"All right," Pat said. "Okay. I will speak to the church staff. I will guard the turkeys. And I will beg the congregation to support the budget. And if that doesn't do it, I will sit in the church door with my hat in my hand." Pat paused, thinking his scorn might drive the treasurer out of the office, but Orin patiently waited. "Yes?"

"Well, I'm trying to cut expenses wherever I can. We give away an awful lot of Bibles. To every child in the church on the Sunday preceding his twelfth birthday. As prizes for Bible reading and memory work. To shut-ins. To people in the old folks' home. Last year you gave away over a hundred Bibles to people who asked for them. Mostly jails and hospitals, I believe. Here's the point. We're giving away good Bibles. I mean, fine-quality, leather-back. We can save almost two dollars a copy by giving an imitation leather, plastic-bound Bible that looks just as good, and will last—"

"Okay," Pat said. "All right."

"One other thing. The Building and Grounds Committee was budgeted two thousand dollars for fertilizer."

"Fertilizer?"

"For the lawn. We've got a big lawn. Of course, that's for the spring and fall, the trees, the hedges around the parking lot and the pot plants in the library, nursery, and so forth. And like they say, it's a witness. People drive by and they see a neat lawn, and a well-kept building and a hedge around the parking lot and they think that's the kind of church they want to belong to. Now, granted, this is good fertilizer. It's clean, it's easy to spread, no odor, and it's enriched. Also it contains an insecticide. You won't find any ants on our lawn. Now we can get a local fertilizer, not quite as good, but at a savings of three or four hundred dollars and I thought—with finances the way they are—"

"Buy it," Pat said.

"Well, that's just it. I can get it, but it's going to make some people on the Building and Grounds Committee pretty sore if I start cutting their budget after it was approved. And we're ordering it through Tom Glazener. You know he's on the committee. So, I thought if you'd—"

"You mean I've got to call all those people and sell them on the efficacy of cheap fertilizer?"

"It could mean four or five hundred dollars."

"Why in the hell do I have to sell cow manure?" Pat

shouted, and was instantly sorry as he saw Orin's face go white. "I'm sorry, Orin," he said. "I shouldn't have lost my temper."

"It's not my money," Orin said in righteous indignation. "It's the Lord's money, but it's still four hundred dollars."

A soft answer inspires abuse, Pat thought, determined not to give Orin the upper hand. "Give me their names and I'll have Mrs. Wright contact them. And if they don't want the local product, I'll go out and talk to them personally. And if that doesn't do it, I'll preach on it Sunday. 'Build your church on a local dung heap.' How does that sound?"

"I was just trying to do my job," Orin said, trying to back down gracefully. "What I thought the Lord would want me to do."

God wanted him to buy cheap fertilizer. There was no way to argue with that, as the Lord had not indicated a preference to Pat. "Who's on the committee?"

"Paul Dudley, Harry Nelson, Tom Glazener, and Virgil Bandelier."

Paul Dudley, a young architect, would be no problem. He was easy-going, wanted to do a good job, and would back the pastor. Virgil Bandelier would follow the path of least resistance. Tom Glazener would have to be handled carefully. There must be no intimation that he had been the one who recommended the expensive fertilizer or that he would in any way financially profit. Tom would retreat if he were given a place into which he could gracefully withdraw. Harry Nelson was such a tightwad he would use human fertilizer to save money. But if he called Harry he would have to listen to the revolving cross again.

"Harry, I've got a great idea," he could say. "Instead of a revolving neon cross why don't you permanently endow the lawn? The Harry Nelson Perpetual-Care Lawn. It would be a great witness to any homeless wanderers who happened to drive past the church. With a sign 'As You Grow So Shall You—' "

"All right, I'll take care of it," Pat said. "Is that everything? Anybody else you'd like me to talk to?"

"I hate to ask you to do it," Orin said, backing out of the office, working his way out as carefully as he had worked his way in. "I know it's hard for a minister to understand, but the way the budget is—"

"It's all right," Pat said, as Orin closed the door behind him. "That's what I get paid for. To run errands. Count change. A pastor is financially responsible. A pastor is thrifty. A pastor is a friend to all and a brother to the rich. A pastor's duty is to be useful and to help others. To pluck gold coins out of sows' ears and to make pearls from swine's teeth."

The intercom buzzed. "Mr. Sorrele would like to talk to you," Mrs. Wright said.

"Okay, and while I'm talking to him would you try to contact the members of the Building and Grounds Committee? Paul Dudley, Harry Nelson, Virgil Bandelier. I'll talk to Tom Glazener myself. Tell them for financial reasons we would like to buy a cheaper fertilizer. For the lawn. A local—product. Tell them it's not as good but less expensive."

"You want to buy cheap fertilizer."

Pat resisted the impulse to tell Mrs. Wright that it was not he who wanted it but the Lord. "Right. Just see if there's any strong objection."

"Mr. Nelson has been trying to get in touch with you. I'm sure he will want to speak to you personally."

"Well, tell Harry that I will call him as soon as I have time but right now all I want is his approval on this—item."

"I'll put Mr. Sorrele on."

"Hello, Sam? If this is about Bob Harkins, I have made up my mind," Pat said. Bob Harkins, an old Negro man, had decided in an unassuming yet obstinate way that he was going to join the church. He was the first Negro ever to have sought membership in the church, and Pat knew that this also was an indictment. Pat thought that Bob Harkins might cause some confusion and disorder in the church, but he believed the congregation would get over it.

Politely, he listened as Sam ranted in his super-charged, emotional, slightly irrational way. There was something captivating about Sam's voice. He had once had his own radio program, until he had been forced off the air because of his attacks on ethnic groups, and he was a popular public speaker. But the attraction wasn't his voice, which was hoarse, nor his mannerisms, which were coarse, nor his ideas, which were both stereotyped and difficult to follow. Pat believed it was the fascination of the unpredictable, that people listened because they never knew when Sam would go over the edge and become completely irrational. Entranced, Pat listened as Sam told of his vision—the world being overrun by colored people. "They're in the schools, in the Armed Forces, in the government. They sit on the highest benches of the land. The church stands as the last citadel of virtue, of morality, of purity. That's why they are so desperate to get in here. So they can destroy civilization. Send us back to the dark ages of Africa."

Pat tried to interrupt, but Sam shifted to a description of himself with his finger in the dike, holding the fort, stemming the tide. "Have you thought who's behind all this?" Sam shouted. "Have you asked who put Bob Harkins up to it? Who would profit most by the mongrelization of our society, the destruction of America, the only bulwark against Communism in the world?"

"No one put him up to it, Sam," Pat said, calmly, remembering the old man standing outside Mrs. Wright's office with his hat in his hand. He didn't want to cause any trouble. He didn't believe in trouble in a church. But he was going to come Sunday, he had made up his mind on it and wasn't nobody going to stop him from trying. Pat had asked him to wait until he returned from the Crusade so he could be there to welcome him, and also to try to control any situation that might develop. "This is something he decided all by himself," Pat said.

"He couldn't have decided it by himself," Sam said. "The smartest nigger alive couldn't have decided. It's too clever. Too diabolically clever. If he decided it himself why did it take him sixty years to get around to doing it?"

"Times have changed," Pat said, remembering the way the old man had said it, more in bewilderment than anger. 'Times is changed.' Pat had only seen the man one time, but he liked him and he believed he understood him. He had been a faithful servant to white men and a respected member of his own community. He had never asked for equal rights for himself, he had never tried to go where he wasn't wanted, he had never tried to be other than what he was. But times had changed. Now people laughed at his ancient dignity and the pride he took in his job. Probably they called him Uncle Tom. Perhaps his own children were ashamed of the courteous and humble attitude that was his sole marketable skill. And now the man's pride and dignity demanded that he ask for what was rightfully his—that he take a stand. "It's not outside agitators who have gotten to Bob, it's time itself," Pat said.

"There'll be trouble if he comes to church."

"There may be. But if someone has to be hurt or embarrassed or humiliated, it's going to be you or me. It's not going to be Bob Harkins."

Sam began ranting again. He knew his power. He knew what he could do. Pat listened unalarmed. Sam's newspaper had already caught the ear of the crackpots in the city. There was nothing he could say that he hadn't said before. The churches were being duped by the communists, used by the devil. Those who read Sam's paper knew it already. Those who didn't know wouldn't learn by reading his paper.

"There are things going on in this church, which if known, would turn this city upside down," Sam said.

Evan! Was that it? Sam had heard about Evan, and he was going to use him as a wedge to keep Bob Harkins out of the church. Unless Pat stopped Bob from joining the church, Sam would expose Evan. Scandal in local church —Services have been disrupted and the membership divided by rumors of—It was reported that—Members believed— The general feeling was—

What could he do? He couldn't let Sam destroy Evan

after he had personally set him up for destruction. Yet to exclude Bob Harkins from the church would not only humiliate the old man, it would also be an affront to most of the world. The newspapers would crucify the church on the altar of public opinion. Was it better to let Evan be branded homosexual by a local scandal sheet or to embarrass Bob Harkins and have the church labeled bigoted by the wire services?

"We give food to deadbeats who disparage our whole way of life. We pay dues to the National Council of Churches, which has denied God and publicly proposed the admission of Red China into the U.N. We have sent medicine to India, where every drop of it goes to save Communist lives."

Pat breathed a sigh of relief. Sam was talking about money.

"And there are others who feel the same way. Who won't give one dime to a gutless church that doesn't stand on the principles that made this country great," Sam said, hanging up.

That could be trouble. Fortunately, there weren't many in the church who agreed with Sam, but there were always some who were looking for an excuse not to support the church, and Red China was a good excuse. Always the first sign of trouble in the church was the loss of financial support. When people didn't feel loved by the pastor and sheltered by the church they didn't give. And the way the budget was— He would have to find some way of shoring up that wall. Reluctantly, he turned to the church files for a copy of the budget. The intercom buzzed.

"Pastor, Jack Merrick called and asked if you could meet him at his club for lunch. He said it wasn't necessary for you to call, that I could let his secretary know."

"Fine. Tell him that I'll be happy to," Pat said, automatically checking to see how he was dressed. The Samaritan Club was exclusive and he didn't want to embarrass Jack. "Would you tell Mrs. Shahan I won't be home for lunch."

Good old Jack Merrick, he thought. An oasis in the demands of the morning. Jack Merrick was president of the local power and light company, a civic leader, a college trustee, and served on the Board of Directors of six different companies. Jack's grandfather had made the family fortune through ruthless and sometimes dishonest practices, but Jack was thoroughly respectable, philanthropic, and of a liberal mind. Pat enjoyed his company because, although he was a member of Pat's church, Jack never required anything of him as pastor. For a time today Pat would be able to escape his image as a pastor and his theological vocabulary, and they could talk about the city and its problems and Jack's political plans.

Jack believed the best way he could serve the city was in politics, and he was planning to run for city council, perhaps eventually mayor. For this reason he had firmly and deliberately identified himself as President of the Power Company. His economy drives had kept the electrical rates lower than those of surrounding cities, the new power plant brought electricity to low-income areas, and opening the company's diversion lake to the public had made a free, unrestricted playground available to all. With these credits in his hand, Jack intended to appeal to the voters as a man who could bring economy to the city government, develop low-income areas, and eliminate discrimination.

For a moment Pat wondered if he should tell Jack of the financial difficulties of the church. Jack would help out if Sam Sorrele and others tried to financially undermine the church. But it would be awkward to ask while eating lunch at Jack's expense. It was always difficult to be a mendicant for the church while taking handouts for yourself.

Of course Jack could afford to buy him a meal, and Dr. James could afford to treat him without charge, and Al Worley could afford to sell him a car at cost, and Mrs. Wright, Anna Mae Rogers, Emily Graham, Marjorie Zinkgraf, and others could afford to give him cuff links, ties, handkerchiefs, and the very wallet in which he carried his money. He had eight suits, seven of them gifts from his parishioners. Three of them had been bought for him, four had been practically new suits of departed relatives. The eighth suit had been a gift from his mother. He owned three watches, a cheap but still accurate Bulova that had been a gift from his parents when he had graduated from high school, a sturdy, ugly watch he had bought at the P.X. when he thought he was going to Korea, and a luxury watch Jack Merrick had given him. Such gifts were tax-deductible, and evidenced love not only for the pastor but also for God, church, and right. Pat found them impossible to refuse without offense and impossible to accept without compromise.

"WHY ARE MY MISSIONARIES FAT, PAT?"

"It's all that pottage we have to eat, Lord."

Pat decided to say nothing of church finances to Jack. Perhaps later if necessary. Instead, he picked up the telephone and dialed Tom Glazener. That could be four hundred dollars.

Taking a chance, Pat explained the necessity of cutting down expenses and asked Tom for a recommendation. Tom, rising to the bait, knew where they could get fertilizer at a cheaper price than they were paying. Commending him profusely, Pat encouraged him to investigate and challenged him to save every cent possible.

With that accomplishment under his belt, Pat pulled the budget out of the files and carefully studied it, determined to save some more. The total budget seemed a staggering amount of money, yet it was all considered essential by the church members. Promotion, telephones (nine of them?), literature, office supplies, insurance, repair of the parking lot (if people could only walk to church, but most of the members lived two or more miles away), building maintenance. The church was still paying for a house they had bought and torn down before he became pastor, just so the church could be seen from the proposed expressway. They used more venetian blinds than a hospital, more folding chairs than a restaurant, more carpet than a movie theater, more paper and stencils than an elementary school. The money they spent on utilities alone would avert famine in a small city, yet the church had to be lighted, and heated, and cooled. The typewriters had to run, the toilets to flush.

"The stained-glass museum," Pat thought. A million-dollar building containing—what? A scattering of fading symbols, a handful of worn legends and dusty relics. A new early American altar, an old Gothic pulpit, a fifty-rank pipe organ, of which less than half the pipes worked and some of those were out of tune, two rows of distinctive pews built by dedicated union carpenters, and emergency food and water supplies for four hundred people in the event of a nuclear attack. "The paradox of the church," Pat thought. "The penniless Jesus on the cross of gold."

Very well, he would meet the budget if he could not cut it. He would ask Jack Merrick in the name of God to buy a little manure for the church. And Sunday he would stand before the congregation and plead with them to support the Lord's work of making the grass grow green. "I'll give them the 'Jesus was born in a log cabin' bit. That'll shake a few shekels out of them. And while they're reaching for their handkerchiefs I'll admonish them to dig deeper until their fingers touch the magic coin that will roll away the stone, and once again we will resurrect the green grass to the glory of God."

The intercom buzzed. "Reverend Gonzalez would like to speak to you," Mrs. Wright said.

"All right, put him on."

"By the way, I've contacted Paul Dudley and Virgil Bandelier and they said they'd go along with whatever you wanted."

"Fine. Thank you."

Leaning back in his chair, Pat listened to the musical, urgent voice of Reverend Gonzalez describing the struggles of the Council to come up with a project. The Catholics wanted to set up a Literacy Center on the south side of town. "But you know who lives on the south side of town," said Reverend Gonzalez. "They're all Catholics. That's not going to help our people any." The Jews wanted the funds for a city Fine Arts Commission. "You know who would be on the Commission, don't you?"

The Protestants had a chance of getting the money if they could only agree on a project. The Episcopalians didn't have a project of their own, but they favored a city Fine Arts Commission. The Congregationalists wanted a Rehabilitation Center downtown that would be open to all races and creeds, and the Methodists favored a Children's Shelter open to all races and creeds, and the Presbyterians wanted a Literacy Center, but on the west side of town. "They want to run it in the church basement," said Reverend Gonzalez. The Baptists were opposed to the government giving the money and to the church taking it. "But the government is going to give it to somebody," said Reverend Gonzalez. "We have to decide who should get it."

Pat listened in dismay. They were all good projects, all worthy of his support; therefore, he would have to choose on the basis of which group should have control. This was a decision he did not want to have to make but he promised Reverend Gonzalez to decide before the meeting began.

"I am not thrifty," Pat said, putting the budget back in the file. "I am not financially responsible. I am not a friend to all and a brother to the rich."

"Now abideth faith, hope, and thrift," said Brother Paul. "But the greatest of these is thrift."

"God is thrift," said Brother John.

"Crap," said Pat. The only really financially responsible one had been Judas. Hadn't he endowed a cemetery for the poor? That was at least as Christian as a church lawn.

Maybe it was time for a fall cleaning, Pat thought. Periodically the money changers needed to be driven from the temple. Throw the rascals out. But he had observed that those who did the cleaning were usually careful not to throw out the money as well, and that the cleaners usually hung around long after the changers had departed.

"Yes," he said, picking up the buzzing telephone.

"I have Mr. Nelson on the line. He thinks he is ready to go along with you on the fertilizer, but he would like to talk to you about it first."

"I was just leaving the office," Pat said. "Tell him I'll call him later," and dropping the telephone he stepped out into the quiet, darkened sanctuary. He stood for a moment listening to the silence and then he sat down in a pew and closed his eyes.

There was something about the place, flawed though the building might be. There was something about the darkness, the silence—Pat did not delude himself about what he felt. Part of it was the height of the ceiling, and the refracted light of the stained glass. Part of it was sentimentality, nostalgia, the association of remembered things—his mother's colorful yet grave hats, the powdered smell of old ladies, the rattle of the offertory, the solemnity of the choir, the familiar songs, the stiff, somnolent reverence. It was like visiting a long-silent battlefield, yet aware of what had taken place there, the drowsy silence imbued with bloody significance. The whispered prayers, the wrestling with angels, the songs of joy, the fleeting visions seemed to give the silence a special flavor, a breath of incense.

And there was a Presence—familiar as death, peaceful as love. He had felt it before. In the rain-threatened wheat field, under the oak trees of a college campus, on the signs and billboards of busy highways, SAVE, HELP, SERVE, on the dreary, sun-baked grounds of a seminary, in the crowded streets and on the beaches of liberty towns, in a park of obsolete antiaircraft guns, in his study as he wrote his sermons, and sometimes even here, in the bomb shelter called the House of the Lord.

"Can I see you a minute?"

Pat opened his eyes. It was Gordon Dean, choir director. "This will just take a minute. You know we've been preparing this special music program? Well, the choir has worked real hard on it and they're going to do a real good job. I'm just real proud of them. Well, I don't think many people from our church are going to come. You know what I mean? They figure it's not church unless someone is preaching, and then on Sunday night a lot of them just aren't going to come anyway. And I'd like for the choir to be heard. You know? They've worked just real hard. Why couldn't we run an ad or two in the paper to let people know about it?"

"Okay," Pat said. They all knew his weakness. Catch him while he was running from something else. "I think after all that work they deserve to be heard."

"Well, I've already talked to Orin and he said no."

When would he ever learn? It hadn't been half an hour since he had promised Orin he would hold down the spending. "How much would the ad cost?" he asked.

"I don't know. See, we're already over the budget on this thing. But if there isn't anybody here to hear them, it's just going to kill the choir after all the work they've done."

"I'll see if I can't find the money some place," Pat said, trying to decide whether he wanted to ask Orin or Jack Merrick for it.

IN THE HOUSE OF THE LORD

"Would you, Pat? That sure would help. I can't get any money at all out of Orin. He acts like it's his money."

"He's just doing his job," Pat said, a bit too sharply. Since he had already criticized Orin for this, he felt obliged now to defend him. "I'll try to get it for you."

As soon as Gordon was out of sight, Pat slipped up to the balcony and sat down. They never looked for him there.

How different things looked from here. How gloomy and empty it seemed. The pews were dusty and worn, the sunlight that filtered through the stained glass faded wearily into the carpeted floor. How small the pulpit looked from here. And how small he must appear standing behind it. "Where is it?" he asked. "Where has it gone?" Where was the truth he had seen in a wheat field, the grandeur he had known in a moonlit field of alfalfa, the significance he had discovered in a tank of drowning bees, the purpose he had sought in a park of obsolete guns?

Where was he who had dreamed of speaking with the voice of God? Singing for pennies. Where was he who had desired to probe men's hearts for beauty, goodness, and truth? Searching their pockets for coins. Where was he who dared to call nations to justice and societies to repentance? Scrambling for crumbs from the government's table. Where was he who wanted to bring forgiveness, to set the captives free? Selling indulgences for the price of a hand-painted tie or a practically new suit. Where was he who sought the mantle of the prophet? Dressed in the coin of the realm.

Once, in Mexico, while trying to take a picture of a church, Pat had discovered a vantage point from which he could see the poor, the crippled, the penitent crawling into the front of the church while burly guards loaded an armored car with money at the back of the church. The poor, the diseased, the penitent crawled into the church and were carried out the back as gold. What the alchemists had sought, the church had discovered.

"WHAT IS MY CHURCH, PAT?"

"Lord, it's a den of thieves. But we're polite. And we do it for You. Lord, it's a storehouse and we guard it well, but we can't keep out all the poor. They multiply like mice. Lord, it's a refuge in the event of a nuclear attack. Four hundred of us will be saved."

"DO YOU LOVE ME, PAT?"

"Yes, Lord, I love you."

"FLEECE MY SHEEP."

Pat Shahan, a man of savings and acquainted with greed, hunting in green pastures, fishing in still waters, helping himself.

GOD IS THE OFFERING I TAKE.

Pat sat nodding sympathetically as he listened to Emily Graham's tale of woe. He had heard it all before many times and he had been sympathetic, understanding, patient. He had shared her agony, he had raged at the injustice of it all, he had wept at her suffering. But he was drained dry. She had milked the last tear from him. She had squeezed the last drop of blood from his heart that had been squeezed, and bruised, and pounded until it had turned to stone. Pat set his face and chewed his lip and shook his head to appear sympathetic, and understanding, and patient. That was the best he could do.

As he listened, Pat tried to avoid looking at Emily. She was a coarse, pear-shaped woman with short arms, whiskers on her chin, and large, ill-fitting false teeth. She sat slumped in the chair so that her massive bosom and broad hips strained the seams of the long-sleeved brown dress, which had lacy cuffs to cover the scars on her wrists. Her puffy ankles stretched the cotton hose and hung over the square-heeled shoes, and her hat looked like a wet dog curled up on a gunny sack. "The Eleventh Commandment," he thought. "The object of mercy shall appear worthy of it."

Pat had been quietly daydreaming in the balcony when Mrs. Wright had found him and told him that Miss Graham was waiting to see him. After apologizing for disturbing his meditations. He had gotten to Mrs. Wright on that, but still he could no longer use the balcony as a place of refuge. Where would he go now? Hide in the broom closet with Mr. Murph? Maybe he should try the men's room again. He had used it for three weeks before Mrs. Wright had found him and stood outside tapping on the door. "Brother Shahan, are you in there? Miss Graham is here to see you." Angrily he had flushed all the toilets in the men's room to relieve his feelings. Six gallons of water down the drain. To hell with the price of water.

To hell with Mrs. Wright. To hell with Emily Graham and the whole damn whining Western civilization. He was sick of it. Nowhere on earth had people had so much and enjoyed so little. The Eleventh Commandment: Thou shalt bite the hand that feeds thee and thy fortune thou shalt curse.

Those who had everything complained because they heard there were some who did not. They wrapped their riches tightly about them and wept bitterly over those who had nothing. Never before had the poor been so loved, so pitied, so talked about. Never before had there been so many tears. Everyone wept over the hopeless and the hungry that they might not need to act. Never before had there been so many tormented, so many persecuted, each man studying his own slights that he might not have to see the stripes of his neighbor.

Pat could not understand it. All his life, no matter what condition he was in, it seemed to him that he was among the most favored of all men. Yet others more fortunate asked for his tears, others more gifted asked for his help.

Emily paused to wipe at her eyes. She had reached the first crisis. Her two older sisters had told her she shouldn't marry and leave their poor father alone, promising that when their husbands were established, they would take him, leaving her free to marry. They had promised. Could they have asked it of her if they loved her?

Well, he didn't know, but he suspected they could. He didn't have any brothers or sisters, but he knew that his father could love him and ask him not to be a minister but to give himself to hanging on to the farm. He knew that his mother could love him and yet ask him not to marry Lillian so she could keep him by her side.

Pat leaned forward in his chair and cleared his throat to indicate he was going to say something. On previous occasions he had discussed A Grateful Child Is A Joy Forever, Honor Thy Father And Thy Mother And They Will Rise Up And Call Thee, but Emily did not feel rewarded.

He had explained To Forgive Is Divine And To Forget Is Just As Good, To Return Good For Evil Is To Show

Your Sisters You Are A Better Christian Than They Are, but Emily had not forgiven.

He had reminded her of those whose pains and injustices were even greater than her own. Omitting only the names, he had told her of Lucy Gillespie, afraid to die, yet painfully aware that each day she clung to life she was loading her family with debts they could scarcely repay. Of Al Worley, who for thirty years had lived with a woman who despised him because he had dutifully married her. Of Ann Ostergaard, who had been the subject of betrayal, then injustice, and now jest. But Emily had not been comforted.

Words were a way of life to Pat. Fulfillment and release. Meaning and method. Words were the tools with which he reached his people, to explain, to express, to comfort. When he was young, he had prayed for opportunities to preach, so full was he of words. He had spoken to Emily, he had explained, and described, and expressed, yet Emily was back again.

What was he to say now? Should he recapitulate? Should he recount her blessings, perhaps discovering some he had omitted before? Or should he make one more effort to find the key? At first he had believed he could help Emily, could save her from despair, but he believed it no longer. He listened, let her cry on his shoulder, and whenever she pressed hard enough he tried to find the words. "Although the Apostle Paul says that love seeks not its own, most of us have discovered the reverse, that love makes demands—"

Emily began talking again and Pat gave up. One reason he had never been able to help her was because she never listened to him. She was always too busy listening to her own whimpers. But then maybe he had never said anything worth listening to—

Pat heard the flat, complaining voice. It was an unpleasant sound—the voice of a woman who lived alone with a deaf and aging father, a woman who talked to herself because there was no one to listen to her, a woman who had no one to whisper with.

"—Eddie wanted to get married right then, he wanted—"

At least not since Eddie had grown impatient and had married a girl he didn't have to wait for, whose father owned a used car lot. Formulating his response, Pat waited for Emily to get to the part where Eddie came driving up to the house in a yellow Buick from the used car lot to tell her he couldn't wait any longer. "Bought off," she would say bitterly. "He said he would wait but he was bought."

He had already covered Be Thankful You Found Out What Kind Of Man He Was In Time, True Love Finds A Way (Liberally Illustrated With Examples From The Narrator's Life), and The Currency Of Love Is Fair Play Not Fore Play. Today he would lecture on: The Aims Of Love Are Sometimes Amiss.

What an absurd thing to say. The aims of love weren't off target, they were in direct conflict. Love for her father demanded that she stay, love for Eddie demanded that she go. Obviously most women would have chosen Eddie over Father, but what did that prove except that one had to choose between the demands of love. One faced the future by turning his back on his parents. Painful but true.

And who was to say that Emily had chosen wrongly? Pat found it difficult to take Eddie seriously. He could not believe that Eddie was a tragic loss or that Emily would have been happier if she had left her father for him. Eddie sounded like the kind of man she should be happy to be rid of.

"Eddie said he loved me. He said he would always love me," Emily sobbed, her large bosom shaking. "Why couldn't he wait?"

There was something incongruous about coarse Emily Graham with her whiskers and big teeth and cotton stockings crying over a lost love like a high-school girl. But life was full of Eddies and love was full of tears and lost forevers. Pat linked his fingers together and thoughtfully, sympathetically nodded his head hoping she would continue, but Emily was waiting for him to put her pain into words.

"Many people have a romanticized view of love," he said, speaking slowly, deliberately, trying to sound gentle yet authoritative while he searched for something to say. "Poets and song writers speak of love as being forever, but the Christian view is that divine love alone is absolute, eternal, and wholly redemptive. Human love is not only relative, it is terminal. That is why marriage vows read 'till death us do part.'"

He knew instantly that it was a mistake to mention death. Scarcely had he uttered the word before she began relating the last days of her father. In many ways this part was the most painful of all.

After a number of years it became necessary for Emily to care for her father's physical needs. She bathed him, carried a bedpan, got up at night to give him his medicine and fed him by spoon. Through all this her sisters were unable to help her, so busy were they with church and club work, and entertaining to advance their husbands' careers. In his last moments the old man had asked not for Emily who had cared for him and was at his bedside, but for his absent daughters—one of them attending a club meeting, the other at the movies.

That had been difficult to accept, and at the funeral, while her sisters wept, and fainted, and clung to their father's corpse, Emily had sat in stony hatred. Two days later one of her brothers-in-law produced a will whereby the old man had left everything to Emily's sisters. Emily had temporarily lost control of her senses and had accused her sisters of killing their father with neglect and robbing her. They in turn had calmly asserted that she had been less than useless to their father, that she had lived with him only because she had no place else to go, and that Eddie not only had never intended to marry her, he scarcely knew who she was.

Blinded by rage and self-pity, Emily had slashed her wrists and thrown herself across her father's grave, wishing to die. Eddie was gone, her father was dead, her sisters had homes and husbands and children. She had nothing left, not even the satisfaction of having been a martyr for her father. She had given her life to care for him and they had belittled that. How could they do that to her? How could they destroy her if they loved her?

Pat didn't know how, but he knew they could. He knew that the world's great lovers had been those who took, not those who gave. He knew that his father and mother loved each other and yet their love did not heal. He knew that he loved Lillian and yet he deliberately caused her pain. He remembered while conducting jail services meeting Winifred Tucker, who had murdered his pregnant sweetheart and lived for three days with her parents while the police searched for her. He believed Winifred loved the girl he murdered and buried in a canyon, and he even came to realize that her parents knew not only the agony of losing their daughter but the horror of loving the man who killed her.

"Emily, everyone dreams of a love that gives, and accepts, and creates—a love that does not defile, but that may be the slipperiest, the most elusive of all man's—"

"I have nothing to live for," Emily said. "There is no one who cares. No one who needs me. What good is a life like this?"

The truth of the matter was that there wasn't much reason for her to live. She hadn't spoken to her sisters since her attempted suicide, she had been too busy taking care of her father to have made any friends, she lived a lonely, useless, joyless life in a small, barren room in a boarding house. Pat could scarcely believe that he would endure such a life, yet Emily waited for him to give her a reason to live. When a man completed his chores, why didn't God let him come in the house?

"That's not an easy question to answer," Pat said, without acknowledging that he had not come up with an answer in over a year, although he had explained Life Is A Book To Be Read To The Last Chapter, Life Is Four Score And Ten God Has Sentenced Us To, and It All Counts On Twenty. That's what they said in the Marines—the career men. "I'm putting in my time. It all counts on twenty." No matter whether it was a Saturday morning Junk-On-The-Bunk inspection or marching from Yudam-ni to the sea. However, that didn't seem like a very Christian answer—hanging on until retirement.

"The Christian view historically has been that life is a gift and while it is not to be held too dear, it is an opportunity and a responsibility. Just as we have the opportunity to live and love and serve, so we have the responsibility of living and loving—"

Yet all his attempts to get her involved in useful activities had failed. She refused to speak to her sisters. She had gone to the women's mission study group and told them her troubles until they began avoiding her. At Pat's insistence she had done volunteer work at the hospital until the doctors complained she was always in the way and the nurses complained that she was not only running the patients' lives but theirs as well. Yet there must be some place for her, something meaningful for her to do.

"Why does God make us suffer so?" Emily asked. "Why does He punish us so? If God loves us, how can He allow it?"

Pat felt tired and he wanted to be alone. He wished for a shade that he could manipulate and make Emily vanish, make questions dissolve, make suffering disappear. Also Evan Moore, falling airplanes, grieving widows, church budgets, and revolving crosses. But he had no shade. All he had was a stained-glass picturization of the Good Shepherd in search of lost lambs. Suffering did not go away, the question did not vanish, Emily Graham waited for an answer.

Quickly he reviewed his previous attempts to explain away suffering. The Law Of Man Is Not The Justice Of God, To Pull Up The Tares Is To Destroy Also The

Wheat, If There Were No Pebbles The Brook Would Have No Music, Where There Is No Night Men Curse The Day, It Takes A Little Grit To Make A Lovely Pearl, Better A Thorn In The Flesh Than A Stone In The Breast, and The Blind Have Eyes That Whole Men Do Not Know.

He didn't know the answer and neither did anybody else, so why didn't he just tell Emily to find out for herself? Who was he trying to impress?

He knew that much of the suffering of which men so eloquently complained was imaginary, like Sergeant Eberhardt, who cried "Why did God let my little girl die?" Pat had tried to comfort and console the drunken sergeant only to discover that Eberhardt's daughter was not dead but in a Wyoming hospital having her tonsils removed.

He knew that much of man's suffering was self-induced. "Why did God take my sweetheart away from me," cried Corporal Lineart, whose sweetheart had married another man when she found that Lineart had syphilis and a wife in Altus, Oklahoma.

He knew that men loved to finger their injustices and tear their slights into sores. He had come home from college for the Christmas holidays, thinking of Christmas trees, girls under the mistletoe, and the forecast of snow, and had run up the stairs to the apartment where his parents lived after they had moved off the farm. His mother met him at the door, not with the hug he expected, since it was the first time he had been away from home, but with a letter.

"You had better read this," she said, and he knew that something was wrong. "It's from your father."

He wanted to run back down the stairs and out of the house where there were Christmas lights, and basketball games, and gaiety, but his mother held the letter out to him and he took it. It was not from his father but from a lawyer, explaining in polite and official language that his father was moving out of the apartment and was filing suit for divorce.

He had hated his parents then, because their world, where love was a tangled web of pain and memory, of shared joys and lost opportunities, of unrealized hopes and unresolved differences, difficult victories and easy disasters, singleness of person and divisiveness of purpose, had intruded into his own world of thoughtless self-interest and easy affection. His world of comfortable answers and pretty illusions, the world of his youth, was shattered forever, and from that time he would know that the price of his education was his father's birthright and his mother's loneliness was the price of his joy.

Pat and his mother sat without speaking in the hot, stuffy room, he exploring his wound, she hers, while outside Christmas carols were carried on the wind and laughing children gathered the first snowflakes of the year on the tips of their tongues.

It had been a little wound and had left only a tiny scar, but he had cried out at his sufferings, had struck out at those he loved most, and had blamed God because the world was imperfect. "An atheist is a man who hates God because he has no one to blame," he thought.

Yet suffering remained. The inescapable agony of humanity remained. And he stood mute before it. And except for its poorboxes, its hospitals, its schools, where men sought new reasons and new drugs, the church could only look on with fear and pity.

He knew that Emily's suffering was exaggerated, that she

enjoyed her tears, that she did not really want to die. He had become the local expert on loneliness, suicide, self-pity, and the death of Emily's father, the injustice of Emily's sisters, the duplicity of Eddie, and the agony of Emily. Yet she was a woman who must attempt to die in order to be important and noticed, who must visibly suffer to earn her sisters' concern. Before that suffering he was mute. The words were gone. There was nothing he could say. "Emily, that's my hand you are nailing to the cross," he thought.

"I don't know, Emily," he said. "I'm sorry, I just don't have the answer."

Emily looked at him. For the first time in the long weeks she had been coming she looked at him—looked and saw him for what he was, a mortal like herself. And what he saw in her face shocked him. She had never accepted his answers before, but apparently she had believed that he had the answer and would give it if she only pressed long enough. He had failed her again, but he did not know what to do. Emily made no attempt to leave. She had come for an answer and she was going to prod and poke at him until she got it, no matter how unsatisfactory it might be.

Vainly he struggled for words, grasping for ideas, for answers. "Pain is a condition of life," he said lamely. "Some have a greater burden to bear but none of us is exempt. But God has promised us that suffering too can be redemptive. 'The valley of Achor,' that is, the valley of tribulation, 'for a door of hope.' Some people let suffering destroy them. Others have used their suffering as a gateway to understanding, as a bridge to humanity, as a stepping stone to—"

"How? Tell me how. I can't go on like this. Tell me what to do."

Pat inwardly groaned, a weary, hopeless groan. Why must they always ask him what to do? Why couldn't they decide one thing for themselves? He was tired of being questioned, of searching his soul for an answer, of failing. He was tired of being poked, and prodded, and pressed, and squeezed, and examined until he had been drained of every human feeling, every shred of dignity. For months he had been beating his head against the wall. What more was he to do? He had answered her question. He had given her the only answer he knew, and given it, and given it. But she did not believe the words and asked the question without hope. And he, because he had repeated the words so many times, no longer believed them and pronounced them with a dulled and stupid tongue.

"Emily, you have to forgive your sisters. You have to forgive your father for dying and Eddie for deceiving. You have to return good for evil. You have to find something good you can do for your sisters, some way to serve them," he said without hoping, or praying, or wishing. "Either kill them and kill yourself, or forgive them and give yourself a chance to live."

Emily appeared not to have heard. Pat racked his brain trying to think of an alternate plan, waiting in silence for her to ask the question again.

"I'll try," she said, hanging her purse over her arm and heaving herself out of the chair. "I don't know how I'll do it, but I'll try."

Pat watched in astonishment as Emily waddled out the door. He wanted to ask if she meant it, if she had understood what he said. He wondered if he should hedge his answer with other solutions in case this one failed. He sat down in the chair and closed his eyes. He did not believe it. Next week, next month she would be back again asking the same questions, probing and squeezing until she had sucked him dry, leaving him nothing for himself, no word or feeling that he could call his own.

"SHE CAME TO YOU FOR HELP, PAT."

"And I gave it, Lord. I gave it, and gave it, and gave it. And Lord, it all counts on twenty."

At least that was over. How much longer until quitting time? He had talked to Emily. He had talked to Evan. He had studied the budget. That left a mess of pottage, a hospital of sick folks, one widow and three fatherless children, and a meeting of the Council, and that took care of the day. And tomorrow, once more up Heartbreak Hill, once more up Golgotha to oversubscribe the budget, gather up the pledge cards, and nail oneself to the cross, and it all counted on twenty.

Pat recalled an atrocity story of two men who were caught trying to escape a Japanese prison camp. They were tied to the gate posts and each day as the work brigades were marched to and from work each man was required to take a plank and hit them. The first blows broke their jaws, and noses, and teeth. Gradually their ribs caved in and their arms and legs were broken, but for four days they perversely clung to life, their bones protruding through the broken flesh, their blind eyes staring, their dumb, swollen tongues hanging from their lips, while their countrymen wept and cursed and shouted at them to die. Why didn't they let go? Why didn't God take them down?

"GET DOWN FROM THERE, PAT."

"Lord, can't you give me a hand? I got up here for you."

Pat Shahan, on the pilgrimage of being, raised above the earth, dipping in the cup, bearing with patience the adversities of life.

GOD IS THE CROSS I BEAR.

Closing the door of his study behind him, Pat walked through the quiet, dark sanctuary on the way to his car, touching the familiar pews, looking forward to the brief respite at Jack Merrick's club. Seeing an obscene word scratched on the back of a pew, he stopped and stared at the desecration. Such mindless, purposeless destruction angered him beyond words. He could understand the man who stole something out of need or covetousness, of the man who struck in anger, or fled out of fear or for advantage, but useless vandalism was beyond his understanding and forgiveness.

Although he was already in danger of being late for his lunch with Jack Merrick, Pat knew he would have to hunt up the custodian, Mr. Murph, and set him to repairing the pew before some of the ladies of the church accidentally read its message. He found the custodian sitting idly, vacantly in the broom closet.

Mr. Murph was a souvenir of one of Pat's ventures into social rescue. Pat had discovered the old man at a jail service and had taken it as his Christian duty to save him from alcoholism, chronic unemployment, and petty crime. He had gotten Mr. Murph out of jail, and unable to place him anywhere else, had brought him to the church and turned him into a sober, law-abiding, incompetent janitor.

"Mr. Murph, somebody has scratched up a pew."

"What say?" Mr. Murph asked, not because he hadn't heard but because it took him that long to focus on anything. Pat repeated that someone had scratched a word on the back of one of the pews.

"What word is it?"

"It doesn't matter what the word is," Pat explained. "Just fix it."

"Well, which pew is it?"

"I don't know which pew it is. It's about half way down on the right aisle. You'll have to look for it. Whichever pew has a word scratched on it."

"What do you want me to do about it?"

"I want you to scratch it out," Pat said in angry sarcasm. "Paint over it. Cover it up some way."

"Well, if it's a deep scratch I won't be able to fix it."

"Would you try, Mr. Murph?" Pat asked. Surely a man should be grateful for freedom, sobriety, and employment. But no, to save a miller was to have a millstone on your hands.

Despite his impatience to be gone, Pat waited to be sure that Mr. Murph got started. Slowly the old man emerged from the broom closet, leaving the light burning, and shuffled off in the direction of the sanctuary, mumbling about "those durn kids."

Pat snapped off the light in the broom closet and closed the door. "A little darkness for the Lord's sake," he said, thinking of the church's enormous utility bill.

Pat left the church, his thoughts troubled by the desecration. It disturbed him that young people were capable of such senseless destruction. But had it been a young person? Mr. Murph blamed every scrap of paper he had to pick up, every misplaced hymnbook he had to return, every open window he had to close on "those durn kids." That was the attitude of a lot of the church members, but it seemed to Pat that an ex-alcoholic, ex-bum should be more charitable.

And who was to say that it had been senseless? Perhaps it was not as devoid of meaning as he would like to believe. Perhaps it was an attempt at speech by a profane and tongueless soul. But if so, what was its message? Was it an expression of rebellion at a carpeted air-conditioned church with foam rubber-padded pews? Was it a rejection of the church's message of love for the rich and hope for the poor? Was it a crude but honest evaluation of his sermons of piety, brevity, and wit? Was it an expression of disgust for man and his ways? A plea for help? A declaration of faith in the regenerative powers of love? Pat believed in words, that no word fell purposelessly or futilely on barren ground. This was a word, a symbol of communication, a declaration, question, or exclamation of faith and morals, a sign of hope or despair—but what did it mean?

Getting into his car, Pat drove slowly past the church, half expecting to see someone painting a swastika over the copper doors. "What a terrible urge there is in man to destroy," he thought. "To trample underfoot and then to turn and rend." He remembered high-school friends who wrote on walls and sidewalks, scratched out or painted over advertisements, removed the reflectors from road signs, threw down tombstones, carved their initials on monuments, tore the arms off statues, and methodically broke bottles, street lights, and the windows of vacant houses. He remembered Marines who had carelessly pilfered, wrecked, or abused any property for which they were not checked out and held personally responsible.

But Pat had never been destructive. He had lost toys but had seldom broken them. He had driven his father's car too fast but had never raced in it. He had never been careless with his clothing, never thrown down the Bible his mother gave him. He had never known the triumph of ruining what belonged to another, the possessive excitement of scratching his initials into unblemished creation, the thrill of destroying something beautiful—except for the white hawk.

The year Pat was fourteen, Leeman Pigg saw a white hawk. At first most of the farmers scoffed at the idea of a white hawk, but soon they began to see it too. Some people thought it was an albino hawk. Others thought it was only a rare type of hawk not usually seen in that locale. Skeptics said that it was not a hawk at all but a white owl. That year everyone talked about the white hawk, and most of the farmers tried to trap or shoot it.

One day when Pat was driving the cows to the barn to milk them, he saw the white hawk soaring above the pasture, its feathers pink in the setting sun. It moved effortlessly across the sky, dipping and rising on the wind. Pat ached as he watched the hawk, yearning to rise above the fields and effortlessly to fly, yearning also to possess the hawk and make it his. He watched, following the hawk across the pasture, running after it across the fields, jumping from furrow to furrow, leaping over ditches, climbing fences until he lost it on the dark horizon. He was so late getting home his father had to help him milk.

All that summer Pat watched for the hawk, stopping in the cotton field to search the sky while the Negro hands chopped obliviously about him. Days, even weeks would pass when he did not see the hawk, and he would fear that someone had killed it and that he would never get to see it again, to hold it and feel its sharp talons gripping his flesh, to examine its wonderful feathers, and look into its brilliant eye. He dreamed of catching the hawk and taming it. It would ride heavily, imperiously on his shoulder, looking fierce, and do as he commanded—fetch things, carry messages, attack his enemies. And it would be the only one of its kind in the world. And it would be his.

Pat spent his fourteenth summer trying to catch the hawk. He set traps with eggs or fresh meat and each morning before going to the field to work he would run to inspect the traps. Sometimes the traps were empty, the bait gone, the steel jaws tightly clamped on nothing, and once he caught a crow.

Late that fall, when shocks of feed were standing in the field, he had taken the shotgun his father had given him and one of his mother's hens and had gone out to the field. Tying the hen on top of one of the shocks of maize, he had laid down in the weeds of the ditch nearby with the shotgun by his side, both hammers back. It was warm in the ditch with the sun on his back, and he had almost dozed off among the weeds when he heard the hen thrashing with excitement.

Looking up, he saw the hawk drop from the sky, sinking its talons with a sound he could almost hear. With its wings beating, the hawk hovered over the hen, fierce and proud and bloody, its beak tearing into the hen's heart. Raising the shotgun, Pat aimed at the top of the shock and pulled both triggers. The hawk and the hen disappeared in a cloud of dust and feathers.

Clutching the shotgun, Pat climbed out of the ditch and walked to where the hen, its feet still tied, hung in bloody strips down the side of the shock. A few feet away lay the hawk. It didn't look proud or stern the way he had imagined it. It didn't look like anything living. It was a mass of gore and feathers and it wasn't even white. It was a dirty gray color and it was undersized.

Pat stood and stared at the quivering flesh and all he could think of was the three large pores in Mr. Pigg's red nose. Once at a school Christmas party he had sat terrified, awestricken as Santa Claus came down the aisle handing out stockings of fruit and candy. Pat was so excited he thought he would cry, and then as Santa Claus handed him his stocking he saw the three large pores that belonged in Mr. Pigg's nose. His mouth fell open in surprise as he realized that Santa's face was rouged, and his costume was shabby and dirty at the cuffs, and the stocking of fruit and candy slipped through his fingers and fell to the floor.

Pat picked up the hawk and carried it to the shop behind the garage where his father was working at the forge. He threw the hawk down on the dirt floor and waited. His father turned from the anvil where he was shaping a red hot rod. "What's that?" he asked.

"That's the white hawk," Pat said, kicking at it with his shoe, turning it over in search of white feathers.

His father wasn't proud of him the way Pat thought he would be. He even seemed sad. But he had given Pat the shotgun, and it was to kill things with, and hawks weren't any good to anybody unless they were dead—or tame. They killed chickens, and pigeons, and rabbits. "Yeah, that's the white hawk," he said, trying to sound proud. "It wasn't good for anything, was it?"

"No, I don't guess it was," his father said, turning back to the anvil. "What are you going to do with it?"

Pat looked down at the hawk. He had hoped that his father would say it could be mounted, that there was some way of putting it back together again where he could keep it and show it off. When he looked down at the bloody feathers and dusty entrails he was not proud of it. He did not want to have it or show it. He did not want to look at it. Picking it up with disgust he walked down behind the barn and threw it in the weeds.

His mother watched him as he carried the shotgun back to the house. She did not like killing and she did not like him fooling with the shotgun. He knew he would have to tell her he had killed a hen.

"You killed one of my hens?" she asked, not giving him a chance to explain. "One of my layers? When you knew I was selling the eggs and saving every penny I could get to pay my pledge to the missionary union? What am I going to do now? What am I supposed to tell them? That I can't keep my word because my son shot my best layer? Ask your father for the money? The way he feels about church? You know I have to save every cent I can get my hands on." Turning away from him in anger, she began to cry.

"But I killed the hawk, Mother," he tried to explain. "It won't ever bother your hens again."

"Why?" she asked. "Why did you have to kill it? Why do you have to play with guns? I told your father not to give you the shotgun."

Pat walked back out to the field, avoiding the shock where the hen still hung in bloody tatters. His mother knew very well why he killed the hawk. To protect her hens. They ran for the hen house every time they saw a shadow on the ground. And also he wanted it to come down so he could see it, and hold it in his hands, look into its golden eye and feel the wild beat of its heart.

Pat flopped down in the ditch and rolled over on his back. His eyes searched the sky hoping that the hawk he had killed was not the white hawk, hoping that some day he would see it again soaring against the sun, its shadow sliding across the ground. He lay on his back and watched, but the hawk didn't sail across the sky because it was lying in the weeds behind the barn, a rotting lump from which he averted his eyes every time he drove in the cows, a stench in his nostrils every night when he milked.

"PAT. WHY DID YOU HAVE TO KILL, PAT?"

"Lord, it was a dream, a cry of wings, a prayer of flight, a shadow against the sun, a promise of morning rising on the wind."

Pat Shahan, holy crusader, aiming his guns against the sky, setting his sights on what is wild and free and above, to bring down, capture, contain, and tame—for order, safety, and peace.

GOD IS WHAT I KILL.

Days of a Hireling

> *Seeing his days are determined, the number of his months are with thee, thou hast appointed his bounds that he cannot pass; turn from him, that he may rest, till he shall accomplish, as an hireling, his day.*

PAT SHAHAN, well-dressed minister about town, harbinger of happiness, making his way to the Samaritan Club through the signs and temptations of this world. TURN. YIELD. STOP. SLOW. NO THOROUGHFARE.

Pat Shahan, prophet to the Samaritans, being assisted from his car, swept past the potted palms of the porte-cochere and ushered through the magnificent carved doors by uniformed Negroes, realizing too late that the doorman who prepared the way was a Negro minister whom he knew, catching a glimpse of the man's stiff, uniformed back as the door closed between them.

"DID YOU SEE HIM, PAT?"

"I'll speak to him on the way out, Lord."

Pat Shahan, bearer of good tidings to wealthy gentlemen, fingering his tie as he stands, an alien at the door, waiting to be recognized and admitted into the good life and the com-

IN THE HOUSE OF THE LORD

pany of the elect, where soft music mutes the buzz of business, the snap of jaws, the click of silver on plate. LOVE ME. LOVE ME. LOVE ME.

Pat Shahan, smiling priest of God-favored people, genial ambassador of good will, being ushered across the broad carpeted room to the nodding approval of this world.

"Hello, Pat, good to see you," Jack said, standing to greet him.

Gratefully Pat sat down to the safety and elegance of dim lighting, cheerful companions, and mood music. TAKE ME. TAKE ME. TAKE ME.

"Well, how was it?" Jack asked with sympathy, and Pat was pleased that he had asked, because he could tell Jack what the Crusade had been like and Jack would understand. He could tell Jack of running errands, calling taxis, arranging travel plans and carrying bags for athletes and actors. He could tell Jack of the long afternoons in hotel rooms, of coffee and donuts ten times a day, of moments of intense excitement, moments of rare and tranquil beauty, and the dead aftermath of empty chairs, littered floors, and numb, emotionally drugged men who flinched from thought, or speech, or prayer. He could tell him of quiet, thoughtful men yielding to the emotional needs of personalities, of planned spontaneity and feigned enthusiasm, of the strategy of idealism wedded to the footwork of expediency. He could explain to Jack the grinding agony of portraying genial patience, exhaustless brotherhood, boundless optimism. He could tell Jack of seeing the banner tangled in the weeds and hearing the crackle and hiss of Ray Elliott's burning airplane amid the vision of NOW. COME. SEE. THRILL. HEAR. SEEK. REPENT.

"Jack, it was—it was awful. It was a—a—"

How could he say it so that Jack could understand? The eternal verities that became lies, self-evident truths used as expedient slogans, mysteries prostituted to clichés. And with what rod could he measure the duplicity of honest men, triangulate the heights of pious pretense, plumb the depths of guilty despair?

"I heard about Ray," Jack said. "That was too bad." Pat could only nod. "Now which one was he? I can't seem to place him."

For a few minutes they discussed Ray Elliott, Pat trying to describe him—he sat in this pew, attended these services, knew these people—Jack trying to establish some memory of him. Then Jack signaled to one of the uniformed Negroes and they ordered lunch, Jack as smooth and polished as ever, polite yet decisive, courteous yet commanding, and Pat was reminded again how comfortable it was to be with someone who was always at ease in social situations, always firm but cordial with waiters and employees, always confident in his position and power.

Pat relaxed, willing to be at ease, eager to pause at a restful arbor and hear of accomplishment, liberality, and success. "That's great, Jack, just great," he said, listening to Jack's ideas for revamping the city government for economy, progress, and social justice.

Jack laced his fingers together and slowly shook his head. "I don't know, Pat. So much depends on chance and timing. Right now things don't look too good."

"What's the matter?"

"Well, there was an accident, Pat. Tragic but unavoidable. But the Power Company was involved and when people think of the Power Company they think of me. Given the right treatment by the papers, it could finish me politically in the city. However, I'll have to say they're being very fair. They recognize it was an accident and that's the way they're reporting it."

Pat Shahan, who had listened to laughing children playing in the snow, heard of a boy who listened to laughter and running feet in the breathless silence.

"—supposed to ring the doorbell and either collect or cut off the service. Usually the people have just moved off without paying their bill, but in this case the people had moved out but had let a woman move in to use up their unexpired rent. This is on the east side, and things are pretty casual over there. Anyway, this woman had a son in an iron lung and when the serviceman rang the doorbell she was across the—"

He who had turned away from the roar and crackle of a burning plane tried to escape the vision before his mind, tried to re-establish the reality of paneled walls, carpeted floors, and soft, languorous music. HOLD ME. HOLD ME. HOLD ME.

"—panicked and chased the truck down the street. Well, the serviceman saw this Negro woman running after him and he stopped, but he thought she was just mad because he had cut off the electricity and he didn't pay too much attention at first. When he realized what she was saying—she was pulling on him and talking so fast he couldn't understand —he went back and turned the electricity on, but by then it was—"

He who had thrown the desecration of a white hawk into

the weeds behind the barn listened as Jack Merrick tried to dispose of an accidental victim.

"—big company. A serviceman has so many calls to make every day. He rings the doorbell, knocks a couple of times—maybe he lights a cigarette, and if there's no answer, he cuts off the service. That's the only way the company can survive. We have five hundred thousand customers. I can't stop and think every time we cut off service that we're leaving people without light or heat or any way to warm the baby's bottle. I couldn't live and think like that, nobody—"

He who had watched a kitten pick its way through stickers watched Jack pick his way between blame and innocence.

"—for them. If you'll remember, we were the first company in this city to adopt fair employment practices. I'm not saying we're perfect because we're not, but, Pat—in a city this size things happen and no one is to blame. You don't know about them because you're not involved. I'm involved with six companies and the Chamber of Commerce, and I can tell you that only last month in this city a woman drowned because road construction had cut off the drainage from her house. No one knew it would happen, no one—"

He who had sought for fairness in the divine plan that doomed bees to drowning searched for justice in human plans that doomed the weak to accidents.

"—discrimination because they have to put up a higher deposit and don't get a second notice or grace period. The truth is since I began requiring larger deposits for the east side we have cut delinquent bills by more than half. And the reason we don't send second notices or give a grace period on the east side is because it doesn't work. Usually they've just moved off without paying. We send a serviceman one time and if they don't pay we cut off the service. It had nothing to do with race or discrimination, it's strictly economics—"

They sat in silence looking at the salads that had been placed before them, keeping their faces pleasant so as not to betray the gentle laughter and soft soothing music. TAKE ME. TAKE ME. TAKE ME. Pat took up his fork and speared one of the tiny shrimp, trying to shut out of his mind the vision of a panic-stricken mother trying to choose between hand-cranking the iron lung and appealing to the source for the restoration of power—of a boy hanging on the thin, pulsing current that gave him the breath of life, hearing laughter and running feet in the sudden, breathless silence, watching the mirrored hope fading from his own eyes.

"God," he said, dropping the fork back in the dish, startled at the sound, aware that other diners were looking at him, offended by his breach of decorum.

It was his hope, he thought. His future. His salvation, daily bread, the grace he lived by. What faith he must have had in it. What reverence. It must have been a part of him, or rather, it must have seemed that he was a part of it. And then someone threw the switch and he was cut off—excommunicated.

I must go to the mother, Pat thought. I've got to help her to understand, to make peace with a world where men have power to kill but not to restore, where things are wrong but no one is to blame. And I must try to comfort her, he thought. And I must stand by that boy's body. Not as a friend or even as a penitent but as one who comes empty-handed to share.

He who had seen the horizon threatening fire and rain saw Jack Merrick searching his face for a sign. "What do you think? Do you think it'll hurt me on the east side?"

He who had aimed obsolete guns at simulated targets longed to point the finger of accusation. He who had dreamed of striking down the forces of evil yearned to throw the first stone. He who longed to call nations to repentance waited to pardon, but no one was guilty. There was no one to blame, no one to confess, no one to pardon. A great crime had been committed and yet no one had done wrong. "I've got to go," he said.

"You don't hold me responsible, do you?" Jack asked. His face was a mask of liberality and good will and his voice was soft and controlled, but beneath the mask, Pat saw the face of fear. "We have five hundred thousand satisfied customers. We have the lowest rates in this area. We have supplied electricity to low-income—"

Pat was surprised that a Christian liberal like Jack should feel no guilt. "Jack, you're campaigning on your economy drive with the Power Company and that economy drive cost a boy his life. If you take the credit, you have to take the responsibility."

"Pat, I can't accept that responsibility. How could I live with something like that? How could I go on being president, making decisions? Pat, there are servicemen out right now cutting off service to somebody. Tell me what to do?"

"I've got to go," Pat said. "I've got to go to that boy's mother."

"You can't leave now. You're my pastor. You've got to tell me what to do."

LOVE. ME. LOVE. ME. LOVE. ME.

Pat Shahan, who had prayed for a vision, saw himself dressed in the vestments of prosperity, sitting in the temple of decorum and civility, in the company of the comfortable, being ministered to by uniformed Negroes, listening to the laughter and music of this world—NEED. ME. NEED. ME. NEED. ME.—too polite to cry out and disturb the digestion of others, too civilized to weep in public, guilt-ridden because in a hungry world his plate was untouched.

He who longed to champion the poor, to defend the dispossessed, to comfort the bereaved, to bear the pain of the persecuted sat in the company of the rich and powerful meeting needs, affecting behavior. USE. ME. USE. ME. USE. ME.

"THEY WHO FOLLOW ME ARE FORSAKEN BY THIS WORLD, DESPISED AND REJECT—"

"It's all right, Lord. I'm used to being accepted."

Pat Shahan, with Greatheart on the way, feeding wolves, restoring power, descending into hell.

GOD IS MY CONNECTION.

Pat drove slowly, picking his way through the quiet residential streets, too preoccupied to notice the signs that slid past the car. FIGHT. BACK THE ATTACK. K.O. COMBAT. STAMP OUT.

He should have gone to see that mother who had lost her son. Surely he had been a cross to bear, helpless, needing constant attention, sucking her life, and yet, in losing him perhaps momentarily she had lost her reason to live. He should have helped her find it. At least stand beside her until she did.

He would try to see her tomorrow after Ray's funeral. But he knew it would not be the same. The moment had passed—the moment of her need for him, the oneness he had felt with the bereaved and forsaken. He had spent that moment ministering to the mighty.

Silently Pat cursed Jack Merrick. Not only had his emotions been torn by the story of the boy's death, but he had also had to forego his desire to go to the mother and to put aside his own outraged sense of justice to comfort Jack. He had been too upset to eat lunch and now he had a headache. "Thank you, Lord, for this headache."

"Do you know Jack Merrick?" asked a cynical, gap-toothed reporter. "What kind of a man is he?"

"Jack Merrick is the epitome of the American dream," Pat said as flashbulbs popped and pencils scratched. "A boy fortunate enough to have an unscrupulous crook and exploiter for a grandfather so that he might live in the best house in the best neighborhood, go to the best schools, belong to the best clubs, and grow up to be a liberal champion of the exploited, thereby returning good for evil—instead of using the poor to gain riches and thus power, using the poor to gain power and thus riches."

"Isn't Jack Merrick a member of your church in good standing?" asked the reporter, grinning cynically.

"Well, yes and no—"

"Wouldn't you say that a man who financially supports the church, attends regularly, and teaches a Sunday School class is a member in good standing?"

"Well, that's a very complex question—"

"How many Negroes do you have to kill to be a member in good standing in your church?" asked the reporter, sniggering with his tongue between his gapped teeth.

"That's not it at all. You have deliberately misunderstood. Jack Merrick has never killed anybody. It is true that Jack is president of an organization that takes heat, light, and refrigeration from widows and orphans, but he does it for the good of the community. And if he didn't do it, he would lose his $50,000-a-year salary and not only would he be unable to support the Jack Merrick charities, he would also have no power or position from which to fight corrupt practices like office parties and employees' World Series pots."

"Then what constitutes being a member in good standing?"

"A church member in good standing is first of all a nice guy. He wears a suit to church, preferably black, blue, or brown, and if he is an outstanding church member he wears a suit every day. His hands are soft and well-manicured for hand shaking and back patting. His breath is free from the odor of alcohol and tobacco for hymn singing and foot kissing. He is polite to equals and well-mannered in public. If he must whisper it is in church. If he must use the name of the Lord it is in a joke. He steals from none but customers. He lies to no one but his competitors. He is humble before his creditors, harmless in the face of injustice, subtle before investigation, and wise beyond care. An all-around candidate for the Chamber of Commerce. And the real saint is he who would give a cup of cold water to a nigger on relief. In a paper cup, of course."

Pat nodded in satisfaction as he drove past the hospital looking for a parking place.

"If that describes a church member, then what is a pastor?" asked the reporter.

"A pastor?" Pat asked in surprise. "Why he's—"

"The pastor in the twentieth century is an administrator," Dr. Hoffman had said, lecturing on the glamorous and rewarding life he himself had declined. "And the church officers are his staff. The pastor is an architect and the Bible is his blueprint. The pastor is a promoter and the gospel is his product. The pastor is a public-relations expert and Christianity is the opinion he shapes. The pastor is a general and the pulpit is the firing line—"

"Bring up the heavy artillery," Pat said. "We're being overrun."

"I think being pastor is the noblest thing a man can do," Mrs. Wright had said when she asked him to repair the office stapler.

"The way I see it, the pastor is the Lord's tax collector," Orin Kilgore had said when Pat canceled the Over The Top Campaign.

"The pastor is, first of all, servant to the denomination," Dr. Espey had said at Pat's ordination. "He is specially trained and uniquely equipped to gear the needs of the people to the program of the church."

"Being the pastor of a church is the most satisfying thing a man can do," had said Billy Bob Cox, evangelist and right-wing activist who owned three cars, a private airplane, and a ranch in Oklahoma. "And it doesn't matter how good or how small. Little churches do a powerful lot of good for the Lord and the man who preaches his heart out in a little rural church will someday have a big city church of his own, or a place on the denominational board."

"I'm not sure I want to be a minister's wife," Lillian had said when he asked her to marry him. "It's not you, and it's not that I'd mind you being a preacher, it's just that I don't see myself that way. You know, walking a step behind and always having to worry about people starving in China in front of old ladies in fur coats."

"Why do you want to be a preacher?" his father had asked, and Pat had said nothing because how could he tell his father he wanted to be a good man, to love God, to help others?

"Why, a pastor is a friend to all and a help to none," Pat said, confounding the reporter. Slowly he drove past the hospital for the second time looking for a place to park. "Because a minister is the unnecessary link between the indisputable past and the unpredictable future. Because a pastor is prisoner to the needs of his parishioners, the programs of the denomination, the budget of the church—and worthy of a parking place," he said, seeing some empty spaces in the lot reserved for doctors.

Driving into the lot, he jumped out leaving the motor running. "Park it close, I'll only be a few minutes," he said authoritatively, turning and walking away before the slow-witted attendant could ask if he were a doctor.

"Not the service you get at the Samaritan Club," Pat said. "Not what a pastor deserves. Especially as he goes forth to battle death and disease and bring comfort and healing to the sick."

Pat had a healthy man's lack of regard not only for the sick but also for the hospitals where they congregated and the doctors and nurses who enjoyed their company. The cheerful way Mrs. Wright said "lots of people are sick" as she handed him the list of church members to be visited always galled him. And it galled him even more to discover when visiting that some patients were not sick at all but only collecting insurance or debts of sympathy.

Once he had rushed to the hospital to stand by a dying Sam Sorrele only to discover that the fearful heart attack was gas pains caused by overeating. At first he had been angry at having to lose a night's sleep because Sam couldn't belch, and then it struck him as being funny. He had laughed at the sheepish, shamefaced Sam, causing consternation among the doctors and nurses because of his irreverence in the hallowed halls of suffering.

Now he made his social and sympathy calls first, carrying optimism and cheer with him, saving something for the tragedies that lay in wait to overwhelm him.

Pat Shahan, miracle worker, striding cheerfully yet masterfully down the hospital corridor, spreading sunshine along the way.

"I just couldn't get any relief from these dizzy spells," said Miss Anna Mae Rogers. "I did what you said but I didn't get any better so I thought maybe I had better check into the hospital where I could get some attention. I've just been so despondent and downhearted—"

"Let the Lord be your umbrella," said Pat Shahan, piercing the gloom.

"You're the first person that's come to see me since I

broke my hip," said Mrs. Weatherby, her sharp eye examining the dark blue suit for evidence of irreverent use. "I've been here almost a week and I expect—"

Pat Shahan, knitting the bones of contention with God for a splint.

"I've got poison ivy where no one has ever had poison ivy before," said Diana Dean, choir director's wife, and she was determined to tell him where.

"There is a balm in Gilead," said Pat Shahan, unguent of the Lord, walking rapidly yet hopefully down the corridor with healing in his wings.

"Everything, I have wasted everything," a drunk admitted cheerfully. "I threw away my youth. I threw away my talent, I threw away the love of the only woman who ever loved me. I have wasted every chance I have ever had. And I'd do it again."

"God is our refuge," said Pat Shahan, leaving the waiting rooms of deliverance for the halls of the shadow of death.

On the first floor he saw a surgeon whom he knew. "I don't know, Pat. I don't think there's much chance of saving her and I'm not sure she'll be any better off if I do. But I guess I have to try—"

"Let the Lord be your scalpel," said Pat Shahan, conditioning his reflexes, walking prayerfully down the corridor, hope and fear greeting each other.

On the second floor he was stopped by a stranger whose wife had just suffered her fifth miscarriage. "The doctors say another pregnancy could kill her, but what can I do? She's Catholic."

"Have you talked to a priest?"

"He told me to put my faith in God."

"And you want me to tell you to put your faith in contraceptives?"

"I don't care about God, or faith, or church. I just want my wife," the man said, unable to face the alternatives ahead. "How can I touch her knowing I may kill her? How can she love me knowing she may die? How can we live like that?"

Pat Shahan, on the curve of probability, steering his way between man's life and men's law. "God is when you love."

On the third floor he met a man whose wife had just given birth to a monstrous child. "The doctors told us we could never have children, but we didn't believe them. We prayed for a child and when Betty became pregnant we told everyone it was a miracle. And it's a monster. The doctors are going to tell my wife. Would you talk to her?"

"Where is your minister?" Pat asked, biding for time. "Have you tried to contact him?"

"I am a minister. And I don't know what to tell her. I don't know what to tell my church. They all prayed for this child. How am I going to tell them this is God's answer? I can't even explain it to myself."

Pat Shahan, serpent-wise and dove-simple, struggling with the tangled knot of good and evil, normal and aberrant, not daring the Alexandrian solution—"God is our abortion."

Pat talked to the minister about the laws of nature and the grace of God. He held the wife's hand while she tried to understand what the doctors told her, tried to believe what her husband was saying, tried to look at what God had sent her. Then he went to sit for a while with Vernon Elmore, a church member who was slowly dying.

"He's slipping," said Mrs. Elmore, pursing her lips and shaking her head with conviction.

Pat looked down at Vernon Elmore's vacant eyes fixed unblinkingly on the ceiling and his toothless and cavernous open mouth through which no breath seemed to pass. "Well, we never know," he said, hopefully.

"Oh, yes, I know," said Mrs. Elmore. "He barely lasted last night and he's worse today. Sinking fast. He won't last another day."

Pat looked uneasily at Vernon, who was staring open-mouthed at the ceiling.

"He doesn't know anything," she said, wearily shaking her head. "He just stares at the ceiling. I don't believe he even knows I'm here."

"Mrs. Elmore, wouldn't you like me to get someone from the church to come and stay with Vernon while you go home and get some rest? I'll stay until we can get someone."

"No," she said, awkwardly resting her head in the palm of her hand. "I'll have time to rest later."

The finality with which Mrs. Elmore spoke, the ungainly way she sat holding her head in the palm of her hand moved Pat to tears. Quickly he looked away. He was here to help this woman face the death of the man she had lived with for almost fifty years. Mrs. Elmore was old and ugly with years, and yet the patient, almost serene way in which she waited for her husband's death seemed to Pat a vision of woman's lot—waiting to be asked to be a wife, waiting for a husband to come home from work or war, waiting for children to come, to go, to return, patiently waiting to bear and bury. He thought of his mother sitting at the bedside of his dying father. "Don't leave me here alone," she said when he started once to step out of the room for a moment. At the time he had thought it was a foolish sense of propriety—because they were divorced. But now he knew his mother did not want to wait alone.

"Mrs. Elmore, would you like me to get someone to come and stay with you?" he asked, unable to stay himself, but not wanting to spend the afternoon thinking of her sitting alone with her dying husband.

"I'm all right."

"Have you called your children?"

"They said they'd come but they all have jobs and won't be able to stay for long. I thought I'd wait till the last minute. I'd rather have them here for the funeral. I don't want to have to go home to an empty house."

Pat was very conscious of the silence. He had to say something, everyone expected it, demanded it of a minister. And no one listened, so it didn't really matter what he said or whether she heard, only that the silence of grief be numbed by the murmur of prayer. Quietly he began to pray.

If Mrs. Elmore heard or was comforted, she gave no indication. Pat began thinking of other things to say, remembering how some ministers developed a habit of mumbling whenever there was quiet, as though silence were a kind of nakedness which they must cover, a mystery which they must veil. Pat occasionally caught himself muttering "yes, yes," to no one for no apparent reason except that he was a pastor and therefore responsible for speech. He had known an untrained fundamentalist preacher who intoned at every pause "Is airy sinless? No, nairy." Once, with Dr. Espey, he had waited with the family of the deceased for the funeral service to begin. In the hush that came upon them in

IN THE HOUSE OF THE LORD

the moment before they entered the church, Dr. Espey had looked around and in the burden of that silence said, "Well, everyone seems to be having a good time." And no one, not even Dr. Espey, seemed to be aware of what he had said.

The recollection struck Pat as being funny, and for a moment he was afraid that he would chuckle in the presence of a dying man and his grieving wife. The tears he had repressed were becoming laughter.

Pat shifted in his chair, forcing his emotions under his control. He was here to comfort and he must do his best. Putting Dr. Espey out of his mind, he began thinking of things to say. Should he comment on miracle drugs? The reputation of the hospital? The competency of the doctors? The attitude of the nurses?

Pat watched Vernon Elmore, who lay, his eyes half-lidded, staring open-mouthed at the ceiling. "How small a man looks in death. How defined," he thought, remembering what a small lump his father had made. Remembering how the father who had taught him to fish, and shoot, and drive a tractor, the father who had taught him to belittle Yankees, and Negroes, and preachers, who had gone away leaving behind a letter from a lawyer, who had laughed when Pat accidentally fell in the horse trough while rescuing bees and wept when Pat, wearing his proud new uniform, had left for what he thought was to be Korea, who had struck a man for showing Pat stark, black and white, barely decipherable photographs and shot a man for stealing tires off the truck, the father who had fought in the trenches of France during the First World War but never spoke of the heavy trunk in the cellar that contained hobnail boots, a moth-eaten uniform, a steel helmet, a German officer's belt, a bit of fabric from Quentin Roosevelt's airplane, the father who had seen Paris and New York and castles in Germany, who had played baseball, killed Germans, hunted for arrowheads, and been enslaved to a Texas farm had become unified and condensed into a single white lump in a charity hospital—a lonely, dispossessed, dying man, so small that for the first time Pat could put his arms around his father and embrace all of him. For the first time Pat could add him up and write down the score. "In death do we discover our father," he thought.

It seeemd to Pat that Vernon's eyelids fluttered. He looked at Mrs. Elmore but she had not noticed. The old woman sat in an attitude of cramped and utter weariness. Pat's heart went out to her. He must do something for her. He had already set the crooked straight, made the blind to see, anointed with oil, commended into the bosom of Abraham, and turned away the angels. Now, like a poor magician, he must do one more number before the curtain could fall. Pat Shahan, great physician, fumbling in his bag of tricks, groping for words, trying to pull comfort and wisdom out of an old shabby hat.

"I always dreamed of having a Golden Wedding anniversary," Mrs. Elmore said. "You know, we ran off to get married. I always felt bad about that. Mama never forgave Vernon because we weren't married in church. I told her we would some day just for her. I always thought someday —I've already made my dress. I don't know where I'll wear it now."

"Mrs. Elmore, wouldn't you like for me to get you something? A cup of coffee?"

"Coffee here is not fit to drink," she said.

Pat bit his lip, not knowing what emotion he was suppressing. There was something so comically trivial, so pathetically human about her complaint. "In the face of death we criticize life," he thought. "Man on the gallows complains because the rope chafes his neck."

"Food's not any better," she said.

Pat's mouth opened into a smile and then his chin began to quiver. Abruptly he got to his feet and left the room, leaving Mrs. Elmore waiting alone.

Pat Shahan, ambassador of good health, running down the tiled and silent corridors, leaving in his wake mingled tears and laughter, fleeing the coffee and cancer of this life.

"DID YOU COMFORT MY PEOPLE, PAT?"

"I think so, Lord. I diagnosed, prescribed, mended, bandaged, salved, purged, overhauled, and tranquilized. But I didn't keep score."

Pat Shahan, humble and obedient servant, trudging through the gravel of the parking lot, past the insolent attendant, past all the empty spaces to the end of the parking lot where his car had been left, the ignition on, the seat belt dangling through the closed door.

GOD IS MY SCOREKEEPER.

Pat Shahan drove hunched over the wheel, watching for traffic signals, trying to avoid the appeals that stretched before him—GIVE. HELP. SHARE.—acutely aware of his failure to bring hope and comfort to those in the hospital. But what more should he have done? And what more could he have said to Mrs. Elmore? "Time as well as prayer changes things? Worry does not rob tomorrow of its sorrow, it only saps the strength of today?"

Remorselessly they demanded that he speak to their needs and the words were never easy to achieve, never cheap to say. Even the slippery, shopworn words with which ministers oiled their speeches were frightfully expensive, paid for out of honesty and self-respect.

Little wonder that he had fled the hospital with its demands for tears and explanations. Still, he should not have left so abruptly. He should have tried to control his emotions, to explain—

"I must be tired," he thought. The shock of seeing Ray's airplane burning on the ground had unsettled his nerves. Seeing Vernon Elmore dying while his wife waited had wrenched his emotions. Hearing that a couple's prayers for a child had been answered with a monster had—. Quickly he turned away from a large billboard showing a crippled child standing upright by the grace of crutches and braces. AID. SAVE. CARE.

It was too much. He had been squeezed and teased and flayed until his tears had dried up, his heart strings had been stretched out of tune, and his pity had turned to ashes. There had been too many curly-haired girls hanging on crutches, too many old men distorted by arthritis, too many bewildered, unwed mothers, too many delinquents begging for another chance, too many orphans, too many jobless ex-convicts, too many hungry mouths, sightless eyes, damaged brains, shirtless backs. He was surfeited. His cup ran over. His concern had been enlarged to the point of non-resilience. His heart had been lacerated until it was as tough and scarred as the shell of a turtle.

IN THE HOUSE OF THE LORD

He had read headline casualty figures of traffic accidents, natural disasters, riots, revolutions, and demonstrations until he had developed a kind of spiritual thermometer. No car accident involving the death of less than three members of one family or six people in all, no air disaster of less than fifty, no natural calamity with a toll of less than five hundred, or revolution with body count of less than a thousand merited pity or concern. Indeed such deaths did not even merit reading about unless an ingenious reporter could ferret out an ironic or bizarre detail with which to garnish the account, add color, and lend human interest.

"No wonder man is so enamored of war," Pat thought. Because war gave life a yardstick. A fire in Arkansas, a murder in California, a famine in India, persecution and injustice in Russia, Spain, Mississippi were all so equally and unbearably terrible and significant that one must ignore them. But in war our troops attack, fall back. A ridge is taken or lost, a bridge is built or destroyed, a division is saved or lost. Bodies and planes and ships can be counted, added up and subtracted like milestones. A road, two ridges, and a hundred and fifty-two bodies forward on the road to somewhere. But without war life had no measuring rod.

A nomadic tribe escaped slavery to find the promised land, but how far was freedom? A man climbed the hill of Calvary, but how high was forgiveness? A man changed his opinion on a trade route to Damascus, but in which direction was right? A girl heard voices in Domremy, but what was the sound of peace? Men measured the distance to the stars but could not weigh justice. Men discovered continents but could not find mercy. Men studied the heavens, men studied the earth, men studied the persecution of a people, the slavery of the classes, medicine, psychology, sociology, law, philosophy, communication. Yet man still stood in chains, in hunger, in rags, in filth, in sores, in sin, in need. How many famines, how many persecutions, how many plagues forward on the road to somewhere?

Pat slumped over the steering wheel, tired and hungry, his stomach gnawing because he had not eaten. His head ached. And clipping across his vision were signs. FEED. CLOTHE. SERVE. CARE.

Sometimes Pat felt the whole world stood before him with extended hand and that he gave and gave until he had nothing left that was his own. He had no thought that was free from a sermon, no emotion that was not demanded for the sake of another, no moment that he did not share, no possession secure from appeal.

"DID HE ASK FOR ASSISTANCE?"

"Yes, Lord, I gave him my soul."

For a moment he thought of going home for a snack. He could take a sandwich into the study, or maybe out in the back yard, and eat gloriously free from the specter of hungry eyes, open hands. But there was too much to be done—a whole afternoon of people demanding words, explanations, encouragement, attention, love—stuck to his veins, sucking his soul.

"DO YOU LOVE ME, PAT?"

"Yes, Lord, but this is a tough territory. These people don't pat back."

STOP. Pat brought the car to a stop before the signal light. Taking a deep breath, he leaned back and closed his eyes. When he opened them he saw a young woman run out of the house across the street to greet her husband, who appeared to have just returned from a trip on the road. While the man got his bag from the back seat of the car, the woman picked up his sample case, and with her arms around him, walked him to the house.

A horn honked behind him and Pat, seeing that the light had changed, drove on, reluctant to leave the small frame house with no front yard, no porch, no garage. He wanted to be that man. He wanted to come home, to be greeted as a hero, to be relieved for a moment of responsibility.

HELP. AID. GIVE.

Pat thought of the excited girls who waited for the final whistle to blow at the high-school football games so they could run to their heroes and walk them off the field, while he, a substitute, trotted to the locker room alone. He thought of the dreams he had once had of coming back from Korea a wounded veteran, to be welcomed home to rest by a girl who loved him. But he had never been a hero, he had never been allowed to put aside his burden for a while, and no girl had ever thrown away her reputation or defied convention for him.

Thin, fragile Joella had given him a pink rose made of tissue paper when he was fifteen, and when she was sixteen she waited beside the chain-link fence for the final gun to sound and then ran across the dew-dampened grass, her long black hair flying, to walk foul-mouthed Melvis Keyes off the field.

Irene had been pure and untouchable, and for two years he had worshipped her from afar, scarcely daring to touch her long, thin hand, but when he had rushed proudly from the high-school auditorium, his diploma in his hand, it was not he whom Irene wantonly and publicly kissed but

Galand Webb, who had received the American Legion Citizenship Award. Ellen he had loved because he was in uniform, in a strange town, and because his days were spent in endless and meaningless cleaning and assembling of obsolete antiaircraft guns and tracking simulated targets across the sky. Because his life was intolerably lonely and without purpose. Because he needed to be important to someone, to be able to share his frustrations and rare moments of joy, to be seen with a beautiful girl on his arm. But when he escaped the routine of cleaning and tracking and guarding the obsolete guns, of marching from barracks to mess hall, to gun park to barracks, of sweeping and swabbing down, of field days, inspections and rifle drill, it was not he for whom Ellen waited, but Glen Asher, who had marched from Yudam-ni to the sea.

He loved Lillian. She bore his children, ironed his shirts, turned his collars, and loved him although it had never occurred to her that he was other than an ordinary man. And when he came home after preaching the word, defending the faith, and risking his church, his career, and the wrath of Dr. Espey by openly affirming a quotation from a theologian who was not only suspectedly atheistic but was also Jewish, Lillian had said, "Do you think it's all right if I hang out the clothes on Sunday? I've already done the wash."

He had never been a hero, never been a great lover, never caused heartbreak, never demanded his own, never pressed advantage. He remembered with pain that a college girl had once thanked him for being "nice."

Sometimes in his daydreams he was remorselessly inconsiderate. Sometimes when he was weary with well-doing, when he had yielded, and given, and thrown away with both hands until nothing was left of him, he dreamed of young, firm-fleshed girls from whom he took. Because he was a moral man he always disposed of Lillian in some way so that he was not unfaithful to her. Usually she was killed in a car wreck and sometimes the children as well, and he, in the blindness of grief and despair turned on the world, lying, seducing, taking, gratifying his whims. But even such daydreams were unsatisfactory. He did not find it enjoyable to use people. He would begin to care, to be responsible, to pay his debts, to leave things better than he found them. Soon there would be RESCUE, RESTITUTION, RESPECTABILITY, and the daydream of taking pleasure faded into the reality of fulfilling need.

Pat Shahan was simply not what the world considered a Great Lover. Still, Pat considered himself to be adept at love, much above average. He believed that if there were anything at which he excelled it was making love, and it frustrated him that he could never prove his talent, never demonstrate his skill and prowess. No one would ever know except Lillian, and how was she to judge as she had no comparison? He thought of telling her but that seemed unsatisfactory, and to tell the world of his skill was impossible in his position. But that was the way the world knew lovers. No one testified to Casanova's prowess except Casanova. His paramours were notoriously silent.

"Who was that old fool?"

"I think he said his name was Frank Harris. Wasn't he disgusting? Every time I walked by he drooled."

Yet in those moments when he was most sure of himself

as a lover, he was most aware that Lillian was more than he would ever know, more than he would ever experience. At such times he was almost overcome with a feeling of hopelessness. The more he gave the more was required. The more he knew the greater the unknown. The more he loved the greater the demand for his love. And there was no totality in anything, no completeness anywhere.

Sometimes the shallow and meaningless repetition of the gestures of love with only the faces changed, with no consideration other than one's own needs and specialties, seemed to him a desirable thing—the freedom from the obligation to give, to discover, to know. Yet, he knew that such liaisons did not add to a man, but reduced him, instead, to a bag of dulled tricks and indifferent souvenirs in which faces and facts did not agree.

But what was the yardstick of love, and who kept the score? Did three casual sexual encounters equal one faded tissue paper rose?

"Justice is the currency of love," said Dr. Espey, who did not believe in racial integration, labor unions, or open housing.

"Love is having a little consideration," his mother said when Pat, home from college for his birthday, had taken Lillian to dinner and then gone home to find the uncut cake, the uneaten dinner, the melting ice cream on the table, and his mother in her bedroom crying.

"Love is appreciation," said Walter Miles, seducer of retarded children.

"Love is yes," said Ann Ostergaard.

"I always worried about you," said Pat's father, who even on his deathbed was unable to pronounce a word that was obscenely quick on the lips of humanitarians and whoremongers.

"DO YOU LOVE ME, PAT?"

"Lord, I appreciate you."

Pat Shahan, on the way to somewhere, giving, yielding, bearing, leaving unquenched the smoking flax, leaving unplucked the tissue paper rose, affirming the world.

GOD IS MY YES.

Pat Shahan, soldier of the cross, storm trooper of the Lord, canon fodder of the church, reporting for further orders.

"A lot of things happened while you were gone," Mrs. Wright said, taking out her notebook and deciphering her shorthand.

THOU SHALT TAKE CHARGE OF THIS CIVIL DEFENSE SHELTER AND ALL OTHER CHURCH PROPERTY WITHIN VIEW.

"I couldn't get Jerry Barnes, but I talked to his aunt, Mrs. Walstein, and she said Jerry had been doing just real well the last she heard which was about six months ago."

"THOU SHALT WRITE A LETTER OF RECOMMENDATION FOR JERRY BARNES, FULL OF SOUNDING BRASS AND TINKLING SYMBOLS SIGNIFYING NOTHING.

"Mrs. Shahan wants you to get a loaf of bread and some kind of cheese on the way home."

THOU SHALT TAKE FIVE LOAVES AND TWO CHEESES, AND AFTER BLESSING THEM—

"Emily Graham called to say that she had been praying

about what you told her and that she was going to do it."

Uneasily Pat tried to remember what he had told her. He had the feeling he had said something foolish like: "If you can't forgive you might as well go hang yourself." No, he wouldn't have said anything like that. But suppose she had misunderstood? "Brother Shahan said I should hang myself."

He said so many things, gave so much advice it was impossible to keep track of it all. Who knew how much of it had been bad advice, or had been misunderstood or misapplied?

THOU SHALT HAVE FAITH IN THINE OWN ADVICE.

He had done his best for Emily. He was certain he had given her the best advice he knew and now he would have to trust her to rightly apply it. It was just that he couldn't imagine Emily Graham—No, that was wrong. It was wrong not to have faith in her. It was wrong to put a limit on what people could do. When would he ever learn that? It wasn't that there was so much to be learned, it was just that it had to be learned so many times.

Emily Graham had found an answer, a way out of the bitterness of her life and he had helped her. There amidst all the wreckage and uncertainty of the day was a certain and shining deed. He had helped Emily Graham. Perhaps unknown to him there were others he had helped. Perhaps at this very moment Evan Moore was—What had he told Evan to do? Perhaps at this moment Jack Merrick—

"Did—uh—did anyone call from the newspapers?"

"No."

They were going to let Jack get away with it. They were

going to report it as an accident. Which it was of course, but they could at least deplore the conditions that made such an accident possible. They could editorialize on the tremendous power modern civilization placed in certain hands. A government contract affected the economy of an entire state. The location of a highway, dam, airfield, school changed hundreds of lives. A military base was abandoned and a town perished. A switch was thrown and a boy died. The press should call such men to an accounting of their powers. The papers should forego for a while their pleasure in prying into the private lives of private citizens and call for responsibility in the use of public power, demand safeguards to protect the defenseless, and point the finger of accusation at those who carelessly or selfishly abused their powers. And by heaven, if they didn't, he would.

"FORGET NOT THE ELEVENTH COMMANDMENT."

"Which commandment is that, Lord?"

"THOU SHALT NOT KEEP SCORE ON OTHER PEOPLE."

That was best. Let every man look after his own conscience. Free from the spotlight of publicity, Jack could correct the situation, create his own safeguards, make restitution as his conscience demanded. Or, he could write it off as experience—

"VENGEANCE IS MINE. I WILL REPAY."

The public exposure of sin really accomplished very little. The innocent were hanged along with the guilty. One man was saved by the public revelation of his sin and two dozen of his accusers went to hell for their pride. Still, a lot of people would go around cutting off the electricity if someone didn't blow the whistle."

"THE WAGES OF SIN IS DEATH."

"Lord, if sin really hurt, preachers would be as rich as doctors."

Mrs. Wright turned another page of her shorthand notebook. "Mrs. Elmore called to say that Mr. Elmore had improved and that your visit just did wonders for him. In fact, she said she thought your prayers just wrought miracles and she wanted you to keep right on praying for him."

Pat thought he noticed a note of respect in Mrs. Wright's voice. Of course, that was to be expected when one could work miracles. He wondered how many other of his prayers were outstanding, perhaps performing miracles at the very moment.

"Copy for the church newsletter has to be in today."

Pat grimaced. Not only did he have to come up with a title for next Sunday's sermon but he also had to write an inspirational column. Among the announcements of births, deaths, marriages, baptisms, meetings, and new books for the library, the parishioners expected to find a couple of paragraphs from the pastor.

Pat hated the column which Mrs. Wright had first entitled *Standing Pat* and which he had changed to *From the Pastor's Desk*. It represented him at his worst, because enthusiasm and good diction might camouflage a dull sermon, and a poor memory might transform it into something better, but thoughtless prose stood naked before the world. Besides, Mrs. Wright mailed copies of the bulletin to shut-ins, visitors, church members who were in college or the armed forces, and other churches, and Pat disliked thinking of his hurried, careless words being sown on the wind beyond recall.

Pleading a busy schedule and a headache, Pat hoped that Mrs. Wright would be able to find an old paragraph in the files that might be suitable for reuse.

Mrs. Wright promised to look but demonstrated little faith that anything he had written would be worth printing twice. "I thought since you were in the Great Crusade and Ray Elliott being killed and all that you might like to say something about the paradoxes of life and death. I remember Dr. Ledbetter preached a sermon on that subject one time. The finest sermon I ever heard. How that man could preach!"

"What did he say?"

"He just told what they were. Were there many people in the hospital?"

"Oh, lots of people are sick. A whole pot full," he said, closing the door of the church office behind him, unwilling to admit he didn't know what the paradoxes of life and death were.

Pat stopped on his way through the sanctuary to check on the scratched pew. Mr. Murph had, in an economy of work, gone over the scratches with a dark stain, the effect of which was to make obvious what had before been merely noticeable. Stifling the impulse to leave the emblazoned word for the ladies of the church to call to Mr. Murph's attention, he went in search of the old man, finding him dozing in the balcony in an attitude resembling prayer.

"Is airy sinless?"

"What say?"

"No, nairy," he said. "Mr. Murph, I want you to get your brush and bucket of stain and block out the entire scratch so that it cannot be read. Do you understand that?"

"I just did what you said."

"Just do it," Pat said, turning on his heel and leaving the balcony, feeling that there was a conspiracy against him. Everyone was going to do what he said and then blame the result on him.

"Jerry Barnes was a member of this church for three years," he wrote in the solitude of his office, composing a recommendation that was not enthusiastic, but not a black mark either. Not strictly honest but neither an outright lie. In short, nearly perfect, a recommendation that didn't recommend. Besides, the Bible said a man was not to judge—

"DID HE ASK FOR A HAND, PAT?"

"Yes, Lord, I gave him a rope. It's not my fault if he uses it to hang himself."

Pushing the letter aside, Pat attacked the problem of his paragraph in the church newsletter only to be interrupted by the telephone. Sam Sorrele.

"Maybe there's something you didn't know. I told you somebody put old Bob up to joining the church and I went out and found who it was," Sam said. "It's Jeremiah Brown, that nigger politician who's so thick with Jack Merrick. It's just a plot for Jack Merrick to get the nigger vote."

"Sam, I don't believe a word of it."

"You don't, huh? Well, here's something else you may not believe. That economy, progress, and nondiscrimination that Jack is campaigning on killed a little nigger boy in an iron lung. The other papers aren't going to say anything about it because it might offend Mr. liberal-minded Merrick, but my paper is going to say that Jack Merrick killed that little boy."

"It was an accident," Pat said, chagrined that in the entire city only he and a rabid bigot recognized Jack's culpability.

"If Jack Merrick can get the nigger vote by getting a nigger into his church, I think I can lose him the nigger vote by telling how he killed that little nigger boy."

There it was. If Pat would keep Bob Harkins out of the church, Sam wouldn't print the story about the boy's death. What could he do? The idea that Jack Merrick was promoting Bob Harkins into the church to get votes seemed preposterous to Pat. He had met the old man and liked him. Whether or not Jack could be hurt by *The Informer* Pat didn't know, but Jack would have to look after himself. Pat was tired of protecting the wealthy and well-fed at the expense of the dispossessed. He would not offend Bob Harkins to save Jack Merrick from the consequences of his own deed.

"You can't blackmail me, Sam. If Bob Harkins wants to come, he can. And if you could do any damage with that outhouse paper of yours, you'd have done it long ago," he said, hanging up the telephone with satisfaction.

For a moment he tried to picture Sam's ugly red face and then he went back to the problem before him. What would he write in the newsletter this week?

PROFOUND: "Last Sunday morning a little girl's purse containing her Sunday School offering was stolen from our church library!!! This is just one more striking evidence of America's downhill plunge with the moral brakes completely burned out—"

HUMBLE: "Next week will mark my tenth anniversary

in the gospel ministry, an occasion I hope will pass unnoticed—"

RIGHTEOUS: "I was in church Sunday night. Where were you? If the trump had sounded and the Lord had appeared would you have been embarrassed—"

BACK PATTING: "I am justifiably proud of my church. The spirit is such that I had no fear in going on vacation with the knowledge and confidence that in my absence, regardless of personal consequences, the church would take the right stand on—"

PROMOTION: "Stage One (Compel them to come) has been successfully completed and Stage Two (Commence the conquest) will be launched this week with every Astronaut (Sunday School teacher) carrying a sign reading: GET IN THE SPACE RACE, BE IN SUNDAY SCHOOL AND FILL UP THE PLACE."

Pat had visions of future archaelogists digging up the bundles of church bulletins and from them determining the kind of religion that was practiced.

"—appears to have been a numerological society which, while not so devout as agnostics nor so contemplative as atheists, exercised an acute interest in illness and a social enthusiasm exceeded only by the ritualistic sports of the times."

All right, he would write something profound that would make his parishioners sit up in their chairs and cause future archaeologists to drop their shovels. Across the top of the sheet of paper he wrote *The Paradoxes of Life and Death* and sat staring at the words. "All right," he said. "What are they?"

Dr. Espey would know what to say. He would drop his

left hand into his coat pocket to show his humanity, raise his chin to show his authority, frown to demonstrate his sincerity, and in slow, measured tones he would say: "The paradox of life is that a man dies, and the paradox of death is that he yet lives." And everyone would think it was great. They would nod their heads and wonder why they had never thought of that. *Life* magazine would quote him in italicized reverence, and *Christian Century* would run a feature article on his Theology of Irreconcilables. If Pat Shahan said it, he would be able to hear groans and snickers from the farthest pew.

Pat was still staring at the blank sheet of paper when the intercom buzzed. "Mrs. Zinkgraf is here to see you," Mrs. Wright said, and even over the telephone he could hear her tone of disapproval. Mrs. Wright sat in judgment of those who came to see him.

"All right. Tell her to come on back," he said, trying not to imagine the curt manner in which Mrs. Wright would inform Marjorie: "Reverend Shahan will see you now." He tried not to think of the embarrassment Marjorie would feel as she heard, the conflicts she would face walking alone through the darkened sanctuary, the shame she would feel as she sat in his office.

Marjorie Zinkgraf was what every church secretary recognized on sight, what every pastor's wife suspected, what every minister laughed about, half-dreaded, half-yearned for—the serpent lurking in the Garden of Eden, the siren lying in wait in the sanctuary, the soprano soloist setting snares in the pastor's study.

But other ministers had Delilahs and Bath-shebas to tempt them, Thais whose souls they sought, whose bodies they reached for, fat Ladies Aid Chairwomen they righteously rejected and hypocritically laughed at. He had Marjorie Lowe Hildebrand Zinkgraf, small-town high-school sweetheart who had at too early an age married a stranger in uniform, been unfaithful to him, and then in a fit of guilt and remorse caused by his death had married Warren Zinkgraf, a wounded veteran who would never be whole.

Marjorie cared for him, worked part-time in a department store to supplement his income (in addition to his pension Warren made pocket money by repairing clocks and cleaning guns), and was lonely, childless, and unloved. And what was to become of small-town high-school sweethearts who failed at love? For what other purpose were they born, for what other reason did they live?

Of course he had dreamed of such things—a beautiful woman stricken with an unholy passion for him. Sometimes she would be a woman of the streets, and sometimes she would be a sweet and innocent child, but in either case he would deny himself the satisfaction of a physical triumph to point her to a higher, purer, more fulfilling love, knowing that although he would never possess her, she would always belong to him, would covertly place flowers on his pulpit, would watch him from a secret pew. She would die the victim of slander, or overwork, a dread disease and a broken heart, and he would stand at her graveside pronouncing the last words, he alone knowing as the earth rained down upon her that she loved him. And he would walk away holding the memory of her pure and undying love for him like a faded tissue rose, full of sentiment and nostalgia but lacking both odor and thorns.

Marjorie's first visit had taken him completely by surprise. He had not known her then, and she had come to him as a mature woman with an unsatisfactory marital life seeking physical fulfillment. He had panicked, making an ass of himself, talking too loudly and too much, flexing his moral muscles and striking self-righteous poses. "She never laid a hand on me, Lord."

Subsequent visits had been less tumultuous but more painful as they tried to communicate through mutual embarrassment and shame. He knew that her life was misery, but he did not know a way out of it. He knew she had a tremendous load to bear, but he could not tell her to drop it, and he did not know how to make it lighter. Not knowing what she would demand of him this time or how he could help her, he awaited her coming.

Hearing her timid knock, Pat self-consciously put on his glasses, rose to his feet, and invited her in. Marjorie appeared to have just come from work, as she was dressed attractively in a businesslike white blouse, dark skirt, sweater and high heels, with her brown hair brushed back from her face. Marjorie was only a few years older than Pat but her eyes were old and tired, and her face, though still beautiful, was taut and strained. She appeared calmer and more composed than the last time he had seen her, but she did not look at him when she came in, and she quickly sat down.

"I didn't know whether you would be back or not," she said and then bit her lip. "I just thought I would drop by—you're probably very busy."

"I got in last night," Pat said. "Things have a way of piling up when you're gone but I'm about to get them under control. What can I do for you?"

"I—I have a lot of trouble with the Trinity," she said.

"We all have a lot trouble with the Trinity," he said, joking to set her at ease. Marjorie smiled and seemed to relax a little.

The last time it had been the immortality of the soul she didn't understand. "We have to believe in immortality, don't we?" she had asked. "Otherwise why would we live like this? I mean, if I thought I were going to live this day only once I wouldn't spend it at work, or here in your office, or even at—I mean, think of all the people who are trapped, who never do what they want to do. We couldn't live like that, could we? If none of it meant anything—all the struggling and doing the best you can—"

The time before that it had been Evil she didn't understand. "But how can God permit it? How can He allow us to do wrong? I don't mean us. We're old enough to know better and should have to pay for our mistakes, but what about children? A person can do something when he's a child—and maybe it's not even his fault, maybe he wasn't taught better—and have to pay for it the rest of his life. How can God—"

Now she wanted to understand the Trinity. Pat placed his palms together to indicate the gravity of his reply. "First, you must realize that the Christian concept of the Trinity does not contradict the Old Testament concept of the singularity and—"

While he answered deliberately, straight from the seminary textbook without thought, Marjorie stared at the stained-glass representation of the Good Shepherd without listening. Slowly her eyes closed. At first he thought she was going to pray, then he realized she was forcing back tears. "A lost soul," he thought. "Equipped for a world that was neatly packed away in the attic with the stereopticon and the butter mold, where unfaithful high-school sweethearts did penance by marrying wounded but poetic warriors." But the butter mold was gathering dust and Warren Zinkgraf was a selfish and contentious cripple.

"Think of it this way," Pat said, trying to get her involved in the abstraction of the problem. "In human terms a person is separate and distinct without any essential connection with other people. But when we speak of the triune God, we mean—"

Helplessly he watched her cry, but her tears were not so unrestrained this time, her grief so wretched. He thought of offering her his handkerchief. He thought of offering his shoulder to cry on. He thought of sympathetically touching her hand. Instead he pretended not to notice her tears. The subtle perfume of her body powder pervaded the office. Her lips parted and her breasts rose as she took a sudden breath. Pat looked quickly away.

"—undivided—uh—essence. Think in terms of functions—distinctions—" She wasn't listening, but at least she wasn't crying any more. She seemed pensive, forgetting he was there. He could deal with that. Anything was better than listening to her crying hysterically and telling of her hatred for herself, her husband, their life together.

Pat did not know why she had chosen him rather than another, nor why she continued to come. He never seemed to help her. He talked of Providence or Revelation because she never invited his advice, never mentioned her previous marriage, and never spoke about her life with Warren except in moments of hysteria and then only in general and emotional terms. Ignoring her tears, ignoring her piteous flirtations, he always plowed doggedly on, talking about corroborative evidence, the laws of probability, the theories of inspiration, the attributes of God, not knowing what else to do.

"—but all being of an equal and undivided essence. Without distinctions or personalities, God is an indefinable essence, and intangible—"

She seemed calmer now and her lonely face seemed to sag as the tension went out of it. Pat had been told that at sixteen Marjorie had been a great beauty. Now, nearing forty, much of that beauty remained but little of the happiness, the joy that must have once been a part of it. The years had added nothing to her prettiness, neither character nor fulfillment.

"—infinite unity and as such 'wholly other,' separate and apart from the finite—"

He had been told that she had known her first husband for less than a week when she married him, that they had been married for less than a month when he was shipped overseas, that Marjorie was living with a young, draft-exempt doctor when her husband was killed, that in the next three months she had been laid by every able-bodied man in the small town and then had married Warren Zinkgraf, kneeling beside his bed for the ceremony.

"—fundamental question of whether these distinctions are immanent or—"

He had been told that for over twenty years she had been faithful to Warren although he was probably impotent, although he was insanely jealous, abused her when she was late from work and publicly accused her of harlotry in the stock room of the department store. She took care of Warren, helping him in and out of the wheelchair, on and off the bed, working in the department store, and delivering the clocks he had repaired, fighting off the charities of gentlemen who wanted to make her happy, relieve her tension, fulfill her need as though she were a machine to be serviced.

"—evidence of the immanence and pre-existence of—"

Pat scanned the bookshelves looking for help. There was Hebrew History, The Life Of Jesus, The Development Of The Church, Revelation and Reason, New Sermon Illustrations, Myth And Meaning, but there was nothing to say to a woman who had thrown away her life first to vanity and then to penance. He leaned forward and stared at his desk, wishing he had an inspirational poem he could read.

"—that man and his world are part of the expression of God—a clue, a sign He had given us that—"

The first time she had been frightened and pathetic, desperate for him to see her as a woman, to be attracted to her, willing to give a little more because she had a little less to offer. And he had retreated into the role of the garrulous, bumptious minister talking about exegetical objections and rational grounds. Her emotional nakedness had been painful for him to see and instead of helping her he had only added guilt and frustration to her other burdens. But despite movies and popular novels there was nothing he could give her that did not dispossess her.

He had escaped her seduction, but he had not been proud of it. His sense of failure at not helping her was complicated by a sense of personal loss because he was sure she would not come back, and a touch of jealousy because he was sure she would turn to some other man. But she had come back, painfully embarrassed, unable to look him in the eye, stammering out her wish to know more about the transcendence of God.

"—some of the marks or signs of the infinite God in the finite—"

He was too young for this. Ministers should be old as serpents, harmless as doves. Even atheists liked old ministers. There was something safe about the old, something neuter. That was the reason God was always pictured as a white-bearded grandfather. Still, Eve covered herself with leaves when she heard Him coming—

There should be some tension between them. After all, he was a man and she was a woman. He didn't want her to think him neuter or effeminate. But each time she came Marjorie seemed less aware of him as a man. She sat in his office, in his presence, not listening to his words, scarcely aware he was there. What was she thinking? What was she looking for in his office? What did she find?

"In the Book of Romans, St. Paul refers to these things, saying—"

What would Brother Paul say to Marjorie? Why, he would quote the thirteenth chapter of First Corinthians. " 'Love suffers long and is kind. Love seeketh not its own. Love never faileth.' " Well, he knew the words too. He could quote them to Marjorie. But where was she going to find that kind of love? He had not found it, not even with Lillian. There were times in his preoccupation with the problems of others, in his anxieties over his pastoral duties when he forgot who was there, and it was not love he made but the gesture without expression, symbol without substance, act without grace.

And Marjorie had not found that kind of love either, in

spite of all the arms and beds she had been in. Or if she had found it, it was with Warren. Certainly her life with him suffered long and was kind, and certainly it was not self-seeking. But she failed, and when she failed she came to him and sat in his office staring at the Good Shepherd while he spoke pious nonsense.

"—love and as Eternal Love, God must have an object which is also—"

Marjorie looked at him sharply. She had heard that. She seemed to be thinking about what he had said as though it had some meaning for her. Probably he shouldn't have used the word "love," but that was the trouble with the Christian religion. No matter at what point you began, you always ended up talking about love and church attendance.

"You mean—in order for God to be love, He has to have someone to love?" she asked.

Her question caught him by surprise. Was that what he meant? Certainly it was an oversimplification, but that was it, wasn't it? It might be more blessed to be loved, but it was more difficult to love. Marjorie had always sought to be loved; was she now able to give love? Pat studied her for a moment. He thought she was.

"—not the object but the source of love, even when that love is unrequited, even when the subject is unworthy, or unlovely—"

She was still listening, but less intently now, and he knew she was composing herself, preparing herself to go home to Warren Zinkgraf, to try once again to find love in the midst of jealous impotence and self-pity. How could he help her?

"Marjorie, the Trinity—"

"I think I understand now," she said, standing up. She even smiled, a careful, strained smile. "It always helps when you explain things."

Pat stood stiffly behind the desk, helpless, left out, an alien to her life, noticing the curve of her hips as she let herself out the door.

"DID SHE ASK FOR LOVE, PAT?"

"Yes, Lord, I gave her doctrine."

Pat Shahan, pious eunuch, encompassed with visions he cannot see, surrounded by people he cannot know, in the midst of experiences he cannot share.

GOD IS MY TISSUE PAPER ROSE.

"Ruby Watson and Lee Jepperson are here for their appointment," Mrs. Wright said.

Thanking her, Pat went to the door to watch Lee and Ruby come down the aisle together. In a few more days he would watch them walk up the aisle together, but on that occasion they would be man and wife. How many couples had he seen coming to his office hand in hand, arm in arm, radiant with happiness, touching in their concern for each other? It was a sight of which he never tired. Such things always bolstered his faith in love, increased his understanding.

But Lee and Ruby did not walk down the aisle hand in hand. They did not even come down the aisle together. Each sauntered along at his own pace, in his own pleasure, seemingly oblivious to the other.

"They've quarreled," Pat thought as they approached his

study as though it were a dentist's office. With a smile of good will that he hoped would soften their temporary displeasure with each other, he invited them in.

Lee and Ruby sat down, slumping in their chairs, bored, looking neither at him nor at each other but waiting with sullen impatience for him to have his fun.

Pat did not like them. They looked immature, untidy, irresponsible. Lee's hair was too long, Ruby's dress was too short. They appeared irreverent, disrespectful, and superior. For the first time in his pastoral career he was about to marry two people he did not like. And what was he going to say to them? He had prepared his little sermonette, the kind of thing he always said on such occasions, but now it seemed oddly inappropriate. He was not sure they would understand it, that he would be able to relate to them. Nevertheless, because he did not know what else to do, with a germ of doubt he began in his traditional, tried and approved way.

Pat Shahan, shepherd of love, cupid of the church, advising a young American couple on the meaning of love. " 'Love never ends; as for prophecy, it will pass away; as for tongues, they will cease; as for knowledge, it will pass—' "

Pat Shahan, plotter of destiny, director of fate, scheduling the lives of others. "Let's put it on the calendar for 7:30 Friday evening with the rehearsal set for the same time Thursday—"

Pat Shahan, matrimonial folk humorist commenting on the rituals of respectability. "I offer three suggestions. Keep it short, keep it simple, and keep the mothers out of it—"

Pat Shahan, moralist, philosopher, and matrimonial consultant, setting forth his theories of systematic bliss. "There are four aspects of married life to be considered—physical, spiritual, social, and financial. Let us first consider the physical—"

Pat Shahan, dispenser of faith, forgiveness, and conjugality, pronouncing his special blessing. "I'll see you on Thursday. God's blessing on both of you. Don't tempt fate, and may the grace of—"

Still they sat—Ruby Watson and Lee Jepperson—bored but waiting. Perhaps he had left something out. Pat looked at his watch. Almost twenty minutes. He had given them the full treatment. Nevertheless, he thought back over what he had said to see if he had left anything out, remembering how Dr. Hoffman had said that when a minister undertook a wedding his obligations were not over until the children had been baptized. "There's a lot more than a fee involved," Dr. Hoffman had said.

Mindful of his lifetime obligation to two strangers who had asked him to make them morally and legally one, Pat sat up in his chair and leaned forward across the desk in a gesture they could interpret either as dismissal or an invitation to ask questions. Still they sat, slumped in their chairs, seemingly oblivious to each other and to him.

Pat studied the straight-haired girl who sat with her knees apart so that he could see halfway up her thigh, her mouth screwed up in an attitude of cynical resignation. Perhaps, despite her assumed knowledgeability, there was something she wished to know about the physical side of marriage. Did she think because of his profession, because of the difference in their ages that there was a communication barrier between them—a gulf? Did she think he wouldn't understand? He who had sat in the damp storm cellar praying that God woud reveal to him who Cain and Abel married so that he wouldn't have to ask his mother?

Perhaps Ruby was afraid. It was only natural. A young girl placing her body, her life, her future in the hands of a man who was yet an unknown quantity. Would he be kind? Faithful? Dependable? Would their love be mature, redemptive, drawing them closer together as the years passed? Would they live happily ever after? Or was that the cruelest of man's delusions and dreams? Did she think he couldn't understand her anxiety? He had taken a young girl to his own bed, with nothing to offer her but a shabby vision of what he wanted to do. In a half-empty church decorated with a single spray of flowers, dressed in a new blue suit he had selected because he could use it afterward to preach in, he had waited with an impatient Dr. Espey beside the altar for Lillian to march down the aisle in the white wedding dress she had borrowed from a friend. Ridiculous ritual enacted by children. Solemn parody of wealth and respectability. Passionate pledging of uncontrollable virtues to the unknown future. What had he seen in Lillian's eyes? Fear? Anxiety? No, he had seen trust. She had believed in him, in his promises, in his petty dream of duty. She had believed in happily ever after.

"Sexual compatibility is based on faith just as surely as man's relationship to God. All human relationships are based on trust, understanding and—"

"We know all that," Lee said.

Startled at the interruption, Pat looked at Lee, a stocky, dark, low-browed, bushy-headed boy of perhaps nineteen or twenty. The superior knowledgeability of high-school graduates irritated him. Of course it was hard to tell any more how much they knew about sex. He had offended some of his parishioners by supporting sex education in the public schools, but he sometimes doubted its value. After two lectures on menstruation, menopause, and contraception, and one on abnormal psychology, some of the students felt they knew all there was to know about love and physical gratification. Pat thought of letting them know he knew a lot of things about sex they had never heard of but decided against it.

It was obvious they wanted to ask something, because they moved not at all, but sagged dejectedly in their chairs. What could it be? Did they want his approval? Did people say they were too young, too immature, that they weren't right for each other, that they couldn't know the meaning of love, duty, responsibility? Did they think he wouldn't understand? He could still remember his mother's polite but condescending words. "Well, of course I like Lillian. I think the world of her. But—do you think she could ever be a minister's wife?"

Dr. Espey, whose own wife was a shy, frail woman who pretended perpetual ill health to avoid church duties, was even more direct. "She seems very nice, Pat," he had said. "But she will have to learn that the will of the Lord and the good of the church come first. Only after you have fulfilled your duties as a minister may you consider your duties as a husband and father."

But the real surprise had come from his father, who loved Lillian. "I wish you wouldn't get married, Pat," his father had said.

Pat had sat beside his father on the old, lumpy pink sofa in the deserted lobby of the hotel, staring at the ruins of ancient Rome painted on the walls, wanting to ask his father what it meant? Wasn't love gentle, kind, redemptive? Wasn't love happily ever after? Later he had sat beside his father's deathbed with the same question on his lips. "What is love then if it doesn't heal, doesn't restore?" But he had been unable to ask it.

Yes, he understood what it was to want the approval and the encouragement of others. He knew what it was for two people to stand alone in a half-empty church and to face the dark and prospectless and unknown future with nothing but trust in each other and a pledge of mutual responsibility.

"It is kind of frightening when you think of all the important decisions you have to make before you're old enough to vote, isn't it?" he said, smiling at them. They did not return the smile. "But love is a pledge of responsibility, to understand and care for each other. To leave father and mother, the security of home—"

That wasn't it either. He saw them exchange a look of patient boredom. They were enduring his counsel the same way they had endured high-school lectures and parental advice, putting in their time until they could get a piece of paper that guaranteed their claim to the American dream of happiness. "What is it you want to know?" he asked.

Lee leaned over in his chair, hanging his head. Ruby chewed a thumb. "How—how do we know we're going to like each other?" Lee asked. He did not smile.

Pat looked at Ruby. She was not smiling either. They were serious, but what did they mean? Were they talking about sexual compatibility? Intellectual agreement? Cultural similarity? Common taste? "You want me to marry you and you don't even know if you like each other?"

"You can love somebody you don't like," Ruby said, scratching at a blackhead on her chin. "My mother says she loves my father but she doesn't like him."

"And even if you like a person, how do you know you'll like them next year?" Lee asked. "Jimmy Green—last year he was my best friend. This year I don't even like him."

"People change," Ruby said. "You think you like people and you find out you don't even know who they are."

Pat stared at them, trying to control his exasperation. They were irresponsible, insolent, making a mockery of his office as a minister. He thought of washing his hands of them, of sending them somewhere else to get married. He was too tired, too busy to put up with such foolishness. Lee and Ruby slouched in their chairs, idly staring at the floor while they pinched at pimples. The future of America, he thought. The hope of tomorrow.

"Why do you want to get married?" Pat asked out of curiosity.

Lee and Ruby exchanged a look that revealed little respect for his intelligence. "So we can live together," Lee said.

"What if you find out that you don't like each other?" Pat asked.

"That's what we're asking you," Lee said.

"We thought we wouldn't have any children. At least until we know whether or not we like being married," Ruby said.

"Have you talked this over with your parents?" Pat asked.

"Yeah, I told them," Lee said. "My mother said not to come around asking her for money. My stepfather hasn't said anything to me since I was sixteen."

"Ruby, what did your folks say?"

"Mother said I should talk to a preacher."

Pat felt the uncomfortable weight of middle age pressing upon his shoulders. For the first time he felt a lack of understanding, a lack of trust in the younger generation. He was a stranger, an outsider unable to judge their experience by his own. He had been born in a day when there was right and there was wrong, and even the people doing them knew which was which.

Pat did not want to marry Lee and Ruby. He did not want to baptize their children, to attend their anniversaries. He wanted to forget them, to ignore their life together. He wanted the luxury of being appalled by their immaturity, their irresponsibility, their lack of manners and respect, but he could not afford it. Either he should send them to a Justice of the Peace or he should make an attempt to help them establish a stable and lasting home.

While they sank lower and lower in their chairs, patiently enduring, exchanging occasional glances of agonized incredulity, he lectured them on: LOVE IS NOT A FOUR-LETTER WORD, MARRIAGE IS NOT ALL BEDS AND ROSES, and TO HAVE A LOVING SPOUSE YOU MUST BE ONE.

At last, knowing that he had failed, that he had not reached them, that they understood nothing of what he said, he decided to punish them no more. "Does that help any?" he asked.

"Yeah, I guess that's all we wanted to know," Lee said without conviction.

"Well, we'll see you at the rehearsal," Ruby said as they left, walking as far apart and as oblivious to each other as when they came.

Pat wondered if he should refuse to marry them. He wondered if it weren't a mockery. He couldn't stop them from getting married, but he didn't have to stamp their union with the church's approval. Perhaps he should try to counsel them again. But nothing he said reached them and they didn't want advice. They just wanted to live together.

But was that any different from what his generation had wanted? They married for love, for a stronger America, a better tomorrow, a safer world. They said that love was the greatest thing in the world, that marriages were made in heaven, that responsible parenthood was next to godliness, that the home was the cornerstone of democracy and the church. But for all their lofty words their record was marred with failure. If Lee and Ruby liked each other after a year of married life they would be ahead of many of their predecessors.

Perhaps the word love had become so commonplace, so commercial, so ersatz that it was no longer respectable. Very well, let them find another word. "Like bears all things, believes all things, hopes all things, endures all things. Like never ends."

"WILL IT LAST, PAT?"

"Lord, I believe in the resurrection of the young."

Pat Shahan, friend of tomorrow, investor in the future, praying for whatever endures.

GOD IS HAPPILY EVER AFTER.

Days of Prophecy

> *And it shall come to pass in the last days, saith God, I will pour out of my Spirit upon all flesh: and your sons and your daughters shall prophesy, and your young men shall see visions, and your old men shall dream dreams . . .*

PAT SHAHAN, besieged commander, writing to Dr. Espey and All Other Christians In The World.

"Sir:

I am surrounded by the enemy. My orders are confusing, my weapons are obsolete, my ammunition is ineffective. My targets were destroyed in the last war. I am facing wholesale desertion by friendly forces. I am determined never to surrender this Civil Defense Shelter nor to retreat into the future. Victory or death! Please advise."

Pat Shahan, vicar of Christ, composing an encyclical to the Chairman of the Program Committee of The Great Crusade.

"Blessings on you, T.F.

"And thank you for allowing me in my small way to participate in the Great Crusade. It was a never-to-be-forgotten experience, and I certainly had a good time. Let's do it again next year and make it a bigger and better success in every way. Say hello to all the gang—the bullfighter, the actor—"

Pat Shahan, exiled apostle, transcribing visions of The Paradoxes Of Life And Death.

"To Mrs. Wright And All The Members Of The Church Who Were, Who Are, And Who Are To Come:

I perceive that—

An Atheist is a person who blames God for the way man is.

A Humanist is a person who blames the world for the way man is.

A Christian is a person who blames man for the way God is.

Dr. Espey is all horse and no rider.

A liberal is a man who hates his overpaid servants.

A conservative is a man who loves his underpaid servants.

A pacifist is a man who has not yet spotted a target.

No one likes a holier-than-thou Atheist.

Children should not be born under air conditioners.

As Methuselah said: 'Old age is no accident.'

Christians are called apart. We are not of this world. We accept contributions from anyone but we give tribute only to God.

The purpose of education is to equip the student to rationalize his preconceptions.

That which is most secret in a woman is most obvious in a cow.

It is easier to sing a lie than to tell the truth. Where were the angels when I was born?

A circumcised child is a happy—"

The intercom buzzed. "I don't want to keep bothering

you, but it's time to take the copy for the bulletin to the printers," Mrs. Wright said. "Is your column ready?"

"I'm sorry, Mrs. Wright, I just haven't had time to do it today," Pat said. "I guess you'll just have to reuse an old one."

"Well, can you give me the title for Sunday's sermon so that I can get that in the newsletter? If I don't get it to the printer's before five o'clock we can't get it in the bulletin, and I think people like to know what the sermon is going to be."

"I'll think about it and call you back in a few minutes, Mrs. Wright," Pat said, hanging up.

In the bottom drawer of his desk were copies of all his sermons, each marked with the time and place of its presentation to avoid the embarrassment of preaching the same sermon to the same audience before they had been given an opportunity to forget it. Now, in his desperation, Pat opened the drawer and began his search for a sermon which was fresh and exciting and also tried and true.

Blind Love—The Story Of Sampson. Had he ever been that young?

On Being A Pillar Of Strength In A Day Of Trouble. Had he ever been that dull?

Will Your Anchor Hold? Had he ever been that naïve?

What Would Jesus Do? When had he been so wise?

I Accuse!! When had he been so righteous?

Who Is On The Lord's Side? When had he been so clear-sighted?

On Being A New Person. " 'To him that overcometh will I give to eat of the hidden manna, and will give a white stone, and in the stone a new name written—' "

There, neatly typed on Mrs. Wright's electric typewriter

were his immortal words. "In every man there is a desire for a fresh start, a better birth, a new name." When had he said that? Only three months ago and already he wanted to wipe the slate clean and start over. Perhaps then he would be able to find understanding for Evan Moore, peace for Emily Graham, forgiveness for Jack Merrick. But would he be able to stop a falling plane, explain a monster child, accept a revolving neon cross, measure the depth and breadth of a couple's love, or find meaning in the signs and banners of his life?

There, stiff and yellow with age, was the first sermon he had ever preached. Curious, he lifted the single, folded sheet of typing paper out of the file and opened it. *The Love of God*. He was still in high school when Dr. Espey had asked him to address the church, and he had been both elated and terrified.

"What will I say?" he asked Dr. Espey.

"Just tell them what you know about the Lord," Dr. Espey said.

Pat thought that was easy enough for Dr. Espey to say because Dr. Espey had been to college and the seminary and knew about all there was to know about the Lord, but he knew almost nothing, and certainly everyone in the church knew as much as he.

"What am I going to say?" he asked his mother.

"Whatever the Lord gives you to say."

"What if he doesn't give me anything to say?"

"Then don't say anything," his mother said, "because if you do it will be a lie."

Pat didn't understand how he could say nothing with the whole church waiting for him to speak. He would have to say something even if he made it up himself. Even if it weren't true.

He had waited as long as he could, wandering aimlessly across the fields and down to the pasture, climbing up on the water tank or the big cottonwood tree in the front yard to look out to the horizon. He sat on the corral fence, he waited beside the horse trough, he lay awake at night listening to the wind in the cottonwoods making the sounds of rain. But the Lord did not give him anything to say and there was no more time to wait. Frantically he began looking for words. What did he know about God?

There on the stiff, yellowing paper, printed in ink by his own clumsy hand were the points of the sermon. God is love. The Bible tells it. Nature proves it. Wise men through the ages have said it. Our own lives reveal it. Because God is love, his children must be love also. Therefore: how a man loves is more important than what he believes.

The sermon had been a failure. As far as he could tell no one loved any more or any differently than before. His mother and father, for the only time he could remember, sat side by side in church, yet on the way home they had quarreled. His father had pointed out that one of the men serving as usher was a bootlegger. His mother denied it. In less than a year his father had moved out of the house, leaving a letter behind.

Dr. Espey had hurriedly corrected any false impression that "young Brother Shahan" had said how a man loved was more important than what he believed. After all, as a man thought in his heart, so he was.

Pat looked at the faded words. Had he really thought

that how a man loved was more important than what he believed? Had he ever been so young? So naïve? So idealistic?

He had been ashamed of his failure and had gone to the barn to be alone. His mother had found him and had tried to console him, to explain his failure, to explain her life with his father by saying that while the love of God was certainly an unmitigated good, human love was quite another thing.

"God's love makes you wise," she said. "Sometimes human love just makes people foolish. I hope you learn, son. I hope you understand. You have to be careful."

He had understood. He had learned that love was sharper than the sword, crueler than jealousy, more heartless than hate. Love aimed its guns against the sky. Love was the prayed-for monster. Love made one vulnerable. Love exposed.

Pat studied the outline, trying to discover some glimpse of the boy who wrote it. What had he been thinking? How did nature prove the love of God to a boy who spent summer days rescuing the drowning bees? How had his life revealed the love of God when he had tortured a kitten, killed a white hawk? Did he know that in less than a year he would sit with his mother in a strange apartment and listen to children laughing in the snow? Pat dropped the sermon back into the file. He couldn't use it.

No, he did not believe that how a man loved was more important than what he believed. He couldn't believe that. Not even if it were true. That would make his education, his study of the scriptures, his sacrifices and self-denial, his thoughts and prejudices, his plans for the salvation of the world, his private bargains with God things of no importance. All the pretty things he said on Sunday, all the splendid thoughts he expressed, all the committees he appointed, all the budgets he approved, all the charities he initiated would be nothing. No, he couldn't believe that. Not even if it were Christian.

"HOW DO YOU LOVE ME, PAT?"

"Carefully, Lord."

Pat Shahan, breathless messenger, exhausted runner, discovering that he has lost the message, unable to go back in search of it because running has become more important.

GOD IS MY EXPOSURE.

Pat Shahan, phantom paraclete, bearing the consolation of religion, the sympathy of the church, the hope of immortality to Rachel Elliott. Driving through planned, restricted, repetitious neighborhoods, past OLYMPIA HEIGHTS, PEACEFUL VALLEY, HAPPY MEADOWS, INSPIRATION HILLS, ENCHANTED FOREST, down streets named SERENADE, MILKY WAY DRIVE, RAINBOW'S END, stopping beside a mailbox made of a dummy bomb. RAY ELLIOTT, 246 FANTASY LANE.

Pat waited a moment in the car in front of the brick, ranch-style house in the middle-income development which, although it was still being developed, was no longer fashionable. He had been here only once before. On that occasion he had been driving through the neighborhood on his way to talk to a widow whose only daughter had run away from home. Seeing Ray working in the yard, Pat had stopped to ask directions.

Ray, lean and tan, with sweat glistening on his smooth face, had given him directions clearly, distinctly, without doubt or haste. "Turn right at the second corner, proceed for four blocks, take the left fork of the—"

After Pat had thanked him and Ray had repeated his instructions for accuracy, Ray had demonstrated his new lawn mower, a powerful model loaded with adjustable accessories. "That's a real fine machine," Pat had said to Ray, a little intimidated by all the intricacies and choices it offered. "A real fine machine."

"It gets the job done," Ray said precisely, without ostentation or pride.

Pat sat in the car looking at the house. What would he say to Rachel? "I'm sorry? Death comes to the best of us? Death is not death but a little sleep? Death is not separation but beautiful island of somewhere? Family reunion in the sweet bye-and-bye? Weep not, for his warfare is accomplished, his iniquity is pardoned? Weep not, for he's over on the other shore?"

And what would Rachel say to him? He knew the desire to strike back at death, to lash out at those closest at hand, to affix blame, inflict pain, draw blood. He had sat with his mother at his father's deathbed, both of them looking for targets of opportunity.

Would Rachel try to assign the guilt for Ray's death? Would she hold herself responsible because he had left her, and home, and children to risk his life? Would she call him to account because he had been the one to mention the Cru-

IN THE HOUSE OF THE LORD

sade's need for a pilot to Ray? Would she hold the Crusade responsible because the need for publicity had caused a man's death? Would she lay the body at the door of the church because Ray had been on church business? Would she accuse God because God permitted accidents?

And what would he say if she did? Should he explain that it was natural for humans to attempt to alter the event by determining the cause—to change the past by labeling the guilt? Should he admit he had referred the Program Committee's request for an experienced pilot to Ray and try to explain why he had done it? Should he suggest that pilots who were not church members also crashed? Should he remind her that atheists blamed God for death, Christians blamed each other. Should he acknowledge that the Crusade was folly climaxed by Ray's meaningless death? Was he called upon to justify God, Crusades, and death?

Pat got out of the car and walked across the neat brown grass checking his equipment—a cup of bitter tears, a sterile compress of humanity, a packet of hope (sprinkle lightly), two faded tablets of reason, a catalogue of nostrums, a last cigarette of remembrance, a vial of ammonia, a packet of dust, and as a last resort a commemorative service for a tranquilizer. He did not go empty-handed.

Pat Shahan, staring at his shoes in guilty impotence, ringing the doorbell with gentle dread, looking at Rachel with the embarrassment of mute sympathy, speaking in flustered commiseration, entering the house with his meager offering of hope.

Pat sat down on the couch in the small, formal living room, aware of his soiled shoes on the white carpet. Surely that was an ostentation with children in the house. Or a gesture. Perhaps a white flag thrown in the face of the world's dirty shoes. A manicured lawn contemptuous of the dogs of this world and their dirty business.

Rachel sat in a chair opposite him, an attractive woman in her early forties, casually yet neatly dressed. She appeared very tired. Her fingers trembled slightly, and there were dark circles under her eyes, but she was composed, without tears. She even managed a smile as she looked at him, waiting for the narcotic of hope, the palliative of religion, the mercifully sharp needle of remembrance.

" 'I am the resurrection and the life'," he said. " 'In my father's house are many mansions'," he said. "I remember the way Ray used to sit in church with you and the children and sing with such joy, such hope shining in his face," he said.

"The children know you're here," Rachel said. "They want to talk to you before you leave."

Pat shriveled a little inside. It was difficult enough explaining death to adults. To children death was incomprehensible. Annihilation was unbelievable. The immortality of memory and heirs was unsatisfactory. Harps and wings was unconvincing. Absorption into Other was unintelligible. "Yes, I wanted to see them," he said.

"How was it, Pat?" she asked with the same tired, strained smile. "How was the Crusade?"

Pat Shahan, apologist for ballyhoo, advocate of promotion, defender of the Crusade, measuring reality and illusion, dividing promise and result, weighing grandeur and disaster.

Not as good as we had hoped for, he thought, but better

than we had expected. Less than we had planned, but more than we needed. Neither an abysmal failure nor a stunning success. Not enough to fly on but enough to live with. A bold campaign expertly executed but falling short of the objective.

"It was about average," he said.

"Did you see Ray before the take-off?"

"Just briefly," Pat said, trying to remember those last moments when he and Ray had shouted at each other over the noise of the bi-winged stunt plane.

"Did Ray say anything?"

Pat tried to remember what they had said, but the shock of the crash seconds later had erased the words from his mind. What did Rachel want? Forgiveness for some petty quarrel in their last moments together? A sign that his last thoughts had been of her? Immortal words of wisdom for his children to live by? Life wasn't like that. People facing certain death might prepare a last word, but certainly no one dying accidentally, instantaneously ever left any memorable words behind. He was sure Ray had not. Their last words had probably been trivia, nonsense. "Is the banner straight?" "Don't fly so high they can't read the sign." "How much are they paying you for this?"

"I don't remember what we said," Pat told Rachel. "I'm not even sure we heard each other. Ray was already in the cockpit, and we had to shout over the noise of the engine."

Suddenly Ray's last words came to his mind. "This is the big one." Was that it? But what did it mean? For a war hero, pulling a banner couldn't be too big. Perhaps he had said: "This is a big one," referring to the record-breaking size of the banner. But no, Pat could remember that at the time he had wondered what Ray meant, had in fact been puzzling over the words when the airplane hit the ground. Ray must have believed that towing the sign over the city was a momentous and significant act.

"Pat, why did Ray agree to tow the sign knowing there was a risk? He was a married man with children."

Pat Shahan, high priest of fate, searching the ashes of events, examining the viscera of failure, giving reason and meaning to the accidents of men.

"Rachel, first of all, I am positive that it had nothing to do with you and the children, or anything that might have happened between you and Ray the last few days. It's human to blame oneself when accidents like this occur, and to think that by acting differently you could have prevented—"

"But why did he do it, Pat? He didn't want or need publicity. He had nothing to prove—courage or skill or whatever it is that men have to prove."

"Well, Rachel, perhaps this was Ray's way of doing what he could for the Lord. Not all of us can be preachers. Perhaps being a flier, Ray wanted to fly for the Lord."

"Ray thought the Crusade was stupid. Didn't he tell you? He said pulling that banner would do about as much good as dropping flower seeds on the city. He said scientists were sending rockets to the moon and the church was waving banners at fifteen hundred feet. He didn't do it because of the Crusade, not because he thought he was doing something important."

Pat stared at his soiled shoes on the white carpet. How was he supposed to know why people did things? Probably Ray did it because Pat had asked him to. Was that what Rachel was driving at? She wanted him to shoulder the blame for Ray's death? He looked up at her.

"Pat, the release was never pulled. Ray could have dropped the sign."

"Are you sure?"

"Don't you think I've checked? That's why I couldn't see you this morning. I had to be sure. The mechanism was working perfectly. But Ray didn't pull it. Why didn't he pull the release when he saw he couldn't get the banner up? Why didn't he drop the sign?"

Again Pat went back to poking with trembling fingers in the refuse of the past, looking for reason. Perhaps there hadn't been time to pull the release—then he remembered how the plane fell and bounced. There had been time. Perhaps Ray had panicked, fumbled for the release and missed it. Perhaps he had believed until the last moment that he could make it, and then, knowing that it would do no good, he did nothing. No, Pat couldn't accept that. If nothing else, instinct would pull the release, even if it were his dying gesture, even if he were already burning on the ground.

"Ray was a good pilot," Rachel said. "He had towed things before. He knew what to do. There has to be a reason why he didn't pull the release. I thought maybe you could explain. I want you to help me understand."

Pat closed his eyes and rubbed his temples with his fingers. Who knew Ray Elliott and who knew what he had done? And who, knowing, could explain Ray Elliott and what he had done? No one. But he had to try.

Pat sifted the ashes through his hands, parted the entrails with his fingers, not sure there was a reason, or that if there were it would be intelligible to him. Taking up the fragments known to him, he began piecing them together, trying to arrive at a picture he could understand.

Ray Elliott, Super Hero, skilled pilot, supremely confident of his ability to lift the banner, even while his pride sent him crashing to earth. Ray Elliott. PATRIOT, having flown banners all his life, SCHOOL SPIRIT, COLLEGE TRY, ESPRIT DE CORPS, DEATH BEFORE DISHONOR, unable to let them go even as they dragged him from the sky. Ray Elliott, Who Flew Higher Than Those Of His Generation, gesturing contemptuously at all man's efforts to save himself, with an upraised finger puncturing the world's balloon of upward mobility.

Having put the pictures together, Pat quietly tore them apart. The pieces fit together too well to be convincing, and their sum was less than Ray Elliott.

"Ray always liked you," Rachel said. "He didn't care for most ministers. He thought they were—not sissies or cowards but—soft-headed. Ineffectual. He always talked about a chaplain in Korea who gave flower seeds to the Communist prisoners because he thought doing nice things made people nice. He thought if they grew flowers they would become lovely too. Of course they just threw them on the ground, but it rained and the flowers came up. The chaplain said it was the miracle of the resurrection. He thought he was going to turn the whole compound into a flower garden. Then, just before they bloomed, while the chaplain was talking to them, the prisoners trampled the flowers into the ground. Just deliberately destroyed them. It really upset the poor man. For a while that was all he could talk about. 'People who destroyed flowers could destroy the world.'

Finally some of the men went out and pulled up his own flower bed to shut him up. You weren't a chaplain, were you?"

"No."

"You know, something happened to Ray in Korea. Korea changed him. I thought since you were there you might help me understand."

"I didn't go to Korea."

"Oh, I thought—I thought maybe you could tell me what happened to Ray."

Pat Shahan, callow apprentice, flawed prophet, alien adviser, trying to examine famine, pestilence, destruction, death, with a beam in his eye, a mote in his vision, trying to see Korea through the fog and damp tarpaulin of a California gun park.

Ray Elliott was a hero in the Pacific. An ace three times. He came home from the war victoriously, triumphantly, with pride in his country, in his outfit, in a job well done. But Korea was different, and although he was decorated he was not a hero, and although he returned home he was not triumphant, and although he had done his job he was not proud of it. It was hard to feel victorious and proud and triumphant, because no one had been declared winner. No one had been declared winner because no one had figured out how to keep score. In the Pacific you could paint the number of enemy planes on the fuselage of your own, you could stick flags on maps, and add up islands. But how did you keep score in Korea? What scale of bodies to yards? What ratio of our ridges to their roads, our bunkers to their bridges? Therefore, Ray Elliott took the banner because it was something he could paint on his fuselage, and went down in flames trying to write the score?

Ray Elliott was born to be a hero, a man who broke up the ball game with one swing of the bat, one long, arching pass. Ray wanted war to be the same way. He wanted one plane, one bomb, one victory. He wanted a war to end all wars, a death to end all death, a wrong to end all wrong. What he got was Korea. Korea was not a hero's war. There were no home runs, only sacrifice bunts. No long passes, only three yards and dust. Thousands of planes, ten thousands of bombs, creating nothing. Therefore, Ray Elliott agreed to tow a banner over the city because he thought it would break up the ball game and he struck out going for a home run?

Ray Elliott was a man of action who did the right thing instinctively, without thought. He was born to be a warrior, a knight errant in an age when men knew who the enemy was and could serve God, defend right, and save civilization by killing him. In a day when evil had a nationality and a name. The Mongol. The Hun. The Redskin. The Saracen. The Christian. The Vandal. The French. The English. The German. But in Korea the enemy had to be found, identified, and defined. He was the enemy only so long as he was on this side of that line and that side of this line, of this sex, of that age, of these nations, between the times of, excepting those who— Therefore, Ray Elliott seized the banner in his teeth and took off to mark the enemy positions?

None of it made sense to him. None of it explained anything, but Rachel was waiting for an answer. "Korea was a different kind of war," he said. "It was dirty, futile, without redemptive qualities." He paused. What was different about that? All wars had been Koreas. Only sometimes there had been a moment for triumph, jubilation, a victory party before dawn revealed the score. "Korea was the morning after," he said, trying again. "It was especially rough for men like Ray who thought they had won a lasting—achieved a final—I don't know, Rachel. I just don't know. I didn't go to Korea."

"Did Ray ever tell you about his vision?" Rachel asked.

"No, I don't think so," Pat said, expecting to hear how Ray had seen God above the Yalu River. But what Rachel had to tell him was not a vision at all but a rather commonplace incident.

Ray's wing was called in to give air support to a unit that was being attacked, but when they reached the area the troops on the ground were being overrun. The Chinese were in the bunkers and trenches and the troops were all mixed up so that he couldn't tell them apart. His guns were loaded and he was carrying napalm, but he couldn't do anything without killing his own men. The other pilots kept asking him for orders and the men in the bunkers were calling for support, but Ray circled until the planes ran low on fuel and had to return to their base.

"He didn't know what to do," Rachel said. "He was in command and he couldn't act. I don't think Ray ever got over that. He said it was like a nightmare—the enemy was all over them and there was nothing he could do but circle and watch. He said if he were in the bunkers and were being overrun and someone were flying cover, he would want them to drop the napalm. Even if it burned him, too. Can you understand that?"

Yes, he too had seen that vision—the barbarian horde overrunning the world. Only he had not seen it from the vantage point of a fighter plane but from walking the streets where men raped, pillaged, defaced public property, carved their names on monuments, destroyed natural beauty, defecated on graves, broke out windows, threw refuse in the streets, littered the highways with broken bottles, tore down traffic signs, shot up mailboxes, wrote obscenities on sidewalks— Perhaps that was why he had wanted to go to Korea. Because in Korea evil had a face, a name, and he could shoot it down, blast it with grenades, burn it with napalm, push it back into a corner and drop the bomb.

Would he then have discovered what Ray Elliott had seen? That evil did not have a name or face, a nationality or religion. Or rather, that evil was of every name and face, of every nation and religion. Men built prisons and discovered that Eichmann was the jailer. They built bunkers and discovered that Hitler was planning the defense. They built monasteries and discovered that Stalin sang the prayers.

Therefore, Ray Elliott, discovering that evil was his co-pilot, wrapped the banner tightly and inseparably about them both and sank from the sky?

Therefore, Ray Elliott, having picked up his shield and lance, and having ridden off to battle giants, discovered that he was tilting with phantoms and, folding his arms, waited to be cast to the ground?

Ray Elliott, having flown too high, discovered that the sun was melting the wax from his wings and—

Ray Elliott, having presumed too much—

It was incomprehensible to him. His head ached, his mind reeled. There was no way he could understand Ray Elliott in terms of what he had done. The pieces did not fit or they fit too well. Either there were not enough pieces to fill out the portrait or there were extra ones left over. And what did Rachel make of all this? Did she understand? Pat looked at Rachel for a sign.

"I think he lost faith in man," she said. "Ray always believed in God, and he used to have such faith in people —that they were good. Faith in his men, in himself. That they could do things. That they could right wrongs. But when he flew over those boys and saw there was nothing he could do to save them—something happened to him."

"But, Rachel, that was years ago."

"That's just it. Before Korea he believed he could change things—that he could make a difference. But after Korea things bothered him—little things he read in the paper, about people he didn't even know. Things no one could do anything about. I think once it was about a girl who wasn't admitted to college because a computer made a mistake. And there was something about a highway that went through a park because—I can't remember now. I try to forget those things as quickly as possible. But Ray was a very direct man. He hated being helpless. When something was wrong he wanted to set it right. He would risk his life to do it. He would bomb a church or a school to do it. But everything has gotten so muddled and confused and no one seems to be able to do anything."

"But why did he pull the sign, Rachel? And why didn't he pull the release?"

"That's what I hoped you would be able to tell me," she said.

Pat felt tired and confused, and the small, neat room with

its blatant white carpet seemed to close in on him. He was certain now that Ray had not towed the sign because he believed in the Crusade, or because his pastor had asked him to. But why Ray had done it, why he had not pulled the release, why Rachel told him about it he did not understand. Nor did he understand how a person could believe in God and lose faith in man. Did he believe that man was incapable of saving himself, incapable of escaping evil? And therefore—

Recognizing that he had a busy schedule, Rachel suggested that he might like to see the children now and led him into the family room where he waited for them amid the tokens and evidences of Ray's life. There were athletic trophies, high-school honors, pictures of a slim, confident Ray Elliott standing beside various types of airplanes, medals and ribbons from two wars, dummy bullets. A photograph of an atomic explosion hung on one wall looking like a dull and out-of-focus picture of a flower. What was it doing there? What did it mean? Was that the answer? The game-winning home run? The Pyrrhic victory? Was that Ray's idea of salvation? Was that the picture of Ray's God? Not with healing but with napalm in His wings? Or had Ray only been attempting to give a name, a face to the enemy? Pat raked through the souvenirs of Ray's life looking for a clue. And as he searched, the words to a blasphemous song came to his mind.

> O, the napalm's connected to the A-bomb,
> The A-bomb's connected to the H-bomb,
> The H-bomb's connected to plutonium,
> Now here is the Name of the Lord.
> Them bombs, them bombs, them H-bombs—

He turned to see the three frightened, wide-eyed children watching him. Vaguely he opened his arms in a gesture that could be a plea of innocence or an invitation to come to him for comfort. The children, a boy and a girl in junior high, another son in elementary school, stood beside their mother without moving.

Pulling the children with her, Rachel walked to the couch and sat down. The children settled around her, watching him, waiting for the words that would restore meaning, release them from guilt, and reassure them of an orderly universe in which men lived by reason and God ruled by love.

Wanting to be close to them, to bridge the chasm with his presence as well as his words, Pat placed a chair before the couch and sat down. "Life is short," he said. "Death is certain. The resurrection is our hope. The soul is immortal. Stars in my crown. Sweet bye and bye. To be with Jesus. To sit at the foot of the throne. Peace in the valley. Over on the other shore."

He gave them all the clichés, all the sugar pills men had gagged on since Abel perished. And still he had not consoled them, not wiped the tears from their eyes, not eased their sorrow, not borne a portion of their grief, not answered the question of why their father had to die. He gave them what he could, what he had, and it was not enough. The children watched him, waiting for an answer. Rachel pleaded with him to give them more.

"Your father was a good man," he said. "He-uh-lived a full life. He accomplished more than—a lot of men. He will be-uh-remembered. The good he has done will live after him. The mistakes he made will be forgotten. It is for us, for those of us yet living to—to carry on the work he—began.

It is for us—for those of us who—who remember, to keep alive those—things which—"

"Why did he have to pull that old sign anyway?" Debbie asked.

Pat Shahan, seeker of truth, picking through the bones of disaster in search of the name of Providence, of the hand of God.

"Debbie, we don't always understand—why men choose to—to do the things they do. We can only trust that—for them—regardless of the consequences, these actions had—uh—meaning and—"

"What did the sign say?" Robbie asked.

"Well, it said—" Pat looked at Rachel, but there was no help for him there. He searched the white carpet, the handsome, smiling Ray Elliotts leaning against airplanes. He studied the medals, trophies, dummy cartridges, souvenirs, a distorted and misshapen flower, but found no answer there.

Pat Shahan, in the Garden of Gethsemane, revealing his wounds, persevering to the end. "It said 'JESUS SAVES,' " he said, draining the cup.

"DID YOU PULL THE RELEASE, PAT?"

"No, Lord, I think I can make it."

Pat Shahan, heavenly pilot, steering his craft for the other shore, past UNDERSTANDING, COMMUNICATION, PEACE IN OUR TIME, WORLD DEMOCRACY, MANPOWER, NEW DAY.

GOD IS THE SIGN I FLY.

Pat Shahan, in the midst of an existential journey, searching for meaning, through rows of TASTE. TRY.

EXPERIENCE. Pat Shahan, honest man, seeking for truth among KING SIZE. ECONOMY SIZE. BARGAIN SIZE. FULL SIZE. Pat Shahan, family provider, groping through TAKE, BUY, BEST, for bread and cheese. Pat Shahan, threadbare savior, searching the shelves of FREE, SPECIAL, SAMPLE, for a bargain.

Pat Shahan in Vanity Fair, wondering what Lillian was doing that she couldn't go to the grocery store herself. "Probably washing," he thought, remembering how she had startled the members of his first congregation by announcing she would miss a meeting of the Ladies Missionary Society. "I have a washing to do," she said.

NEW. POWERFUL. DIFFERENT.

"First my husband and then the heathen," she said.

FANTASTIC. SENSATIONAL. FABULOUS.

"Let she who is without washing be First Vice President," she said, gathering another armload of leper's rags.

MIRACULOUS. REVOLUTIONARY. SUPREME.

"First the washing and then the world," she cried from the rooftops, her arms dripping WONDER WORKING, FAST ACTING—

Pat Shahan, feeling the actual, differentiating between fifteen kinds of enriched, natural process, guaranteed, new, different, bargain, fortified, flavor-added bread in convenient, comfort-fitted, customer-approved bags.

Pat Shahan, contacting the environment, standing in the check-out line, vainly hoping the shoppers with full baskets would let him ahead of them. No one noticed him. In fact, they seemed to notice nothing. After a day of making decisions, solving problems, watching for expressway turnoffs, and elevator stops, remembering names and telephone numbers, being bombarded by sights and sounds, being warned, threatened, appealed to and directed by signs, symbols, and flashing lights, they seemed to notice nothing—oblivious even to SURPRISE. EXTRA. BONUS. OFFER.

Ahead of him a man carrying a carton of milk slipped deftly into the line, and no one seemed to see or care. "That's what I should have done," Pat thought, staring at the man, angry because he didn't have the nerve to do it nor the flair to carry it off. The man glanced arrogantly over his shoulder and Pat turned to look at the book and magazine shelves so he did not have to confront him.

RAPE. SNIPER TERRORIZES. MOB TAKES. STRIKE. SUICIDE CLAIMED. TROOPS OCCUPY. TEENAGE MOTHER KILLS. THE DAY JACKIE. WHY LIZ. LSD AND. SHOOT OUT IN.

Horror, disaster, rumors of war, glimpses of doom hung over the world, but nothing definite that you could understand, or stop, or make up your mind about.

STUDENTS PROTEST. NEUTRALISTS TAKE TOWN. LOYALISTS KILL THREE HUNDRED. LIBERALS BOYCOTT POVERTY MEETING. REBELS BURN VILLAGE. TEACHERS STRIKE. KILLER GOES FREE. PRIESTS CHALLENGE. DOCTORS STRIKE. PROFESSOR ADVOCATES. PACIFISTS INJURE. PSYCHIATRISTS OPPOSE.

The old labels, the old yardsticks didn't fit any more, and who knew what was right, or even what was happening?

"Will this be all? Did you find everything you wanted? Did you check our bargain counter? Here is your change and your Lucky Letter Card. Spell out the word CASH and win a thousand dollars worth of gift certificates. Do you save?"

"What?"

"Do you want the stamps? Redeemable in over a thousand stores across the country."

Pat Shahan, collector, escaping through the electric door with his bag of daily bread, his chance for tomorrow, and his negotiable tokens for a guaranteed reward, walking to his car with his relics clutched tightly in his hand, confronted by a smiling confidence man passing out tracts.

SALVATION IS FREE. JESUS PAID IT ALL. LIFE'S GREATEST BARGAIN. A GIFT FOR EVERYONE. DISCOUNT PRICES. ALL FOUR TRACTS 10¢.

"Are you saved? Are you a Christian? Do you know Jesus? Have you been washed in the blood of the Lamb?"

"Yes," Pat said politely, trying to escape around the man. "Yes, yes, yes."

"How do you know?" the man asked, catching him lightly by the arm.

Pat Shahan, bearing the fruits and rewards of this life, caught in the grip of fanatical circumstance, groping for the bones of verity in the soft underbelly of faith.

"I believe that I am," he said.

"That's not enough," the man said severely. "Even the devils believe. But are you free from doubt? Are your garments spotless? Do you have the peace that passeth understanding? Have you placed your hand in the nail-scarred hand?"

"You cut ahead of me in the check-out line," Pat said,

recognizing the smooth arrogance, and wrenching free, he threw his bread and cheese in the car and got in, slamming the door on JESUS SAVES. CHRIST IS THE ANSWER. SALVATION NOW.

Starting the motor and putting the car in gear, he drove haughtily away with magnificent disinterest, steering between ETERNAL DAMNATION and INFORMATION THEORY.

"ARE YOU A HUMBLE MAN, PAT?"

"No, Lord, but I'd be proud to be one."

Ahead of him, between QUICK RELIEF and DEAD END, he saw a shaggy, ragged man of indeterminate age bearing a homemade sign, PEACE PILGRIM, across his stooped shoulders. Pat slowed in passing him and waited for the man to appear in his rear-view mirror. Across pilgrim's chest was a similar sign. WALKING FOR PEACE.

Pat watched the man fade from view in the mirror. There was in him a yearning for such a pure, simple, single-minded mission. To walk for peace. Or dance for joy. Or sing for love. Or pray for— But what direction did you take, and down which street did you turn? How far did you have to go? And what equipment did you need? A lantern? A divining rod? A compass? A litmus? A trial balloon? A straw in the wind, a Wasserman, a Binet-Simon, barometer, ink blot, gauge, caliper?

But it was so easy. He could take up his banner and set off down the road and never have to serve at Crusades, confront Evan Moore, counsel Emily Graham, worry about Ann Ostergaard, comfort Jack Merrick, console Rachel Elliott. He would never have to bury friends or marry strangers, approve budgets, oppose revolving crosses, measure progress, deliver Thanksgiving turkeys, or pray in a Civil Defense Shelter.

What banner should he wear? UNITY? JUSTICE? EQUALITY? PERCEPTION? MEANING? POWER? CONNECTIONISM? LOVE? COMMITTEE? STUDY GROUP? STRUCTURE? FREEDOM? SALVATION? BEHAVIOR? PEACE?

"WHAT IS PEACE, PAT?"

"Why, Lord, that's the thirty-eighth parallel."

Pat Shahan, in Egypt, driving for peace, steering for love, cornering for joy, turning for hope, braking for faith, dragging for freedom, racing for salvation.

GOD IS MY ROAD TEST.

Pat Shahan, one of the army of the saints, returning home from the wars, steering his way to safe harbor through parked cars and playing children.

Pat Shahan, lonely pilgrim, who had cast his bread upon the waters, divided his garments with beggars, and walked the second mile with opportunists, arriving at the gates of sanctuary.

Pat Shahan, humble man of God, making his way into the house through the throng of happy children.

"Daddy, can we stay up late if we're good?"

"Anya said 'hell.' "

"No, I didn't."

"Yes, you did too, while Daddy was gone. You said 'hell.' You did too, you said 'hell.' "

"All right, Penny, that's enough."

"Penny got a spanking for spitting in the flowers."

"Daddy, look at what I drew at school today," Penny said, holding up a finger painting of chaos and violence.

"Yes, that's very pretty."

"It's a picture of things eating other things. Miss Prince said everything eats something else. Mother's going to hang it on the wall."

"Good."

Pat Shahan, in evangelical poverty, returning home with bread and cheese.

"What time is the meeting tonight?" Lillian asked, turning her cheek to receive his greeting.

"Seven thirty," he said. It had always been seven thirty.

"I guess I'd better get busy," she said, brushing past him. "How was Rachel?"

"All right, I guess," Pat said. He took off his coat and threw it over a chair, then stretched out on the living-room couch. "I don't think I helped her much."

"You probably helped her more than you know," Lillian said from the kitchen. "A Mrs. Loomis called, and we got a letter from your mother. It's on the coffee table."

"Who is Mrs. Loomis?" Pat asked, picking up his mother's letter.

"She's Emily Graham's sister. She wants you to call her. Her number's there by the telephone."

"Oh God," Pat said. "Did she say what it was about?"

"Something about Emily."

"Oh God."

"I wish you'd stop saying that," Lillian said. "Is it something I can help you with?"

"No," Pat said regretfully. Other men came home from

the office to tell their wives of the disappointments and victories of the day, but he could not. He was a prisoner to confidences, secrets, privileged information. Besides, Lillian had the right to know people on her own terms, her opinion untainted by his knowledge of their secret and perfidious hearts. This he would have to do himself.

"Don't you think you should call?"

"I don't know why I can't have one minute to myself to read my mother's letter," he said bitterly, putting the letter aside. He picked up the telephone and dialed the number. "Hello, Mrs. Loomis? This is Reverend Shahan. You asked me to call?"

"Are you Emily Graham's pastor?"

"Yes."

"Well, I'm her sister and she's over here right now and says she is supposed to serve us—that you told her to serve us. She's trying to rearrange my house, plan my meals, everything, and I'm not going to have it. I'm not going to have her ruining our lives the way she ruined father's life."

"Mrs. Loomis—"

"She wouldn't let him do one thing for himself. She made an invalid of him. She ran that poor man out of his mind."

"Mrs. Loomis—"

"I'm not going to have it, Reverend Shahan. I am simply not going to have it. I want you to come over here and get her right now."

"Mrs. Loomis, Emily is trying very hard to forgive. Won't you give her—"

"Forgive? Forgive who? Forgive what? She is the one who should be asking for forgiveness. She ruined our father's life. She lived in his house, ate his food, took his medicine. She just sucked the life out of him. He never had a moment free of her. She made an invalid of him and he hated her for it. Oh, how he hated her."

"Mrs. Loomis—"

"I'm not going to have her over here. I think she's losing her mind. Either you come get her or I'm going to have her committed."

"Mrs. Loomis, I cannot come get Emily due to a previous engagement, and I seriously doubt your ability to have her committed. However, you may tell your sister that I'll be happy to see her in my office in the morning. Not later than nine o'clock, because I have a funeral. I would be happy if you would come with her, Mrs. Loomis, but in any case, I shall pray that you may be delivered from your ignorance and hardness of heart," Pat said, hanging up.

"Damn bitch."

"Is it something serious?" Lillian asked.

"Why in the hell did I have to call now? Why couldn't I have waited until morning, then I wouldn't have to see Emily before the funeral. I have enough to do before then, but no, you have to insist—"

"I was just trying to help you so you didn't forget."

"You really have to work at it, don't you? You have to go out of your way to make things difficult for me."

"I was not trying to make things difficult for you."

"No, nobody tries," Pat said. "It comes to them naturally."

Pat waited, but Lillian, who was making housekeeping noises in the kitchen, did not respond. "It's nobody's business to make me unhappy, it's just a hobby with them," he said, sharpening his barb, but Lillian did not reply.

IN THE HOUSE OF THE LORD

Pat looked at his mother's letter, written on pink stationery with a large embossed carnation at the top. He knew what to expect. A catalogue of activities, church meetings, luncheons, a list of people she had seen who had asked about him (none of whom he would be able to remember), one or two recipes he had liked as a child (all of which, like butterscotch pudding, he had outgrown), a recital of family births and illnesses, including weights and symptoms, and a parting complaint that she did not see enough of her grandchildren. All legibly written and logically organized.

But when he began to read the letter he noticed with surprise that it was not dated, did not begin in the usual fashion, appeared to be written in haste, and was almost incoherent.

After reading the letter through once and going back over it slowly, he was able to piece together the story. His mother had given a party for her Sunday School class of girls in the small house she had been renting since Pat and Lillian had gotten married. A group of boys crashed the party, behaved in a loud and obscene manner and when asked to leave had become rude and disorderly. When they did leave two of the girls went with them without her approval or their parents' permission. Since the occasion she had been receiving obscene and threatening telephone calls.

"Everything is going to pieces around here," she wrote. "The young people are completely out of hand and the police won't do anything about it."

His mother, who had lived through prohibition, the depression, and two world wars was afraid to live in the town where she was born, one of those small, quiet towns where nothing ever happened. The brave, all-sufficient woman he had known as a child was frightened. She who had faced the demands of marriage, the pains of childbirth, the stigma of divorce, the terror of loneliness without flinching was now afraid.

Pat could still recall the days of the depression when hobos walking the roads or riding the freights would stop at the farmhouse and ask for handouts. His father was usually working in the field or perhaps away from the farm entirely, but his mother had never showed any fear of the men, although they were ragged and dirty and many of them were rough in appearance. Instead, she instructed them to wash up at the windmill and sometimes required them to do small chores before feeding them and giving them whatever clothing she could find.

Pat wondered if it could have been the farm that gave her courage—that safety and stability had been there. Had he, in dispossessing his parents of home and land, robbed them of permanence and strength as well?

Pat stared at the letter in disbelief. He did not believe that young people were essentially any different from what they had always been—selfish and cruel, idealistic and kind, immature, impatient, indolent. He did not believe that the town had reverted to anarchy, or that the police were helpless and corrupt. His mother had lost faith—not just faith in young people, or law, or herself—she had lost her grip on life. "The Ray Elliott syndrome," he thought. The fixed belief that the world and the people in it were essentially different from what they had always been—the belief that history was dead and totally irrelevant to present life. When he looked up, Pat saw that Lillian was watching him from the entrance to the kitchen.

"Did you read your mother's letter?" she asked, although it was obvious he had. "Don't you think you ought to call her? I would if I were you."

Pat watched as Lillian went back into the kitchen, angry because it was so easy to say he should call his mother and so difficult to know what to say.

What was he to tell her? That God was not the U.S. Cavalry coming to rescue Christian women from the red-skinned barbarians? That Robert E. Lee had surrendered the sword of chivalry, gentility, and hypocrisy? That corpses in Germany, California, Mississippi, Israel attested to the fact that God did not stay the oppressor's hand, did not smite the blasphemous tongue, did not offer refuge to women and children, did not reward the meek, did not temper the wind for shorn lambs?

How should he advise her? Should he suggest that she buy a tear-gas pencil? Carry a hatpin in her hand? A gun in her purse? Take karate? Move to Australia? Fort up with other women? Come to live under the protection of his roof?

How should he comfort her? Would she be comforted to know that people had not changed? That the boys who invaded her home were the same kids who volunteered for the Peace Corps, who turned back Hitler, who marched from Frozen Chosen to the sea—the same kids who served the ovens at Belsen, who jeered Negroes in Mississippi, who terrorized towns in California?

Would she be comforted to know that history was not

dead? That St. Augustine had returned to Africa? That Hitler made speeches at the U.N., that Rome was still besieged by barbarians, that the Great Wall of China was nearing completion? Would she be comforted to know that St. Francis tended birds in a quiet New Mexico town, that last month Martin Luther created a furor in theological circles by declaring that the just shall live by faith, and that today in California, Galileo was startled to find a new star? That what was would be? That the hell we faced today was the heaven we had hoped for yesterday? That the sign of the future was the vision of the past?

Pat slumped on the couch, feeling beaten and tired. It seemed a million miles and as many years back to that moment yesterday when he had stood to watch Ray Elliott flash the All-Conquering Banner across the waiting sky. He closed his eyes, trying to recapture some of that glory, even if it were false, some of that hope, even if it were feigned. Lillian touched his arm. "Do you want me to place the call?" she asked.

Pat was filled with a silent, unspeakable anger. He did not want Lillian to place the call. He did not want to speak to his mother. He wanted to cry. He wanted to curse and gnash his teeth. He wanted to strike and destroy. He wanted to be alone. He thought of leaving the house so that Lillian would have to talk to his mother herself. Instead he did nothing. He was a mature person, a responsible Christian, a dutiful son. He waited while Lillian completed the mechanical ritual of ringing the number and handed him the telephone.

"Hello, Mother? This is Pat," he said. "I got your letter—"

He waited for her to reply—a sound of relief, of satisfaction, of pride that he had called. Instead she was cautious, distant, doubtful. "Who?"

"Pat. Pat Shahan, your son," he said, trying to laugh. "I got your letter and thought I'd call to see if everything is all right."

For the next few minutes he sat bent over the telephone, listening to his mother's voice, trying to understand. "All right, Mother, all right. Just calm down. Just take your time and tell me slowly. Don't let this upset you so. Slow down. What? What?"

Helplessly he looked at Lillian, who was sitting beside him on the couch. "Mother, you've always been so calm—Mother, Mother, you've always been so strong. Don't lose control now. Mother—"

Pat bent lower over the telephone and closed his eyes. He was hearing a voice he hadn't heard since he was a little boy. It was a confused voice, a strident voice full of hurt and pain and it brought to his mind all the terrors and uncertainties of his childhood—dreams of desertion, fears of failure, of being lost, of being helpless and alone, of being pursued by some unknown dread.

"Mother—I can't come now, Mother. I have a funeral. Appointments. I've been away for a week, Mother. I have—I just can't leave now."

He felt Lillian touch his arm but he could not look at her. "Ask her to come here," Lillian said, but he hesitated. If she left now would she ever be able to go home—back to the small frame house she rented two blocks from the city square? Would she ever again be able to live alone? He must not let this momentary fear cripple her.

"Mother, you can come here for a few days if you want, but I think it might be better—Mother—Mother, don't lock yourself in the house. You have to lead a normal—Mother, please—Have you talked to Dr. Todd? He could help you. Maybe he could give you a mild—Mother, please—"

He was succeeding in calming her. She was still crying, but controllably now, and her restraint made her appeals for help more terrible than all her tears.

"Yes, Mother, I'll pray for you. I always pray for you. All right, I'll pray for you now. I am praying for you, Mother, I'm just not saying the words out loud. Mother, please—

"Our Father which art in heaven, we ask your blessings upon—my mother who needs—courage and—uh—strength. We pray that you will—renew her faith that she might be—str—strong and—useful in thy service. And may the grace—"

Abruptly he handed the telephone to Lillian and left the room, walking down the hall to the bedroom. Falling across the bed, he buried his face in the pillow. He tried to think of nothing—to isolate himself from thought or feeling. He could hear the muffled sounds of Lillian's soothing voice coming from the living room, but he was careful not to make out the words.

"Why didn't Lillian talk to her in the first place?" he thought. Women had a whole lifetime of practice. Soothing colicky babies, teasing away cut fingers and stubbed toes, loving away the smart of battered egos and punctured dreams, clucking over unfortunate marriages and misbegotten children, sighing over tangled finances and twisted alliances, singing over death and disaster.

IN THE HOUSE OF THE LORD

"They are naturals at it," he thought. "Men try to explain the unreasonable with logic. Women talk about the senseless with nonsense."

He heard Lillian hang up and although he did not want it, he knew she would come and talk to him. He closed his eyes and composed his face to give her as little opening as possible.

"What do you think?" she asked.

"God," he groaned aloud. He wanted to scream. He did not think anything about it, he did not want to have to think about it, he did not want to discuss it.

"Did she tell you about the telephone calls?"

Pat sighed helplessly. He knew. He did not want to know any more, and he knew Lillian was going to tell him.

Actually, it was not as bad as he had been ready to believe. There had only been three calls and one of them—the caller had hung up when she answered—might have simply been a wrong number. The other two were unmistakable. The first time she had listened in disbelief while one boy made obscene remarks and the others giggled and snickered in the background. The next time she had hung up immediately, but not before she heard a young voice saying, "We're going to get you, Mother."

"That's why she didn't answer at first. She thought it was one of them," Lillian said.

"Did she call the telephone company and report it?"

"Yes, they told her to hang up if she got any more calls. She called the police, but they said there wasn't much they could do unless they caught the boys in the act."

"Is she going to come here?" Pat asked.

"She hadn't decided," Lillian said, "but I think she was

really pleased you called. She was awfully upset. You just lie there and rest a minute and I'll put supper on the table."

"I have to shower and shave."

"You'll have time for that after supper. Why don't you just not go to the meeting if you don't feel well?" she said.

"I have to go to the meeting," he shouted.

"All right," she said. "All right. I was just asking." And giving him a pat on the arm she left him with his anger.

Pat did not want to go to the Council meeting. He had had his fill of fighting for one day, and tonight at the meeting there would be a hassle over federal funds, endless arguments over committee reports, motions, points of order, nominations—

Tonight he wanted to stay home with his family. He wanted to listen to the children laugh and play, to watch Lillian iron or sew, to look at a book or television. Hadn't he earned a rest? Didn't he have some obligation to his family? Didn't he have enough battles of his own to fight? He had to prepare himself for Ray's funeral. And what about Emily Graham? Didn't he need to spend some time thinking of how to help her? And what about his mother? Hardest of all things to accept was that one's parents were vulnerable, that they needed help, and that one could not help them.

His fearless mother was afraid. She was confused. She was human. But what could he do? He couldn't go to her now, he had too many obligations to the church. There were so many people asking for help and he could not even take care of the members of his own congregation. He was trapped with the good and the affluent, shackled to his position, prisoner to his own need. And what of the others?

Those outside the area of his responsibility? Those who were truly lost, in bondage to poverty, to apathy, to guilt, to sin? Did he do nothing for them?

All day people had come to him with their problems and he had fought their battles, sought their answers. All day he had fought alone, in an exposed position, outnumbered, without encouragement or support, with no shield except a callused heart, with no weapon except blame. He had returned at the end of the day weary, used up, defeated. And now he had to go back again.

For a moment Pat did not think he could do it. But at the meeting he would not be alone. He would not have to fight empty-handed, but could have at his disposal all the weapons of organized power—the mouth of the press, the prestige of the pulpit, the purse strings of the committed, the ears of public opinion, the moral weight of reports, committees, study groups, research teams. When he shouted the foundations would tremble. When he swung his arm the forces of evil would fall back. When he returned home again decisions would have been made, answers found, changes effected.

He would have things to say that the city would listen to. "Suffering is not a private thing," he would say. "The rejection of one old man diminishes all of us," he would say. "The suffocation of a boy is the excommunication of us all."

When he opened his eyes, he saw Penny standing beside the bed.

"Mother said for you to come to supper," she said.

"Okay."

"I'll help you up."

"Thank you," he said, letting himself be tugged and pulled.

"Mother said we had to be real quiet because you weren't feeling well."

Pat Shahan, silent sufferer, lifted from the bed of his pain and led to the head of the table, visions of feasts dancing before his eyes.

"I hope you don't mind sandwiches," Lillian said. "I didn't have time to fix anything and I knew you had a good lunch. Who's going to say grace?"

Pat Shahan, humble guest, hiding in his heart the truth that he did not have a good lunch, that he did not like sandwiches, and that he especially did not like cheese sandwiches.

"It's Penny's time. I said it last."

"Uh-uh, I said it last."

Pious Pat Shahan, offering his sincere gratitude for the meager gifts from God's storehouse of blessings.

"God gives us toys too, doesn't He, Daddy?"

"Uh-uh, that's Santa Claus."

Pat Shahan, patient theologian, long-suffering sage, answering the questions of his children. "One of the most common and most grievous misconceptions of the Almighty is that God is Father Christmas, the jolly, gift-giving, white-whiskered, rosy-cheeked—"

"Don't you like cheese sandwiches, Daddy?"

"A good Christian eats what is placed before him without murmur or—"

"If Penny was my cousin, what would that make me?"

"Illegitimate."

"Pat," Lillian cautioned.

"No, really, Daddy. What would that make me?"

"Relationships are relative; therefore, in the question you have asked, the antecedent is determined by the square of the—"

"What does it mean when you throw up spaghetti? Today at school I got sick and threw up spaghetti."

"It means you had spaghetti for lunch."

"No, we didn't. We had roast beef, cream potatoes, and slaw."

"You are not to throw up at school."

"There really are witches, aren't there, if you believe in them? There are owls, too, but you don't have to believe in them."

"There are things that exist because they are real and things that exist because they are believed to exist. Witches belong in the latter category, owls in the former."

"Why do old people live in crooked houses?"

"You have an undistributed middle term in your equation."

"Why do I feel crooked when I sit down?"

"Sit up straight at the table."

"Why do things eat other things? Miss Prince said everything eats something else."

Pat Shahan, exposed expositor, searching the balance of nature, survival of the fittest, tooth and claw, nature is red, for the love of God. "It seems to be the nature of life for everything to eat something else. For example, we eat animals—"

"Skunks don't eat anything, do they?" asked Anya, whose favorite toy was a soft, stuffed skunk.

"Yes, they eat baby chickens."

"They do not," Anya said, bursting into tears.

"Yes, Anya, they do," he said, kindly. "Everything eats, even butterflies. But it's not so terrible in a way. Baby chickens eat worms and grasshoppers. Everything feeds something else. Mother and I feed you and that's not so terrible, is it? All children live off their parents. I guess you could say that all men disinherit their fathers—"

Pat Shahan, confused churchman, fleeing the chaos and predacity of eating and drinking to the ritual and reason of showering and shaving and combing his hair. "Is that it?" he wondered. Was the whole of man's knowledge and revelation summed up in the fact that things ate other things, that children lived off their parents, and that every man dispossessed his father?

Over the sound of running water he could hear the children's voices calling from the other bathroom. "Mama, Anya's drinking the bath water."

"No, I'm not, Mama, I was just pretending I was."

So they lived off him. Did he care? So they crowded their way into his home, into his heart, into his life and then crowded him out of their home, their heart, their life; was that injustice? If so, then so be it. So they changed his plans, thwarted his dreams, warped his ambition, he did not care. He fed them but they also fed him. Wasn't that the truth of the matter? Wasn't that the way it was with him and Lillian? They fed each other so that both were filled and neither was devoured. Wasn't that the higher truth?

Going to the closet he picked out a new shirt and his best suit. He didn't want to look shabby tonight. He didn't want to look unsuccessful. John the Baptist might do all right in the wilderness, but he would be thrown out of the Council.

Standing before the mirror to tie the dark blue, all-silk

tie Dr. Espey had given him for Christmas, he addressed the National Council of Education.

"Truth is not always harsh," he said. "Fact is not always more accurate than myth, and mystery is not always delusion. The laws of nature are not completely devoid of mercy, the life of man is not completely devoid of sanctuary. Justice does not always belong to the quickest eye nor truth to the longest tooth. The whole of man's knowledge and revelation is not summed up in the proposition that things eat other things," he said, and his audience was struck with wonder and admiration. "Love is the fire that does not consume."

But what about Winifred Tucker? He had murdered his sweetheart. He said he loved her and Pat had believed him. Was there no sanctuary in love? No refuge?

"We encouraged her to go with Winifred because, well, we thought we wouldn't have to worry about her, that she would be safe," the girl's father had testified.

"She was always a headstrong girl. We couldn't tell her anything," the girl's mother had testified. "And Winifred was always so kind to her, so gentle. We thought he was the answer to our prayers."

Pat Shahan, well-groomed prophet, listening to his children's laughter as he put on his best shoes and buffed them to make them shine.

He had been spared deformed, twisted, retarded children. His children had been spared wheel chairs, cleft palates, asthmatic attacks, and yet ahead of them were pitfalls and disasters from which he could not protect them with diets, vaccines, supervision, fairy tales, or myths. His children were vulnerable, and he was unable to guarantee their safety or his desires for them.

He wanted so much for them. He wanted that hope might never die in their hearts. He wanted them to be children of faith—not to dogma, or to rules of ethical behavior—but to believe in life, and yet not hold it too dearly, or take it too seriously, nor believe it was the only gift. He wanted for them to be loved for their own sake. The right to be loved without being devoured.

With what pride he and Lillian had presented their children to friends, relatives, church congregations, total strangers—always with the hope that others would see what they saw—children of hope, of promise, children born under a star, of intrinsic worth and value. And each time the girls had been valued for their beauty, their behavior, their health.

"They look like fine children," his mother had said.

"Angels," said some. "Dolls," said others. "Sweet. The picture of health. Cute. And so well-behaved."

But he searched the faces in vain for a sign that they saw what he saw—that these were children to be given, not taken—to be prized, not used.

"How many parents have these same dreams, and how few ever see them realized," Pat thought. He tried to imagine what a father must feel when at the end of the day what he brings home is not enough to feed his family so that he must divide his bread in bitterness of heart. He tried to imagine what a father must feel when he hears his child coughing in another room and cannot afford a doctor or medicine. He tried to imagine what a Negro father must feel sending his little girl off to school for the first day, not knowing what jeers and insults and humiliations she must endure before she can come home again, yet knowing that no matter how confused or broken-spirited she might be, he must send her back the next morning, and the next. And perhaps next year would not be any better. And perhaps ten years would not be any better.

He tried to imagine what a mother must feel—a mother who had suffered, and worried, and deprived herself for her sickly son—helplessly watching that child suffocating because someone had thrown a switch, erected an impassable barrier between her child and his breath, excommunicating him from life. What insane hopes must have passed through her mind. That the electricity would leap the obstruction. That miraculously the machine would continue to run without power. That somewhere was a Hand which could restore life and breath to her son. That somewhere there was Help, and Help would come.

"God, I'm going to help them," he pledged. "I'm going to see to it that they have food and justice and the right to breathe," he said, and he was not thinking only of his own children.

Feeling the importance and power of a just and righteous cause, Pat slipped into his coat and started to the meeting, stopping at the girls' bedroom to kiss them good night. The girls, fresh from their bath, were playing quietly in their nightgowns. Penny, scarcely stopping her play, put up her mouth to be kissed, but Anya clung to him for a moment, offering forgiveness or reassurance, or perhaps asking it.

Lillian was washing dishes when he started out the back door, but she stopped to dry her hands on her apron and give him a kiss. "I wish you didn't have to go tonight," she said.

Pat clenched his teeth, feeling irritability rising in him. How amazed he was that Lillian couldn't understand why he had to go to the meeting. Why couldn't she just once realize that he had important things to do? He was trying to fight poverty, and injustice, and wrong, to create a more just and rewarding life for children. All children. They must have the freedom to live as they desired, not as victims, as objects of prey, but as children of promise. "I have to go," he said.

"All right. All right. I'm sorry I said anything. I just thought it might be nice if you had an evening at home."

Pat Shahan, fearless crusader, righteous reformer, choosing duty over leisure, putting first things first, and getting in his licks on his wife. "It might surprise you to know that these meetings are rather important, not only to you and the children but to some other people in this town, and I am expected to be there."

"I didn't say they weren't important."

"It might also surprise you to know that I did not have a good lunch. In fact, I did not have any lunch at all. And that I detest sandwiches."

"I'm sorry," Lillian said. "Let me fix you something else."

"I don't have time now," he said, turning on his heel and starting to the car. It was a small victory, a minor triumph, but it was the only one he had had all day and he enjoyed it as he marched righteously out to the car. Lillian followed him.

"I'll have something for you when you come home," she said. "What would you like?"

IN THE HOUSE OF THE LORD

"Just forget it, I'll do without. I'm used to it."

"I'm not a very good wife," she said. "I was just so busy all day, and I couldn't get the washing machine to wring out the clothes, and Mrs. Elmore called—"

"What did she want?" Pat asked, dread seizing him.

"She just wanted to tell me how much good your visit had done Mr. Elmore. She said you were just a saint. Mostly I think she was just so relieved that he was better that she had to talk to someone. I didn't know you didn't have lunch. I'll have something for you when you come home. How about a cake?"

"No, I'm all right—"

"It won't take but a minute," Lillian said, going back to the house.

It had only been a small victory and now even that was bitter in his mouth. When he hurt Lillian, he hurt himself also. Yet, there was something in him that would not die— the sickness that gave pleasure in torturing cats, in killing the wild, free spirit of a hawk, in hurting those he loved.

"Why?" he asked. "Why do we do it? Why do we give pain?"

"Why do we hurt and kill? Is there no kindness, no gentleness, no refuge in the world? No tempered wind for shorn lambs? No Jesus of the bleeding heart? Does no one weep for Jerusalem? Is there no safety in love? No guarantee? No safe conduct? Is there no love that does not consume? Is that the cruelest of man's delusions and dreams?"

"WHY DO THINGS EAT OTHER THINGS, PAT?"

"Why, Lord? Because everything is so good?"

Pat Shahan, bent under the weight of his love, his feet tearing at the bottom of the treacherous river, his hands clutching for support, while grasping fingers tore at his heart.

GOD IS MY HOST.

Days to Come

> *He calleth to me out of Seir, Watchman, what of the night? Watchman, what of the night? The watchman said, The morning cometh, and also the night: if ye will enquire, enquire ye: return, come.*

PAT SHAHAN, defender of the faithful, soldier of cross purposes, armed with the shield of RIGHT and the sword of CAUSE, riding past COMFORT, EASE, PAINLESS RELIEF, to the no man's land of the American Legion Hall, where no church was entrenched and no creed held the high ground.

Pat Shahan, lead scout, arriving early to test the cross currents of controversy, to taste the troubled waters of circumstance, to mark the enemy's positions.

"Look, Pat, we've got to know if we can count on your vote," Reverend Gonzalez said. "The Protestants have agreed to a compromise Rehabilitation-Literacy Center downtown—that is, except for the Baptists, who are opposed to any kind of federal aid, and some of the Episcopalians who like the Fine Arts Commission. Will you go along with us on this? We're going to need all the help we can get."

"Reverend Shahan, I'm the Protestant representative on the Social Action Committee in charge of Dial-A-Prayer. As you know, we have three Dial-A-Prayers, Catholic, Jewish, and Protestant. There are recorded prayers that may be dialed any time day or night from any telephone in the city. But we like to change them every week, so could you record a prayer for us next week? We try to limit the prayers to ninety seconds as that is the average attention span for recorded voices. Ask for Frank Ibetta at Station KCRV. He'll take care of everything. Shouldn't take you over five minutes."

"It's called *For the Love of Christ* and it's a real good movie. Real professional. You know this TV actor—Rex Hamilton—well, he's the star. They're bringing the film here and all they want out of us is cooperation. We give them publicity, provide transportation for those who want to go, take up an offering after each showing—that kind of thing. Maybe put out some banners and posters. Now, you know the Jews are just going to ignore it. Some of the high-church Protestants aren't going to like it, but they won't start trouble just to stop it. We've gone along with them plenty of times. What we need to do is work the ecumenical thing so that the Catholics don't tell their people not to go. Now if I go to Rabbi Jacobs and tell him this is a little infighting among Christians, he'll keep his people out of it, and if you would talk to Father Rhodes and the other liberal Catholics—"

"You're Brother Shahan, aren't you? Well, I'm Brother Thornton. Pleased to meet you. I've been talking to a few people here tonight who are a little fed up with this Thanksgiving basket mess and all this giving to people who are too lazy to work when it don't do our churches any good, and I just wondered what your feelings were."

"I hear Bob Harkins is trying to join your church, Pat. Maybe I should tell you who is behind that. Now wait a minute before you get that righteous look on your face. We accept Negroes. We have five Negro families in our church, which is more than you can say. But Bob Harkins is something else. He's a member of a Baptist church on the east side. The first church he tried to join was Episcopalian. Then he tried the Presbyterians, and then us, and now your church. You wouldn't accept a white person under those circumstances."

It was all too complicated. Pat could understand none of it. In order to save Bob Harkins from rejection by the church he had sacrificed Jack Merrick to the scandal-mongering *Informer* only to discover that Sam Sorrele might have been right. He had acted on the highest motives, the best information he had, only to find that what he had done was entirely different from what he thought he had done.

Pat saw Dr. Espey making his way across the crowded, noisy hall, speaking cordially, warmly to those he met, but not going out of his way to greet people. "How does he do it?" Pat wondered, because Dr. Espey had the ability to get people to accept him at his own estimate—a man of power, of dignity, of virtue. He was not a big man, but he seemed large, he was overweight, but he did not appear soft, his head was bald and his face was wrinkled and lined, but he did not seem diminished by age. When Dr. Espey walked into a room everyone knew that here was a good man, but a good man who couldn't be pushed around, a good man who was dangerous to cross. When Pat walked into a room everyone saw a target—a soft touch for a loan, an insult, a handout of sympathy, a favor.

"How are you, Pat?" Dr. Espey asked, warmly and personally, gripping Pat's hand, and as always Pat felt drawn to him, attracted to the strength and sincerity in the man.

"Fine, thank you," Pat said, taking a step back, resisting the call to discipleship, but Dr. Espey put his hand on Pat's shoulder, restraining him. It was an old hand but its grip was firm and intent.

"Pat, I have just learned something I think you should know. Jack Merrick is the nominee for the Protestant Brotherhood Award—I believe because the Power Company opened the diversion lake to the public without regard to race or religion. I don't think that is sufficient cause, because the law requires nondiscrimination in public facilities. And I don't think Jack Merrick should get the award. For one thing, he is not politically sound. For another, morally he is not the best man our church has to offer.

"Granted, it would be a feather in our cap. It's been seven years since one of our people received it. I think there's discrimination right there. But anyway, I feel the award should honor a man who has served the cause of Brotherhood and should not be used for personal or political gain. I would like to see the award go to a little man—someone who is not rich or politically powerful—a common man who has served the Lord in an uncommon way, perhaps even a heroic way. I intend to offer a substitute motion."

It was easy enough to understand how Jack Merrick had become the nominee. He was a rich, successful public figure —the kind of man the nominating committees always favored. But it was also clear to Pat that Jack Merrick must not receive the award. That was greater irony than he could accept. Nevertheless, it disturbed him to be on the same side as Dr. Espey, who opposed Jack for purely political reasons.

"Pat, I've talked to the chairman and he agreed to recognize me before he makes the committee's nomination," Dr. Espey said, sensing Pat's resistance. "This will save Jack from the embarrassment of defeat. If people go along with our candidate the public will never know who the committee's nominee was."

"Who is your candidate?"

"Ray Elliott."

"Dr. Espey!"

"I've been thinking a lot about that young man today, Pat. That was a tragedy. A real tragedy. Here was a young man, a husband and father, a hero of his country, who died in the cause of the Lord."

"Dr. Espey, there are a lot of people in the Council who think the Great Crusade was a ridiculous spectacle—a mistake—a farce—"

"I've never been afraid of opposition."

"Dr. Espey, they're not going to believe that a man who crashed trying to tow the world's largest banner should get a Brotherhood Award."

"This was more than a man towing a banner, Pat. This was a man giving his life to the service of God, to the service of other men, and that's the meaning of Brotherhood."

"You know Ray may have killed himself," Pat said, expecting to unload a bomb in the temple of fabrication.

"Even his wife suspects it. He made no effort to release the tow rope."

"I've seen the report," Dr. Espey said calmly. "I know there will be some who will try to make something of it. There will be some who will try to use this to hurt the Crusade, and to hurt the church, and to hurt God. But I'm not a cynic, Pat. I'm not an iconoclast and I have no wish to hurt the cause of God. I'm just a simple country preacher," said Dr. Espey, who hadn't been a country preacher since Pat was a boy, "who believes in God, and believes in his fellow man. And I prefer to believe that Ray Elliott died accidentally while serving his Lord. You think it over, Pat."

Pat Shahan, cause bearer, thinking it over as the gavel pounded. If he did not oppose the committee's nomination, Jack Merrick, who was not blameless in the death of an innocent boy, would receive an award for Brotherhood.

Pat Shahan, God's gunman, unlimbering his weapons as order spread. If he did oppose the committee's nomination it was possible that Ray Elliott might receive the award, and not only would Dr. Espey have the Council's tacit approval of the Crusade, but he would also have a banner for next year's campaign. A banner that Pat Shahan would have to wear around his neck like a millstone.

Pat Shahan, half-cocked weapon of the Lord, searching the sky for targets as the meeting began, trying to choose between an ostensible killer and a possible suicide.

He had come to do battle. To attack no matter the risk, no matter how desperate the situation. He had come to point the finger of accusation, to shout THOU ART THE MAN while the pencils scratched and the cameras ground, to cleave between right and wrong with a flaming sword, to make the guilty tremble and the powerful bow their heads. He had come to hold the fort, stem the tide, to take the castle—just once to be heroic, just once to be fierce with decision. And he could find no place to stand. He had come to slay dragons and found only phantoms. And the weapons he had so carefully gathered, and oiled, and polished were not only obsolete but inoperable.

As the first order of business, a coalition of Episcopalians, Jews, independent evangelicals, and Catholic liberals passed a resolution to approve the City Fine Arts Commission as the recipient of the federal aid, leaving the unorganized Protestants and the hard-line Catholics to rage impotently about power politics and underhanded chicanery. The victors sat in sleek and silent martyrdom. Pat watched them as their heads bowed modestly under bigotry and discrimination, the persecuted majority, knowing that he was forever cut off from that company. He too would like to be numbered with the persecuted powers, overwhelming martyrs, but he was a member of a forgotten minority—the man who had no banner to wave, no flag to fly.

A special investigating committee reported that three months of intensive investigation failed to show any negligence on the part of the two church-operated hospitals that had turned down an indigent patient who died a few minutes after being admitted to the city hospital. "Both hospitals have rules of conduct clearly and specifically stating that any patient, regardless of race, color, or creed shall be admitted to whatever services the hospital offers without regard to ability to pay. In both instances on-duty doctors determined that the best interests of the patient would be served by sending him to the city hospital."

The Chief of Police reported an upsurge in the incidence of glue sniffing among teenagers, described its dangers, and recommended that every pastor, priest, or rabbi warn the members of his congregation, particularly the teenagers and their parents, of this danger.

This report was followed by a recommendation of the Social Action Committee that the first order of business of the newly formed Fine Arts Commission be the purchase of a dramatic, educational film vividly portraying the hazards of glue sniffing.

The chairman of the Fine Arts Committee pointed out that there was no provision in any of the proposed budgets for such a film.

Brother Thornton rose to express his opinion that such devices only attracted the attention of young people to an evil of which the vast majority were unaware.

After further discussion of innocence versus information the Council voted to request the local newspapers to run a feature article on the dangers of glue sniffing.

The Committee on Civil Rights reported that two students, one of them the son of a well-known layman, had been suspended from high school for improper grooming— long hair and eccentric clothing. Protestant and Jewish liberals resented this invasion of basic human rights but spoke cautiously for fear of offending the Catholics, who required uniforms in the parochial schools. The report was referred to a committee for further study.

The Social Action Committee brought a recommendation

to file charges against Milford Jones for selling pornographic literature to juveniles. Reverend Wolle objected that Milford Jones was blind and couldn't tell the ages of the boys, that Jones was a member of a minority race, that Jones had to take whatever magazines the dealers gave him, and that to attack Milford Jones was to attack the symptom and not the disease.

"And I don't believe it is very Christian—" Reverend Wolle paused to apologize to the Jews and whatever Unitarians took offense—"I don't think it is very religious to put a poor old blind Negro out of work."

The Council agreed to give the recommendation further study.

The Emergency Relief Committee, which had been formed during the summer to deal with local flood victims, reported that the emergency had passed, that the food and clothing had been distributed, and that fifteen hundred dollars remained of the emergency budget. They further reported that the committee had received excellent and expert help from firemen, policemen, city officials, newsmen, and most of the cooperating churches but that two churches had volunteered their gymnasiums as dormitories for the flood victims and then charged a dollar a night for cots.

The Council found such action deplorable but agreed that it was an internal church matter in which they could not interfere and voted to spend the surplus relief funds in paying the churches for the use of their cots.

The Public Relations Committee reported that the Council would again be represented by a booth at the county fair and recommended that the theme be "BROTHERHOOD —THE WAY TO PEACE FOR OUR TIME," with displays exhibiting Brotherhood at work—such as the four chaplains who gave away their life preservers and went down with their ship, interfaith projects in the slums—

The evangelicals argued that Christ was the only way to peace in our time. Others complained that Brotherhood had been the theme for the past three years. Some felt that "peace" would be offensive, and some thought that "peace for our time" sounded like Chamberlain and appeasement.

Dr. Espey suggested as a theme "THE OPEN BIBLE IN THE OPEN MARKET," with an exhibit of Catholic, Jewish, and Protestant Bibles and a narrated history of Bible censorship, but the Catholics demonstrated no enthusiasm for the idea and some of the evangelicals wanted the history of censorship to end with the King James Version.

Rabbi Isaacs suggested the theme "SYMBOLS FROM THE PAST," with a display of religious symbols and their meanings. Father Donner suggested that the theme be changed to "SYMBOLS FROM THE PAST, GUIDELINES FOR THE FUTURE," to avoid any suggestion of obsolescence. But the evangelicals felt left out, as they had no symbols of their own.

Reverend Hutto declared that any kind of a booth with any kind of exhibit or display would stand as an everlasting example of ghetto Christianity and recommended that the Council sponsor a coffee house with free refreshments and free entertainment, including dancing, poetry reading, folk singing, and personal testimonies regarding the spiritual life.

Certain members of the Council were worried about the cost of a coffee house. Others were worried about the quality of the entertainment. Some warned that the commercial enterprises would object to the competition. Others warned that their parishioners would object to the night club atmosphere. Some felt that the coffee house would be too limited in its appeal, discriminating against those under fifteen and over twenty-five. Others felt it was no place for a man to take his family.

The president of the Council warned that if the Council could not agree on a theme of Brotherhood then public demonstrations of brotherhood such as booths and exhibits were hypocritical if not impossible. Unable to agree on the theme of Brotherhood, a resolution was passed urging the churches to seek independent representation at the fair.

The Public Affairs Committee reported an incident of concern to Council members. An independent service-station owner named Frank Evans had been forced out of business when the street in front of his station was torn up and the entrances to the station barricaded so the city could repair the curb. For ten months no work was done on the project despite the repeated appeals of Mr. Evans. Mr. Evans, due to the loss of business, was forced to sell the station to a chain owned and operated by the brother of one of the members of the city council. Two weeks after the sale became final the street was repaired and the barricades were removed, although up to that date no work had been done on the curb. In a fit of rage Mr. Evans broke in the plate-glass windows of the station and was arrested, and at the present time was in the city hospital with a broken rib and facial lacerations suffered when he fell down the steps of the jail.

After a heated debate the Council agreed to a resolution expressing sympathy for Mr. Evans's cause but deploring his methods of protest. Copies of the resolution were to be distributed to the newspapers. Furthermore, the Council agreed to send a one-man "conscience vigil" to stand silently and prayerfully at the service station holding an enlarged copy of the resolution, remaining so long as his conscience required.

At the insistence of Reverend Hutto, the Council also requested the Chief of Police to conduct an investigation to determine if the arresting officers exceeded their authority or used improper force.

Pat was appalled at the triviality, the inconsequence of it all. A man lost his business and life savings and the Council deplored his method of protest. City officials conspired to rob one man and the Council requested an investigation of two policemen. An indigent patient had died for lack of treatment but doctors had acted in his best interest. Flood victims were charged for the use of donated cots and it was an internal church matter. The Council that had been formed by city officials and was supported by industry and monopoly concerned itself with blind news vendors and the civil liberties of long-haired boys. And who represented the poor and homeless, the dispossessed and excommunicated? Scientists sent rockets to the moon; the church could not agree on the theme of a banner to fly over the county fair.

The chairman of the Brotherhood Committee took the floor to announce the nominations for the Brotherhood Awards, but readily yielded to Dr. Espey.

Dr. Espey complimented the committee on its fine work and happily admitted that heretofore the committee's nominations had been accepted without question. It was for that reason that he wished to make his statement before the

Protestant nomination was announced so as not to embarrass the committee's nominee. He wanted to tell them of a young man, a member of the community, a layman and war hero who had demonstrated the highest kind of brotherhood, giving his life for others, refusing to pull the release and save his own life for fear of dropping the banner on hundreds of viewers crowded below.

For a moment Pat almost bought it. Then he remembered how far the crowd was from the plane, and that even if by chance the wind had caught the banner and had blown it into the crowd it was not heavy enough to seriously injure anyone. He looked at Dr. Espey and there was no trace of doubt in his face. Espey had bought it because it was convenient, and useful, and because it fitted neatly into his other systems of belief, and once he had believed it there was no way to shake his absolute conviction. Even now he was expounding it as fiercely as the other dogma he professed. Pat saw warning signs out. To challenge Dr. Espey's evaluation of Ray's death was as dangerous and as heretical as doubting any other part of his doctrine, which he had tightly knitted into a fabric that could not be unraveled at any point.

Pat looked at the other members of the Council, seeing their lack of interest. They did not care who received the award but had always followed the committee's recommendation. They would follow whatever leadership appeared. Dr. Espey had claimed that position.

The vote was taken, the hands were counted, and Ray Elliott became a sermon illustration, a story of self-sacrifice, a theme for next year's Crusade, while Pat Shahan circled, his guns unfired.

Pat regretted not having acted. In the name of truth he

should have done something, even if he had to expose both Jack Merrick and Ray Elliott. He should have attacked even if he could not tell the friendly forces from the enemy. He should have fired his guns even if it was overkill.

Other items of business were transacted, committees were appointed to investigate a price increase at a church furniture factory, the suppression of an underground newspaper at a local university, and rumors of inflated charges at a local hospital as Reverend Hutto and other young activists sought causes to support, but Pat was scarcely aware of it.

"AREN'T YOU CONCERNED, PAT?"

"Lord, problems are like turtles. If you don't pick them up they won't wet on you."

Alone, he was almost helpless in the face of overpopulation, organized greed, political oppression, world-wide starvation, and yet when he joined organizations to extend his voice and increase his power he found himself involved in trivia, manipulation, the use of power for personal gain, the abasement of men to create causes. The Council built no bridges, bound no wounds, fed none of the starving. In the face of world evil, while the reformers played politics, the sociologists measured dirt, the psychologists trained mice, and the police arrested drunks, the church recorded Dial-A-Prayers, picketed here, paraded there, and posed for surveys.

It seemed to Pat that the church was a giant turtle, dragging around a shell full of empty words, quaint customs, old candlesticks, musty relics, dusty Holy Books, and forgotten symbols. "We don't win many races," he thought, "but we're always at home."

Perhaps it was all too complicated for a religion spawned by the nomadic tribes of the mystical Middle East, simplified by the prophets, spiritualized by Jesus, universalized by the Christians, corrupted by the power and wealth of Rome, humanized by the Reformation, demythologized by modern scholarship, and disregarded by most of its professors. Or perhaps the church should not take up arms against oppression. Perhaps the church should just stand aside and deplore. Act as referee to see that the oppressed used proper means to protest their oppression. Declare itself noncombatant and pick up the wounded and bury the dead.

The church had power, of that Pat was convinced. The church couldn't always fill its own doors, but it could control governments, levy tribute, and launch crusades, inquisitions, reformations, and wars. The church had such power that it was no longer necessary for a man to believe in God. The church could give him what he wanted—political favor, social status, moral indulgence. All that it asked in return was that a man be loyal, faithful, and socially approved.

Yet, with all its power, all its wealth, the church could not save a Negro boy from suffocation, could not save Ray Elliott from the cross of popular myth, could not tell a husband how to love his wife without killing her, or explain to a mother why she must bear a monster child. "So what good is it?" Pat asked, "except to save four hundred people in the event of a nuclear attack."

Pat was aware of the hush around him and knew that the time for adjournment had come. As prescribed by custom, each member prayed in his own way, those who finished first waiting patiently for the vain and repetitious. In a few minutes it would be all over and he could go home with his guns unfired. Go home to another night of listening to the voices of doubt. Or perhaps, like Mac Winston, he should cut himself free and drift from job to job, always looking for a place free of sham, a place where he could serve with meaning.

Pat Shahan, messenger, clothed in the sackcloth of religion, wrapping his hair shirt about him, girding up his loins, disturbing the prayers and meditations of the righteous.

"Mr. President, I wish to say that suffering is not a private matter, that the death of one innocent diminishes us all, that today in this city a young boy died because the power that gave him the breath of life was cut—"

For a moment there was confusion as Pat was ruled irreverent and out of order. However, although the meeting was officially adjourned, and all statements would be off the record, the chairman of a committee especially appointed to investigate the incident would make a preliminary report.

"This is in the nature of a preliminary report, since our investigation will continue for some time to come. However, I do wish to state emphatically that this committee has uncovered no evidence whatsoever that would indicate that the Power Company was in any way negligible or in any way departed from its usual policy. The company has cooperated completely with the committee and has offered to discharge any personnel found to be derelict in their duty. This committee intends to make a full report of the incident in the next three or four months."

"What can you say to that?" asked Reverend Landman, east side pastor.

Pat Shahan, on the long journey of this miserable life, being ignored as the meeting dissolved into shouts of greeting and convocations of joke tellers. Pat turned away, shying from contact. He felt a hand on his shoulder. Dr. Espey.

"Too bad you didn't pull it off. There are too many people here who have accepted favors from Jack Merrick," said Dr. Espey, whose church had a stained-glass window with Jack's name on it. "Anyway, we got the award for Ray. I promised myself I was going to do that for Ray Elliott's widow and I did. And what it will do for the Crusade next year I haven't begun to imagine."

"When did you decide that was the reason Ray didn't pull the release?"

"Well, it was right after talking to you. I thought to myself: 'Why must we always assume the worst about people? Why can't we believe that like our own, their motives are good?' And then I realized. He was trying to save all those people. I think next year at the Crusade we'll have a special service for Ray Elliott. Tell his story. I can tell you I wasn't at all pleased with the Crusade this year, and I intend to suggest some changes that ought to be made."

"Dr. Espey, it was a disaster."

"It wasn't as big a success as I had hoped, Pat, but it wasn't a failure. In many ways it was better than we could have expect—"

"Dr. Espey, it's all wrong. We bring out the football players and television actors and think it's going to change the world."

"But the Crusade is just one aspect of our work, Pat. We do other things. We sponsor schools, orphanages, hospitals—"

"That's right. The poor need specialized training so they can get jobs, and we sponsor colleges with football teams and ballrooms and fraternities and sororities that only the rich can afford. We offer them paved parking lots, and they need transportation to work. We sponsor orphanages, and what is needed is a clean place to leave the kids a few hours a day. We operate this big hospital, and you have to have cash in your pocket to be admitted.

"The poor don't need a hospital; they can go to the city hospital free. They need lawyers so they have a chance against organized money and power, so they have the kind of protection you and I were born with. They pay more for rent, for food, for insurance. They get inferior service from utility companies, the telephone company, the banks, the police, the board of education, the city council, the garbage collectors, the street cleaners, the health—"

"We all want those things, Pat, but I'm talking about the Crusade."

"That's what I'm talking about. We ask a man to tow the world's biggest banner, and they can't even see the sky."

"Pat, I don't understand you. You didn't use to feel this way. The Crusade wasn't all I had hoped for, but it was a success. And it would be absurd for us to change the methods that have proved so successful in the past, the very things that have made us what we are today. I recognize the need for taking a stand on social issues at the right time and in the right way. That's the reason I'm a member of the Council. But I am convinced that a lot of this talk about social issues is just a cowardly attempt to avoid the difficult work of evangelism."

Pat watched Dr. Espey walk away. It was the straight-backed, head-erect walk of a man who was certain of his cause, unaware that all about him were molecules in motion. "Well," Pat said, "you can't shoo turtles."

"Reverend Shahan?"

"Yes."

"Pete Harder, *News*," said a small, dull-eyed man. "I'm the reporter assigned to cover the Council meeting. I was told you could help me."

"All right."

"Who was Ray Elliott?"

"Well, he was a member of my church. He was a pilot. Fought in Korea and the Pacific. Won quite a few medals. Actually, he was quite a hero."

"That why they gave him the award?"

"No, no. You see he flew a banner at the Crusade—that is, he was asked to fly a banner, only he couldn't get it off the ground. Crashed."

"Why did they give him the medal?"

"He was in this airplane and he saw all these people— Well, see, they wanted to give it to a little—they wanted to give it to a common man who served in—He was just—"

"This award is for doing something, isn't it? The guy that got the Jewish award gave this old house for kids to play in. What did this Elliott do?"

"He served his country in two wars, isn't that enough? He was a husband and father and a church member. Ask somebody else," Pat said, turning away.

The Clean Up Committee was rearranging the chairs and the parking lot was almost empty when Pat left the Legion Hall and drove down the brightly lighted streets, busy with young people and automobiles at play, past FAST ACTING, QUICK RELIEF, LASTING BENEFITS, GUARANTEED RESULTS.

"DO YOU LOVE ME, PAT?"

"Yes, Lord, I love you."
"LOVE MY CHURCH."
"Lord, there are so many things wrong with the church it takes a Christian to put up with it."
"DO YOU LOVE ME, PAT?"
"Yes, Lord."
"FEED MY SHEEP."
"How, Lord? With candles? Banners? Revolving crosses? I can't do it alone, Lord, and you know what the church is like. A new organization? Is that the answer? Call it by a new name? Change the motto? Raise the dues and entrance requirements?"

Pat was tired of all the self-interest, and sentimentality, and the piety that invariably fixed the blame on someone else. He did not want to be Sam Sorrele's pastor. He did not want to minister to Walter Miles, Harry Nelson, Jack Merrick. He wished he could drop the compulsion to help, the urge to save, the need to heal. He wished he could strip away all the clichés, all the phony motives, all the dirtied, mutilated words and walk clean and alone. To lie down beside a stream and be fed by ravens. Not to have to walk the roads where men were beaten and robbed and left for dead, where the indigent were left to die unattended and children were denied breath. Not to have to visit the city where every man was a beggar in the name of God. Not to have to go to church, where the cross represented profit and every man a cause.

He did not see the Lord high and lifted up, His train filling the temple. He saw Him low and cast down, His need filling the world. There was something that called to Pat out of the splendor of the moonlit alfalfa fields, out of the necessity of drowning bees, out of the compulsion to feel what Evan felt, to know what Ray knew, out of the pain of tortured kittens, out of the noise of running, in the dreams of peace pilgrims and the guilt of Thanksgiving baskets. Out of revolving crosses and iron lungs and flaming airplanes there was something that spoke to him, and when he wished, he could give Him a name.

Pat Shahan, great mother of the world, offering love in one breast and hope in the other.

GOD IS THE NAME I GIVE.

Pat Shahan, night watchman, finishing his appointed rounds, seeing through the overwhelming darkness the lights of home.

Pat Shahan, long distance runner, swinging down the last turn, churning down the home stretch, head down, heart pounding, arms and legs beating the air, seeing parked in his driveway a strange car.

"Damn," he said, "started my kick too soon." Pulling into the driveway, he looked over the car but did not recognize it. Not Dr. Espey's sleek Oldsmobile standing in reproof. Not Jack Merrick's sporty Thunderbird, crouched and waiting to pounce. It was a vintage Buick, expensive and cared for—class without ostentation. Emily Graham's sister! She was leaving Emily here for him to look after.

"To hell with that," he said, getting out of the car. But no, the Buick was too heavily masculine. Not Evan Moore either, or Marjorie Zinkgraf. Ewing Harrison Ledbetter come to get his church back? Or Sam Sorrele with some new scandal to exchange for the humiliation of Bob Harkins?

Lillian met him at the door. "Harry Nelson is here to see you," she said. "He's been waiting almost an hour."

Harry Nelson. Better than he had expected but worse than he had hoped. "I have been avoiding him all day and you invite him into the living room," he said angrily under his breath.

"I told him you wouldn't be in until late but he asked if he could wait, said it was very important."

"It's that damn cross. That's how important it is."

"I always do the wrong thing," Lillian said. "I baked you a cake."

She really did feel contrite. And when he saw the cake he would be able to accurately measure the guilt. A fifteen minute pre-mix was no more than a mustard seed, but his favorite, a lemon do-it-yourself that took preparation and supervision—that was the second mile.

"I'll bring you a piece," she said.

"Okay, don't wait too long and maybe after Harry has eaten he'll leave."

Lillian returned to the kitchen and Pat prepared his face —haggard, long-suffering, but still able to smile at his parishioners, still willing to hear their complaints. "Hello, Harry," he said, greeting the neat little man. Harry always looked prim and slightly old-fashioned, with his hair parted down the middle, his double-breasted suits and high, stiff collars. Pat shook Harry's small, crablike hand and sat down with a sigh of weariness. Being with Harry always made him feel like an oversized Epicurean. "What a day," he said, shaking his head and sighing. "I haven't had a minute. What can I do for you?"

Harry pursed his thin, bloodless lips in disapproval of

Pat's forgetfulness. "I wanted to talk to you about the cross," he said, and once again he began telling of the religious experience he had had in Los Angeles seeing a neon cross revolving above the streets. He had followed the cross to a little chapel and had talked to the man waiting inside, the only person he talked to during his entire stay.

But it seemed to Harry that here was the purpose and meaning of his life—to purchase such a cross for his own church, a cross that would call men out of the sordid world of pleasure and vice to a life of sacrifice and service.

Pat listened, disenchanted with the dull, listless life the cross was going to call men to, but Harry was excited. His eyes were bright and his lips were trembling. Harry, who had never enjoyed a meal, a drink, a naked dip in the pool, a belly laugh—whose senses were too dull to lure him into adultery or marriage, thrilled at the idea of a cross revolving aimlessly above the roof of the church. "Give me a fat bishop any time," Pat said to himself.

When Harry had finished, Pat leaned forward in his chair and stared at his shoes, pretending to be lost in thought. "Harry, I'm afraid this is going to cost a great deal more than you believe. I have been talking to some people and I don't want you to get involved in something way beyond your means—"

But Harry had the figures with him—cost estimates, operating expenses, and he laid them out for Pat to see. Pat looked at the figures, pretending to study them closely although they had no meaning to him. "I don't know, Harry. I don't want us to get involved with some fly-by-night cross builder—"

But this was the same company that had designed and

built the cross in Los Angeles. They had other crosses in Minneapolis, New York City, Atlanta, and Electra, Texas. They were reputed to be the nation's finest name in electric crosses.

Pat pretended to study the figures some more, then nodding his head thoughtfully, he folded the papers and handed them back. "Then I think the next question is this—bearing in mind Jesus' concern for the poor, the hungry, the sick, is this the best possible use to which the money could be put, the best possible way in which it can be spent?"

God said it was. Harry was certain of that. For a moment, Pat considered the argument that God told him it wasn't, but gave it up as fruitless.

"Then I suppose we have to consider the question: is this the best possible time? Considering the high cost of labor, the season of the year, the busy schedule of the church, the personal involvement this will require on your part—"

This was Harry's mission, the purpose of his life, his God-appointed task. He was sixty-seven years old and he could not afford to wait. He must see the cross finished before he died. "This is my mission," Harry said. "And until it's finished, I'm not ready to go—"

"Before you go I want you to try some of this cake," Lillian said, bringing in a tray of cake and coffee. It was Pat's favorite lemon cake.

"Harry, don't you think that cross would be a waste of money?" Lillian asked, handing him his cake and coffee with a smile while he went white in the face. "I do. Who is going to see it up there on top of the church? What good is it? There are just too many good purposes to waste money on foolishness like that. Did you know that seventy-five cents will cure a leper? That ten dollars will supply a family with food for a month? That five hundred dollars will set up a baby clinic? I have an article right here," she said, placing a pamphlet in his lap. "Do you use cream or sugar? No?" And she was gone, leaving Pat alone with a livid saint.

"The Fourteenth Commandment," Pat thought. "A man who has ears for God has no mouth for laughter."

"I don't believe you are taking my offer seriously," Harry said, tight-lipped with anger. He pushed aside his cake, from which he had taken two bites, being careful to avoid the rich icing. He had scarcely sipped his coffee.

"I do take it seriously, Harry, but you'll have to admit there are some humorous—no. But I have to consider not only your wishes but also the wishes of the other members of the church. I have to think of what's best for all. And I have to consider it from all angles. For example, is this the best place for the cross? Now, you'll have to admit it, Harry, that cross will be seen by very few people from atop our church. But there are other churches in town where it could be seen by hundreds of people. Now, on a purely cost per viewer basis, you'll have to admit—"

Harry had been a member of the church for years, since long before Pat came, and he had always wanted to do something for his church. On the streets of Los Angeles God had shown him the way. Since that time he had carefully saved his money. He had given up movies and desserts so he could buy the cross. He had made his own lunch and carried it to work.

"Harry, it just doesn't make sense."

"I promised God I was going to put that cross on top of

the church, Pat. It was a sacred oath. Now I want to know if you're going to try to stop me."

Pat could, he knew that. As a minister he had debts he could collect whenever necessary. The hours he had spent counseling the confused, consoling the bereaved, sitting with the sick—the friendship, the encouragement, the concern, no matter how freely given, how professionally done, these were considered debts of honor by the recipients to be expiated by church attendance, small gifts, and future favors. He had cast his bread on the waters and he could demand its return. He had never collected these debts because he had never wanted to—never needed to. But he could. There were people in the church who would do things for him they wouldn't do for Jesus Christ.

"Care for any more cake or coffee?" Lillian asked, coming in to get the trays. "No? Well, I think I'll go to bed then. It's getting late. Good night, Harry. Good night, Pat," she said, kissing him. "Don't stay up late."

They waited politely until she was out of the room. "Harry, I'm your pastor. I can't tell you what to do. I can only say that I think what you are doing is wrong and that I will advise the church that in my opinion it is a mistake. But that's all I'll do. I, personally, am not going to stop you, but I think the church will."

Despite his lack of regard for Harry's plan, Pat could not repress his pity for the man who seemed to wither as his dream died. "What the hell," he thought. It was no worse than a lot of other extravagances. No worse than two thousand dollars worth of fertilizer. "Harry, does it mean so much to you?"

"You're a pastor. People know who you are. I've been an accountant all my life. I'm sixty-seven years old. I don't have any family. I don't have any friends. No one knows who I am. I just wanted to do something important before I die."

"Harry, can't you see you'd have been better off living for your church? Can't you see that this money gives you the chance to do something for others, to help somebody out? Can't you find some way to do something for people? Isn't that better than—"

"No, it's my money," Harry said, his thin voice trembling. "I've sacrificed. I've done without so I could give this cross to my church. I walk to work every day. I've never had a telephone. I've never had an air conditioner or a television. I use a razor blade for a week. I've sacrificed these things to honor God, and I'm not going to give it to somebody who'll spend it on liquor and cigarettes."

"And you enjoyed every minute of it, Harry," Pat said, appalled that Christianity could ever have this result. "You did without because you wanted to. That cake didn't cost you anything and you were afraid to eat the icing. The only reason you've never married and had a family or friends is because you're not willing to give anything. And you're never going to be anybody or live until you realize that all this sacrifice and all this talk of doing something important is just selfishness, and give up all this crap, and do something for others."

"That's a very unbecoming word in the mouth of a minister of the gospel," said Harry, tight with self-control. "I'm not sure such a man as you can understand self-sacrifice."

"Yes, I think I can, Harry, but can you understand why

you have scrimped and saved and carried your lunch to work and never allowed yourself to enjoy anything? You're not doing this for the Lord. You're a miser, Harry. You love to save nickels and dimes, and that cross just gives you something—"

"I'm sorry to have troubled you at home. Please offer my apologies to Mrs. Shahan and thank her for her hospitality. I'm going to take my plans before the church board," Harry said with great dignity, picking up his papers and leaving the room.

"You do that."

"I shall," Harry said, jerking the door closed behind him.

"If you're going to slam the door, then slam it," Pat called after him. "It's free."

"WERE YOU RIGHT, PAT?"

"Yes, sir."

"WERE YOU KIND?"

"You can't be both right and kind, Lord. This time I was right. Next time I'll be kind."

"HOW DOES IT FEEL TO BE RIGHT?"

"Well, it's no fun unless people know it."

Pat sat down on the couch knowing he had failed again. He pulled off his coat and tie and leaned back. He was supposed to help Harry, not tell him off. There was something to be said for frankness but not very much. Honesty was not the best policy. Silence was the best policy.

Lillian came in cautiously. "Did I help?"

"Oh, you were a big help."

"Did he slam the door when he left?"

"He wanted to but he was afraid he'd enjoy it."

"That bad, eh?"

"That bad."

"Would you like some more cake?" Lillian asked, starting toward the kitchen.

"No, thanks, but it was very good."

"You didn't eat all of yours and Harry barely tasted his."

"He was afraid he might like it, and I felt like a glutton eating in front of him."

"How did the Council meeting go?"

"Okay, I guess. They gave the Brotherhood Award to Ray Elliott."

"Ray? Why?"

"Dr. Espey said he crashed his plane to avoid the crowd, therefore exemplifying the highest type of brotherhood."

"Did he?"

"I don't know, I don't think so. I told Dr. Espey off."

"How does it feel to be famous?"

"It's no fun if no one knows it."

"I had an idea you'd fight with him before the day was over," Lillian said. "You were so upset and he is so mule-headed."

"One has the suspicion that lurking beneath that mule's head is a horse's ass."

"Mrs. Elmore just called. Vernon is much worse and they don't expect him to live through the night."

"Oh no," Pat said. All afternoon he had held on to a bit of hope. He didn't believe for a moment that his prayer had changed God's mind and snatched Vernon from the jaws of death, but he hadn't given up hope either. "I guess I ought to go to the hospital."

"She said you didn't need to come. She knew if you prayed for him he would be all right."

"Thanks a lot."

"Are you coming to bed now?"

"No, I want to think over the funeral."

"The girls want you to kiss them good night."

"Okay."

Pat walked down the hall to the girls' room. He made no effort to conceal his presence, not minding if they woke up and knew he was there. They seldom did and then they never remembered it the next morning, but it always pleased him when they opened their eyes and knew their father was standing over the bed watching them.

Their faces were open, guileless. Time and practice had not yet formed the masks of pretension that adults were unable to lose even in sleep. Pat kissed them and covered them up, having to straighten the cover for Penny, who always managed to kick it into a wad at the foot of the bed.

"Daddy, I can't get to sleep," Penny said drowsily.

"Honey, you are asleep," he said.

Leaving the warm room, friendly with dolls and horses and pictures of woolly lambs and protective dogs, he walked down the hall to his study, which looked cold and uninviting. Switching on the light, he went in and sat down.

Before him on the desk were the notes he had made that morning. " 'Oh that I had wings like a dove: for then I would fly away and be at rest.' " That didn't seem right for a funeral, especially the funeral of a man who might have decided to chuck it all and fly away to rest.

" 'But they that wait upon the Lord shall renew their strength; they shall mount up with wings as eagles . . .' " That didn't sound apropos for Ray Elliott, whose strength wasn't renewed, who came down instead of mounting up.

"'The days of our years are three score and ten; and if by reason of strength they be four score years, yet is their strength labor and sorrow; for it is soon cut off and we fly away.'" That might do. It had flying in it. Ray had died at the height of his powers, thereby being spared who knew what terrors and sorrows.

"'So teach us to number our days, that we may apply our hearts unto wisdom.'" He could make some points with that. Begin with "man's days are full of sorrow" to give everyone a chance for a little tearful release, throw in a dash of terrors and calamities that Ray had escaped so they could rationalize their self-pity, and sprinkle lightly with admonitions to the living to number their days, to remember that life was passing as quickly as a dream—that the good works they failed to do now would go undone, that the visions they did not see today would be unseen, that the God they avoided today would be forever unknown.

"'Make us glad according to the days wherein thou hast afflicted us, and the years wherein we have seen evil.'" He would remind them that the sorrow and the pain of the moment, insomuch as it was a portion of life, also was the gift of God.

For the obituary he would stick to the facts, with an emphasis on Ray's life and only a brief mention of the method of his death, with absolutely no comment regarding motives or martyrdom. And he would read it himself. He would be honest but he would be kind. Kind, honest Pat Shahan.

Pat pushed the notes aside. He would look them over tomorrow to see if there were any ideas he could use, and while he still had the pen in his hand he would jot down his preliminary ideas for the Dial-A-Prayer.

"Hello, there, glad you rang my number. This indicates that you seek God's aid. I am going to pray for you. If you wish you may pray with me. 'Our Father, which art in heaven—'" Not very original. What if some of his minister friends dialed the number just to see how well he prayed? Would they think he was taking the easy way out—ducking the job? But how did you pray for someone you didn't know? Make it general.

"Our Universal Creator, help this man or woman, boy or girl, to find your will for his or her—"

Broader and more universal. "Give us, O Universal Spirit, the power to be spiritually successful in a property-conscious society, the courage to be mentally independent in an institutionalized land, the strength to be morally good in an unsound financial community, the grace to be humble in a status-structured—"

That looked pretty good on paper. A little ponderous. Perhaps he should save it for his pastoral prayer Sunday morning. He couldn't imagine it doing much for a man listening over the telephone. A recorded prayer to be played over the telephone should be personal, intimate, man to man. His voice should be warm and friendly, his words common but not folksy, down to earth but not— Hell, he didn't sound warm and intimate over the telephone when he talked to his mother.

Perhaps he should form a mental picture of the one he prayed for. Who was at the other end of the line, guilt-stricken, tear-streaked, desperately hanging on his words?

Perhaps dialing over and over as long as his or her money lasted, grasping for hope. A lonely widow, forsaken by all, who every night rang his number to hear him pray— "O Lord, remember those we have forgotten—"

An alcoholic who with trembling fingers discovered a single coin remaining in his pockets and called for help. "Assist, O Lord, the one we have failed."

An unwed mother, rejected by those who professed to love her, dialing his number as the last alternative to abortion or suicide— "Give strength, O Lord, to those we have made helpless—"

Pat tossed the pen on the desk in despair. What did he say to such people should they call? What words of his could restore hope, courage, self-respect, and where would he find such words? What telephone could carry such a message? "How do you pray for anyone?" he asked. "How do you pray?"

Who knew what was best for Vernon Elmore? Or Mrs. Elmore? And was it the same thing? What should he ask for Rachel Elliott? Or Emily Graham? Should he pray that Marjorie Zinkgraf find love and that Jerry Barnes get a job? What should he ask for Harry Nelson—charity? And for Mr. Murph—zeal? What was The ideal for Evan Moore? Jack Merrick? Sam Sorrele? These were his people and he cared for them. When he awoke at night to the sound of rain on the roof he knew who was wet and cold. When the market fell he knew who was sleepless with fear, and when death came he knew which tears were real. But where was the wisdom to know what was best for them?

And what of those he scarcely knew? Those who came almost stealthily into the church and sat at the back. "Hello,

Ann, how's your mother?" "Hello, Carl, how's the team this year?" How many tears were secret? How many hungers hidden? How many cries unheard? And what did he ask for them? For Ann Ostergaard, Mrs. Clark (that her son return?), Jimmy Nevins, Lee and Ruby (that they like each other?), Tom Glazener? And what of the others? Those outside his congregation? Mac Winston, who could not find a place in the ministry or a peace out of it, Dr. Espey, Winifred Tucker, Bob Harkins, his mother?

Other ministers seemed to have magic words that wrought miracles. Other men seemed to have formulas that would open the drawstring of God's grab bag and release a shower of gifts upon those they favored. But he knew no such words or formulas. He had only himself to offer, only himself to pledge. Bowing his head, he made that offer. Closing his eyes, he made that pledge.

The day was over and he was glad. He for one was through with it. Let it go back where it came from. But first, how should he sum it up? A successful retreat? A disastrous victory? A tactical success? He had floundered and failed, but he had also polished his weapons and guarded them well. He had not convinced any atheists, but he had waved his banner. How did he score Emily Graham and on which side of the ledger did he put Vernon Elmore?

"WHAT ABOUT THE BOY?"

"Just an accident, Lord. Jack Merrick was just trying to save the company money and that's a virtue, Lord. If he had killed that little boy to save his own fifteen cents, that would have been little, mean-minded, and reprehensible, but greater love hath no man than that he risk lives to save the company money. I'm going to score that a net ball."

Had he helped Marjorie Zinkgraf? Was Evan Moore—what was the ideal? Better? Happier? Stronger? Good intentions should count for something and he intended the best. Score those moral victories. Vernon Elmore—game called on account of darkness, but he was way behind. Dr. Espey—he would have to wait for the body count on that one. Harry Nelson—a temporary truce. Orin Kilgore—he had saved five hundred dollars worth of manure—a clean-cut, decisive victory. That one should tip the scales.

"Every day is Korea," he thought. "A little music, a little blood. Nothing big. And it's not the gains, or losses, or bodies that count, but how long you can maintain the stalemate." He had held the line all day. That should count for something. He had fed no hungry, clothed no naked, visited none in jail, set no captives free, but he had kept shop for the members of his congregation. And that should count for something.

Was that it then? Was it all over for the day? Nothing more to be done until morning? No futile gestures? No desperation passes? No reckless charges? Could he quit the watch now without neglect, could he leave his post without dereliction of duty? And did it all add up to the love of God?

What were the points to that sermon? Nature proves it. Wise men have said it. Our lives reveal it. When had his life revealed the love of God? Surely not back in that teenage hell, where he knew everything and understood nothing, nor in the days of his parents' separation, nor his days of purposeless expectation in the Marines, nor the seminary days of cant and futility, nor the days of his ministry, filled with hundreds of shards and signs out of which he could not make a single vision. Or was that the vision? That in each day he must discover again the message? Find anew the love—

He had forgotten to get the money for the choir program and he had promised Gordon Dean. Well, he would do that tomorrow. Where would he get it? Not from Harry Nelson or Jack Merrick. Well, he would think of someone tomorrow. If not. "I'll pay for it myself," he said.

Switching off the light, Pat walked down the dark hall to the bedroom where Lillian was reading in bed. Seeing him, she put down her book and raised her arms to him.

"Have a rough day?" she asked.

"Yeah."

She held him, but not in any special way. To her he was no hero, no prophet, no great lover. He was just a man. To her the only thing special about him was that he was her husband. "Well," he thought, "that's something. Maybe that's enough." Prophets were so old-fashioned. Heroes were out of place. Great lovers were uncomfortable in the kitchen.

She would never know all there was to know of him either, but she took him as her husband a day at a time, accepting him with grace, laughing at the surprises, bearing the shocks and disappointments with patience, believing even when he gave pain that he intended love. And that was something. Maybe that was enough.

The telephone rang in the den. Restraining Lillian, he went to answer it. This late at night it was either for him or a wrong number.

"Hello. Who? Evan! What's the matter? Who beat you up? Where are you?"

The voice was muffled by pain and perhaps by tears as well, but Pat was able to understand that Evan had been badly beaten, that he needed help, and that he knew no one else to turn to. But above Evan's voice he heard something else. He heard the still, small voice, the silent sound, like the faint buzz of bees' wings. Calling to him. To try. There was his appointment, there was his sign. His people called him to minister. They appointed him to speak to them of God.

When he looked up, he saw Lillian standing in the door. "Trouble," he said. "I guess I'll have to go."

"Can't it wait until morning?"

"No. You might as well go on to bed. I'll probably come back by the hospital to see how Mrs. Elmore is doing."

"Good night," Lillian said, giving him a warm kiss, which he resented. There was no point in it if she were going to be asleep when he got back.

Pat waited until Lillian was back in bed, trying to think what he should do. He did not know what to say. He did not know how to help. He would go and sit with Evan for a while. Maybe that would help. If Evan wanted to blame him he would take the blame. If Evan wanted him to help, he would try.

Evan had a life—lonely perhaps, guilt-ridden—but with some moments of peace, of happiness, and he had shattered it. He had destroyed the little world that Evan had made for himself, had driven him out of it. Now he would have to help him build another one. Perhaps it would not be one that Pat would care to inhabit, nor one that he would approve, but it must be one in which Evan could find a measure of repose and beauty. "Well, I can live with that," Pat thought. "Nothing is perfect."

Again he heard the voices of carping doubt. "Who made you a minister?" They asked. "Who set you a judge over Israel?"

"Evan," Pat said.

There was his authority. They were his people and they called for him. They anointed him with their need. Their desire called for him to speak for God as best he could. Their need was his scepter, his rod, his sword, his caduceus. Their need called him and he was bound to go.

Airplanes still fell from the sky, bees still drowned while wasps floated, children of prayer were sometimes born monsters, neon crosses still revolved for unseeing eyes, and somewhere a recorded prayer was being dialed. There was darkness in the world, but there was also a light.

He had only one more mile to go. One more attack in force up Heartbreak Hill, one more cross to bear, and then he could put aside his burden and lie down to love, to forgetfulness, to dreams of drunkenness and power, of moonlight and alfalfa fields, of fire and rain, of a place where heavily laden bees could walk upon the water, of a love that did not defile.

Pat Shahan, near-sighted prophet, feeling his way down the dark hall, past a drawing of things eating things, past the open Bible and a worm-eaten crucifix he had bought in Mexico, to the coat and tie he had left on the couch.

It was given to other men to see visions and dream dreams. He saw only signs. To others it was given to speak truth, he only waved banners. Other men saved cities, converted nations, built cathedrals, established orders. To him it was given to put his faith on the line every day and each time to find God there. In the place of death, in the face of evil, in the sickness of life, in the midst of his days to find God. Even if he failed. Even when he failed.

"DO I LOVE YOU, PAT?"

"I guess so, Lord, but nature does not always reveal—"

"DO I LOVE YOU, PAT?"

"Well, most of the time, Lord, but my life doesn't always demonstrate—"

"DO I LOVE YOU, PAT?"

"Yes, Lord, you love me."

"LOVE MY SHEEP."

Pat Shahan, whose reason asked what was beyond reason to answer, whose faith asked what was beyond faith to believe, whose love asked what was beyond love to do.

GOD IS THE SIGN I SEE.

A NOTE ABOUT THE AUTHOR

ROBERT FLYNN was born in 1932 on a farm near Chillicothe, Texas, and served with the Marines during the Korean War. Mr. Flynn teaches in the Trinity University Drama Department in association with Paul Baker and Gene McKinney, who first encouraged him to write. He is the author of *Journey to Jefferson*, a play adaptation of Faulkner's *As I Lay Dying*, for which the Dallas Theater Center under the direction of Paul Baker won the Special Jury Award at the Theater of Nations in Paris, 1964. In 1967 Knopf published his first novel, *North to Yesterday*. Mr. Flynn lives in San Antonio with his wife and two daughters.

A NOTE ON THE TYPE

THE TEXT of this book was set on the Linotype in Janson, a recutting made direct from type cast from matrices long thought to have been made by the Dutchman Anton Janson, who was a practicing type founder in Leipzig during the years 1668-87. However, it has been conclusively demonstrated that these types are actually the work of Nicholas Kis (1650-1702), a Hungarian, who most probably learned his trade from the master Dutch type founder Kirk Voskens. The type is an excellent example of the influential and sturdy Dutch types that prevailed in England up to the time William Caslon developed his own incomparable designs from these Dutch faces.

Composed, printed, and bound by The Book Press, Brattleboro, Vt. Typography and binding design by Kenneth Miyamoto.

Carnegie Public Library
Robinson, Illinois